# After Dark

A PARANORMAL
DARK ROMANCE

# KIRA BATES

PB ISBN: 979-8-9920302-0-4

EBOOK ISBN: 979-8-9920302-1-1

Cover design and art by: Austin Drake at Bottle Cap Creative

Copy Editing and Proofreading by: Alexa at The Fiction Fix

LLC Published by: Kira Bates

*For every serial hobbyist that finally found their place.*

# Dear Reader

Welcome to the vampire-infested town of Georgetown.

This is a paranormal dark romance with sexual and explicit scenes. This novel is a thriller that includes depictions of violence, gore, and to state the obvious, blood.

This novel includes the death of family members, the death of animals, and touches on infertility.

Proceed with caution if any of this makes you uncomfortable.

You can find the full CW list on my website.

www.kirabates.com

# Chapter One

## ROWAN

Lights dance in my vision, and the sounds of The Top 100 Disco Hits fill my ears.

"Wow, Rowan Watson! Leather pants. You're trying to take my cowboy tonight, aren't ya?" Liddy says, swinging an arm over my shoulder. Her boyfriend, Sylas, chuckles and keeps his grip on Liddy's hand. They look like a magazine cover. Her long blonde hair always shines more than should be humanly possible, and her rugged cowboy protects her. His dark blond hair peeks out from his Stetson and curls around his ear lobes. His tidy facial hair makes him look older than he is.

Sylas and Liddy have been together for six months now and are almost never apart. He's all cowboy while she's the small-town princess. He runs the Loughty Ranch at the edge of town with his two brothers, Harris and Noah. They graduated high school years before us, but everyone knows the town cowboys.

"You know I'm not into blonds, babe. I have my eye on something tall, dark, and handsome." I wiggle my brows, and we burst into laughter. I tug her loosely into me and plant a kiss on her temple, pressing down the twinge of pain that starts in my chest.

The Georgetown Fall Carnival is in full swing for opening night. They pull out all the stops this time of year, and this event brings in a large amount of revenue for the city. It's held in a large open field that gets muddy and trampled down just in time for tractors to plow once clean-up is done. Rides line the perimeter, food trucks and unwinnable games between them. The Ferris wheel, our favorite—and the only reason we come—is at the very back. The rides are old and shaky, and the air smells like funnel cakes and sweat, but that never stops the town from showing up. The life these Carolina nights breathe into you is something to hold close.

I take in all the people and joy around me and lift my head back to see the barely visible stars. The crisp air brushes against my nose to let me know fall is here to stay. I jog up to one of the funnel cake stands and wait in line. Once it's my turn, I put in my order and sway to the music blasting high above the screams and chatter.

"Hey, Rowan. I haven't seen you around in a while," Travis says, suddenly up in my space. I've known him since high school, the typical star quarterback. He wasn't the brightest, and he always had a hoard of girls following him around. His baby blue eyes littered with flecks of gold and his short dark hair made him the most sought-after.

"Hey, yourself! What have you been getting into?"

"Well, I have my own construction company now. It's new, but I think we'll get a lot of business," Travis boasts.

I don't doubt that. There aren't a lot of small businesses around here yet.

"With the way I see these cougars looking at you, you'll

get some business," I laugh. "They look like they'll bang down walls just to have you come fix them up."

Travis gives me a full smile at that one.

The food truck worker hands me my sugary treat just as I get a text from Liddy.

"Well, this is my cue to go. I have a date with a pretty lady and this funnel cake. It was good catching up, Travis."

He catches my arm before I can jog off. "Do you still have the same number?"

"I do. Call it sometime." I walk off and try to cool my expression even though I'm giddy.

I haven't had a real relationship in a while. It's not hard for me to find a man to warm my bed, but Travis has a steady job and respects women. Going out with him wouldn't be the worst thing in the world.

I spot Liddy standing in line for the Ferris wheel and squeeze my way past the line of people behind her. Some grumble, but Liddy's excited waving and shouting makes them too distracted, and no one tries to stop me.

"I got the goods," I call out once I reach her side. Liddy takes a bite off the side of the cake and moans. There's no good way to eat these. She has powdered sugar on the corner of her lips that I wipe away with a napkin.

The ride operator calls us up, and we hop inside a cart.

"This is always the highlight of my night here," Liddy says. Laying my head on hers, I agree.

We gossip the first loop away.

"I saw you talking to Travis. What was that about?" She wiggles her eyebrows at me.

"He's cute! I told him he could call me, but who knows if he will. You know my streak with men isn't the best," I confess.

"You're so stubborn. Your streak with men is bad because you don't let anyone in." Liddy huffs.

"I've lived here long enough to date everyone in a five-mile radius. No one here is the one for me."

"If you don't try, you won't ever find the one. Your dating history is based on one-night stands and closing yourself off to the world." Liddy's pointed judgment stabs me where it hurts but remains true.

"Travis will be good enough for right now, and he seems decent." I wrap my arms around myself.

Liddy gives me a sharp, knowing look. "Give him a chance."

We gobble down the rest of our funnel cake just as we make it to the top of the Ferris wheel once again. This is our second time around; we always go twice for good measure. This time, we look out at our small town and its beauty, the lights that spread far and wide but stop just before reaching the outskirts of the Loughty Ranch. Mountains surround Georgetown, closing us off to what I call the real world.

My body jerks forward as the Ferris wheel comes to an abrupt stop. What used to be my favorite ride now feels like a death machine just as it has reached its peak. It's never terrifying to go around in a loop, but being stopped this high has panic racing through my head.

"What do you think is going on?" I breathe out.

"This happens all the time. It's okay. They probably just needed to help someone get off," Liddy reassures me.

I know she's being reasonable, but I don't like being stuck this high up. I'm usually so in control of everything around me, and when I'm not, my head starts to spin and my palms slick with sweat. I want my feet back on the ground. I search below us, my eyes moving back and forth frantically, looking for the culprit.

"Liddy, look down there. Do you see that?"

Lights flash, and paramedics rush toward the entrance of the Ferris wheel. They weave through the crowd, gathering around the bottom cart. The chaos and loud, muffled voices make it hard to tell what's happening from up here. Two police officers push the crowd back, and paramedics lift a limp body from the ride below.

"They're putting someone on a stretcher." Liddy's hand grips my arm tightly.

"I hope it's nothing serious. They're not dead, are they?"

Liddy is in a full panic next to me, and I no longer have hopes of being reconnected with the ground. I can't help but wonder if I'm safer up here or down there. I run my eyes over the crowd forming around the paramedics. Parents are pulling their children away from the crowd, and loud gasps erupt in sheer panic. That's when I spot a man running from the crowd, blood clinging to his skin. He looks back to the crowd with glowing red eyes. Or is it a trick of the light? I try to follow his path out of the sea of people, but he moves so quickly into the tree line, I don't see where he goes.

"Did you see that guy? He ran into the woods. It's like his eyes were red, glowing." I look over to Liddy.

"That's ridiculous! We're way up here. I think you're

panicking." Liddy's breathing is heavy in my ear.

"Me too."

Once the Ferris wheel begins spinning again, I let out a small breath. The relief of having my own feet on the ground quickly wavers when I think about what could be waiting for us down there. Piercing red eyes are now burned into my memory. Will whoever that was come back for more?

Our feet hit the rusted metal stairs, and my heart rate picks up. We have to push our way through the cluster of people still crowded around the ride. Lights flash ahead of us at the fair entrance as paramedics make their way out. The police officers try to bring the chaos down, shouting directions over the music that was never turned off. The screams fill my head, and my breathing turns ragged, I can't seem to get my footing or thoughts straight. I know I'm moving through the grass towards where Sylas is meeting us, but it doesn't feel like I'm in my own body. Someone else has taken over, and I'm just watching. I can't hear Liddy when she tells me the plan for leaving the fair. She pulls on my arm so I can keep up with her. I barely register the sharp pain in my shoulder from her dragging me along.

We make it to the exit, where Sylas meets us.

"Come on, let's get you both out of here," Sylas says. He wraps his arm around my waist and guides us through the fair gates to the parking lot. I take his hand and let him pull me into the tall cab of the truck. The cold leather of the seat hits my legs, and the sudden silence helps me catch my bearings.

"What are we doing?"

"Rowan, you're staying at Liddy's place tonight. Everyone's

in a panic about what happened. They still don't know who did it or what caused it," Sylas says in a rush. Liddy slams our doors shut, and Sylas starts the engine. People run past the truck, trying to get to their cars. The traffic leaving the parking lot starts to build behind us before we turn onto the road towards Liddy's house.

"Liddy, I know you said it's ridiculous, but I know what I saw. That man's eyes were practically glowing." The memory of his gaze still burns through me.

"Tell her what you heard," Sylas whispers. Liddy turns and meets my eyes.

"There's nothing to tell. It wasn't anything. Everyone is terrified and seeing things tonight. That's why we're going to stay together. Someone did something to that man, so it's better to be careful tonight." Liddy gives me a terrified and apologetic look.

She knows how my parents' deaths affected me, how hung up I was on finding their killer. I don't care how scared everyone is, I know what I saw. That man has something to do with what happened tonight. I know it in my gut—this was no coincidence.

We pull into Liddy's driveway, and Sylas cuts the engine.

"Thanks for the ride." I reach for the door, but Sylas locks the truck and faces us.

"Listen," he starts, "you need to go inside and lock all the windows and doors. Shut the blinds and don't be blasting music tonight. I know it seems like overkill, but just stay in tonight. Please."

"Yes, sir!" Liddy salutes him, and he rolls his eyes.

"Rowan?" I guess he needs acknowledgment from me too.

"Yeah. You got it." I can't meet Liddy's enthusiasm.

"Call me if anything happens or if you don't feel safe," he says as we head straight inside.

Liddy shuts off the porch light and locks the front and back doors. I check the windows and close the blinds. Everything seems normal in the neighborhood, and there are no signs of panic or hysteria. My muscles loosen and my breathing comes easier. I was probably panicking over nothing. Why would a random man be after anyone in this town?

I decide to chalk it up to shock and get started on some food for us.

"Hey, I'm going to make us a snack. I don't feel like sleeping. Should we watch TV?" I call over to Liddy.

"Yeah, that's a good idea. I'll turn on Buffy," she practically cheers. We've been catching up on reruns of the show whenever we're together, which is pretty much always. Whenever Sylas joins us, he groans about our choice of entertainment, saying, "You need to watch something with more substance." We never do.

We settle into the couch, a plush gray sectional with a chaise overflowing with pillows and blankets, and I place the tray of snacks I made us on the coffee table. Liddy has the coziest couch out of the two of us. She takes the chaise, and I lay with my head near hers as I spread out over the mass of pillows. We feel normal again after the events of tonight and settle into our smooth routine of Buffy the Vampire Slayer. Buffy is such a badass that it gives me a confidence boost and a false sense of protection.

Liddy busts out laughing, and I look at her like she's lost it. "Remember when you dressed up as a vampire for three Halloweens in a row?"

I roll my eyes before lifting my hand to cover them. "And that's exactly why I was never prom queen. I can't believe you let me do that."

"Let you? I tried to burn that costume."

"I always knew you were up to something. That's why I hid it in your mom's closet." We laugh so hard, Liddy ends up bent over crying.

"I love you, but I'm so glad that obsession is over." She pops a grape in her mouth, and I smile at her. The obsession is far from over, but I don't give her any more ammunition for this humiliation.

Liddy dozes off after two episodes, and I pull my phone from my pocket when it starts to vibrate. The screen flashes with a number I don't know, but I answer, just in case.

"Hey, it's Travis. I didn't get to see you before you left tonight. Are you okay?"

"Yeah, thanks for checking in. Did you hear about what happened tonight?" I head to the kitchen so I don't wake Liddy. There's a wall of windows behind the sink looking into the backyard, and I shift the blinds open to gaze deep into the woods that back up to her fence.

"I saw a crowd of people around the Ferris wheel, but once I saw the paramedics show up, I high-tailed it out of there. Didn't want to get stuck in the middle of all that. What happened?"

"I don't know, actually. Some guy was hauled off the ride,

and they took him out on a stretcher." I decide to leave out what I think I saw after that.

"That's crazy," he says, leaving the conversation short.

"Yeah, it was a real mess getting out of there. I'm glad you're safe."

There's a slight pause in his voice. "I was thinking maybe we could meet up tonight. It was great seeing you, and I wanted to take you up on your offer to give you a call."

A small smile plays on my face. I look toward Liddy, who is still asleep on the couch. I know she would be pissed if I left, and Sylas told us to stay in tonight.

"Uh, yeah, thanks for thinking of me. I think after tonight, I really should stay in with Liddy," I say in my most pitiful voice.

Travis sighs. "I get that. Listen, if you change your mind, I'm grabbing a drink at Bluebird Coffee House. I'll save you a seat."

I end the call with a polite goodbye and set my phone on the counter. My eyes take in the yard as I grip the edge of the sink. It looks so peaceful outside, with no signs of imminent death or ruin. I look at Liddy again, fast asleep, the TV shining brightly through the living room. I guess I could grab a coffee and come back. It doesn't seem like a killer is out there, lurking in the shadows, waiting for me to leave. Everything feels normal. There was a freak accident with a man who might not even be dead. I won't pretend it's insignificant, but I won't let it hold me back from getting out there.

I put my jacket on and slip a pocket knife inside the left breast pocket. I don't want to feel completely defenseless, and this gives me a sense of security. I won't let Buffy go unnamed in my newfound bravery. At least there's no such thing as vampires.

Bluebird Coffee House is close enough to Liddy's that I can walk. It's one of our favorite spots; we would stop there anytime we made a trip to the library. It ended up being quite often. I close the front door quietly behind me and check the streets. Thankfully, I see no one.

The air has a real bite now. I wrap my jacket around me and head into town, stopping when I see the bright blue door to the Coffee House. It sits on a cobblestone road downtown next to shops and restaurants.

Travis sits at the best table in the house—the only window seat Bluebird has—on a single platform looking out the big window onto the street. It's the best spot for people-watching and gossiping. It also looks like the most romantic spot right now. Strings of lights have been hung up throughout the place, and their soft glow puts my anxiety at ease.

"Hey! I decided to get out," I greet Travis as I walk towards him for a hug.

"I'm so glad you did. Was everything okay? Liddy didn't mind?" He leans in closer.

"Oh no, she was asleep. I'll just catch up with her later. I'm sure she'll understand," I explain to him, unsure why I feel the need to convince him, or if I'm trying to convince myself.

"I don't think it'll be a problem." Travis gives me a sly grin.

I smile back. "So, a construction company, huh? What else have you been doing? High school was so damn long ago now." I shrug my coat off and hang it on the back of my chair. Our waitress takes my order, and Travis and I get to catching up.

"Yeah. I wasn't sure what I wanted to do for a while there, but I love working with my hands, and I wanted to give back to the community." He is practically puffing out his chest with pride. I understand why. It's hard to get a foothold in such a small town already set in its ways. Most people end up leaving Georgetown in hopes of finding their big break. Not me. Growing up here came with its challenges, especially after my parents' death, but this town has its claws in deep and has been good to me. I get to brag about my time at the Georgetown community college and how I landed my job with the local news outlet. I beam when he tells me he'll look for my by-line.

The night draws out as we sip our coffee laced with booze. The perfect nightcap, he told me. On drink number two, we laugh so hard, the owners threaten to kick us out if we don't settle down.

"Alright, alright," I laugh out. "I'm too old to be kicked out of a coffee house. We should get out of here."

Travis laughs. "Twenty-six is still young. I'll grab the tab. We can head to my place."

Giggles bubble out of me, and no thoughts are quite sticking in my head. Travis pays the tab and then loops his arm through mine. We walk a short distance to his house, and when we arrive, I look up in awe.

"Wow, wow! Look at you, Mr. Construction. This looks gorgeous!" I'm practically yelling at this point. I feel myself getting significantly drunker by the minute—my vision blurs. I'm starting to think there was more alcohol in the drinks than I was led to believe. Travis grabs me before I trip onto the front steps and leads me inside to the couch.

"Okay, let the fun begin!" I shout, but the fun doesn't begin, because the moment my head hits that couch, I black out.

# Chapter Two

## ROWAN

The sun shines through the window, waking me. I groan and rub my eyes, adjusting to the bright morning light. I press my palm into my temple. My head is killing me. I don't remember what happened once we made it to Travis' house last night. I look down at my clothes to find they're untouched, my coat still on. I don't feel any different, but I shift on the couch, paying attention to any soreness. There is none. I let out a relieved breath; Travis and I didn't do anything.

Begrudgingly, I lift myself off the couch and head towards the kitchen, where the smell of freshly brewed coffee lures me. Travis is cooking pancakes and pouring me a mug of liquid gold.

"Hey, sleepy head. How are you feeling?" he says with way too much enthusiasm.

"I've been better. What the hell happened? Remind me never to order what we had last night again." I place my head in my hands, collecting myself before I look back up.

He looks at me from the corner of his eye. "Those were strong drinks. I'm glad we made it back in one piece. You passed out as soon as we got here; I couldn't even convince you to take your coat off. You fought me over your shoes, but I won that one." He gives me a playful wink.

I reach into my coat pockets, feeling for my phone, but I come up short. Retracing my steps back to the couch, I see it lying on the coffee table. I flip it open and check to see if I have any missed calls from Liddy, but there's nothing. Concern starts to race through me; she would be up by now, and I'd hate for her to feel like I abandoned her. She should be bitching me out. I *did* mean to go back to her house after meeting with Travis, but I didn't expect to be couch-ridden for the night.

I need to check on her and apologize.

Travis' voice makes me jump. "Are you staying for breakfast?"

"No, I really should get going and check on Liddy. She didn't even call this morning. She must be upset with me." I feel so guilty.

I gather myself and say goodbye to Travis. He says he'll call me later, but something doesn't feel right. He definitely isn't hungover, and we had the same drinks. I might be reading too much into this, but I want to get out now while I can.

I'm still wearing last night's clothes as I jog to Liddy's house, the hangover I'm nursing making sweat roll down my back. I strip off my coat as I make it to the front door and step inside.

It's eerily calm. "Liddy?"

The TV is still on, and I see the snack tray from last night knocked onto the ground. Pieces of food have been stepped on, caked into the rug, and sickness turns low in my gut at the sight. I move around the couch to turn off the TV and set things straight when I see her arm hanging off the side of the couch. I step closer to my best friend's body, holding my breath scanning her limp form. Her clothes, hair, and nails—she's covered in blood. Streaks of red are matted in her golden hair, and my eyes instantly fill with tears as I feel my body shake. Dried blood is caked under her fingernails, showing me she tried to fight back.

"*Liddy! Liddy!*" I scream. "Help! Someone help me!"

Her body looks hollow, her pale skin tinted purple. Her eyes are open wide in terror and sunken in. I can't gather my thoughts—I can't breathe or think. My hands frantically search her body for any sign of life, for any sign of what happened. My fingers run across a small puncture on her neck. Tears stream down my face in a flood of panic.

After what feels like forever, her neighbor bursts through the front door.

"What's going on? I heard a scream. Is everyone okay?" His words are panicked and rushed, and with his baseball cap in hand, I see him wipe sweat from his brow.

I sob, not fully sure he can understand me. He moves around the couch, and that's when he sees her. Without another word, he runs back to his house to, presumably, call 911.

I hug her body and rock her in my arms violently, not able to form any words. Tears flow down my cheeks, and I can't bring myself to let go. Her body feels weightless and wrong.

"Liddy, baby, please! I'm so sorry. I'm so, so–sorry," I cry into her. I don't understand who could have done such a thing. It looks like she was bled dry.

Everything that follows is a blur, with the deafening sound of police cars and paramedics pulling up to the house, blaring their sirens. All I hear are loud voices shouting orders, and my eyes blur, going in and out of focus. My head pounds as panic runs through me. One of the officers drags me off her body, but I scream and sob and fight to keep my hold on her. I know she's gone forever once I'm forced to let go.

I kick the officer, trying to break free from his grip, but I'm shoved to the ground and cuffed. The bitter cold of the hardwood floors presses into my cheek as I watch the paramedics lift my best friend onto a stretcher, her body covered and hauled out of the house.

The room is spinning, and I sob so hard, I throw up. I feel the burn in my throat and nose. I don't hear the officers as they speak to me, their voices are muffled and melting into white noise. They don't know what happened, and I can't talk to them, the words stuck in my throat. I'm pulled from the floor and settled into the back of one of their cars, where I sit frozen for the entire ride.

The station is in a frenzy when we arrive, and I'm placed in a room I shouldn't be in. They don't need to interrogate me.

"Ms. Watson, I'm Officer Perry. I just want to ask you a few questions, and we can let you be on your way. First off, my condolences on your loss. You've been through a lot, and I want you to know we were all affected by the loss of your parents." He hikes up his pants by the belt loops and drops to the seat across from me.

His chair scrapes across the floor, echoing off the walls. There's nothing in here except the chairs we're sitting on and the cold metal table between us. The walls used to be white but look as if they haven't been cleaned since this place was built. I watch as he takes a notepad from his pocket and flips it open to an empty page.

I stare at him blankly. Truthfully, I don't think there's anything left inside me. They could leave me here to rot, and I wouldn't care. Liddy was all I had left in life, and she was ripped away from me—everyone is always ripped away from me. She's gone because I couldn't stay home for one goddamn night. It's my fault she's dead, and I won't fight it.

"Now, I just need you to tell me exactly what happened," he states with no empathy in his tone.

I don't meet his eyes. The grief washes over me in waves, but between those waves, a fire starts to burn and my blood begins to boil. It's nothing the waves can put out.

"Rowan-"

I look up to match his gaze and see the fire burning in my eyes reflected in his muddy brown ones. "The only person I had was just stolen from me, and you want me to blab about it? How about you go find who did this?" I can tell my outburst has startled him, because he softens and motions for the officer behind me to remove my cuffs. The bite of the cold metal releases its grip on my wrists.

"I'm sorry we didn't get those off you sooner. It was for everyone's safety," he starts. "We have a team at the scene, but it would be helpful to know what happened before you found her."

I pull my shoulders back, trying to steel my spine and put up a tough front, but my lip begins to quiver. "It's my fault.

I left Liddy's house to go on a date last night. I should have stayed with her. I got back this morning and found her dead on the couch." My head falls into my hands as quiet sobs leave my shoulders shaking. My head is spinning, my hands trembling.

Before I'm released, Officer Perry gives me his contact information and says he'll call with any news, but I don't have high hopes. Memories of my parents flash in my mind. Liddy was all I had left, and she was murdered just like they were: in cold blood, just like the man dragged off the Ferris wheel.

A shiver wraps around me as goosebumps litter my skin. I look over my shoulder obsessively the entire walk home, feeling like someone is watching me. The winding road out of downtown is unusually quiet. The leaves rustle in the wind, the strong force making my hair whip around my face. I feel a gentle caress on my arm, as if someone touched me. I pause my steps and look towards the empty tree line before picking up my pace. I make it to my house with no leads other than her being murdered.

Stepping inside my house feels cold and distant. The bright greens in my rug now feel muted and gray. I hang up my jacket and keys before walking into the kitchen to fill a glass with water from the tap and turn to set it on the kitchen island. Liddy helped me flip this house into a home. Her touch is all over this place—dark brown kitchen cabinets, the pops of gem tones on the rugs and pillows, the deep blue accent walls. All of this was so comforting until now.

I pick up the water, feeling the small inset bumps on the glass, and it takes my mind back to Liddy's body—the small incisions I felt on her neck. The only explanation I can think of seems too impossible. I was bullied so much in middle school for my fascination with vampires that I almost gave it up entirely. Liddy and I loved going to the library and reading as much as we could on the subject. The librarian, Asta Dyani, always knew what we were there for and pulled all the best books on vampire history for us. We would go home and pretend we were vampires ourselves, using ketchup as blood. Pain fills my chest, and I take a sip of water, knowing my mind is spiraling in the wrong direction.

I walk down the hallway towards my bathroom, touching the framed pictures of us that line the walls that now fill me with grief. I start the shower and turn to the mirror above the sink. I don't recognize the reflection I see, disheveled and beaten down. I undress and step into the shower before sitting, unable to keep myself upright. The water washes over me, down my back and through my hair. I rest my head between my knees, shielding my face from the falling water, and let my tears flow down my cheeks.

I replay the day I lost my parents on a constant loop, trying to find anything I missed.

My parents died when I was eleven; I remember it like it was yesterday. It was the most exciting Friday night. They were going on a trip to a cabin in the mountains to celebrate their anniversary, and I would get to spend the entire weekend with Liddy.

I always stayed with Liddy when my parents needed a sitter. We'd been friends since birth. Our parents met in the hospital waiting room, and our mothers shared a maternity wing room. I remember Mom telling me shared rooms were cheaper than private ones. They bonded in their pain and excitement, and our dads had the chance to share the same fear and awe that comes with becoming a father for the first time.

My mom would blab about how they'd change our diapers at the same time and that they learned how to breastfeed together. Everyone had someone to lean on in those first few precious days.

They became best friends after that, never spending more than a day apart. Thanks to our mothers, Liddy and I became inseparable too. I like to think fate brought them together, knowing how much I would need Liddy. We were attached at the hip and grew up sharing the same brain wave. It was nice to have someone to lean on, just like our mothers did. It was nice to always have a home away from home—until my home was no more.

Until they were found dead outside their cabin on that same wretched night.

I woke up at Liddy's house that next morning to find out my parents had died trying to escape a cabin fire. Officials said they were found dead from smoke inhalation right outside the door, and the cabin was engulfed in flames when they arrived at the scene, their bodies pale and eyes sunken in. I overheard the officer saying their bodies were mangled, likely from an animal searching for food, and continued to whisper details I couldn't hear. Everything was so confusing, and honestly, still a blur. I think part of me learned to block out the details of their death. The Thomas family took me in, and that was that. They were kind enough to give me space, but when I was 11, I needed more support. I fought her parents over the details of their deaths for a while. I never understood why I couldn't see them or say goodbye. After the funeral, I begged Sheri, Liddy's mother, to tell me everything they knew.

"It would just hurt you more, Rowan," she would say.

I threatened to run away, but I never had the guts to abandon my best friend. I gave up the fight after a while, but the pain of not knowing stayed deep in the back of my mind.

I felt lost and alone, even with Liddy by my side most days. Unlike her parents, she made me talk about my feelings. It's the only way I moved through grief instead of letting it swallow me whole. I would have let it.

I might let it swallow me now. Liddy is no longer here to save me from myself. I don't know if I'm strong enough to do the saving on my own. No one could have prepared me for my best friend's death. She was the rock who kept me grounded, the glue who held me together.

The memory serves no purpose other than fueling my grief.

I shut off the water and remove myself from the shower with an unwavering ache in my bones. I slide a large t-shirt over my head and climb into my bed, wrapping the cream comforter tightly around me as I lean against the rigid headboard. My phone has been ringing nonstop, but I can't stand to talk to anyone about this right now. I know they mean well, but this time, I need space. I need to get a grip on these feelings. As I slide deeper into bed, a number flashes across my screen— Liddy's mom. I know this is a conversation I should have with her now, so I accept the call.

"Hi, Sheri."

"Rowan, hi. I tried to catch you at the police station earlier, but you left before I could." I can hear the defeat in her voice.

"I'm so sorry. I should have stayed and talked with you and David. I just had to get out of there." The tears start to swell in my eyes.

"Officer Perry said you were taking it pretty hard. They shouldn't have cuffed you or questioned you like that."

The tears begin to roll down my face once again.

"I wanted to see how you were doing and remind you you'll always have a place with us." I can hear her muffled sobs across the line.

"I'm so sorry. I knew I shouldn't have gone out. I can't believe this happened." My shoulders shake violently, and I cover my mouth to hide my cry.

"This isn't your fault, Rowan. If you hadn't left, it could have been the both of you," Sheri says. "I'll let you get some rest now, but please check in with us."

"Of course, I will." I hang up the phone and turn it off before I bury myself in a pile of pillows.

Sleep comes easy.

I wake up what seems like days later. I turn my phone back on to check the time—9:23 a.m. on Sunday and 25 missed texts and calls. There's a text from Sheri with funeral details for Monday. I wipe away the tears that start moving down my face and put my phone back on the nightstand. I always get brunch on Sunday with Liddy and Emma Bishop. It was the one thing that stuck when she started dating Sylas. I could always count on Sundays to catch up and gossip with my girls. We met Emma on our first day of high school and quickly became best friends. Her family moved back here from Stanton, a few towns over from Georgetown. Emma never judged me for my paranormal love—she would tell us ghost stories, the tales of the first vampires, and all about magic—I loved her imagination. She talked about it so vividly, it could have been real. She stopped telling us stories around senior year, said it was time for us to grow up and move on. I never found out why she suddenly changed.

I make my way to the bathroom to freshen up but skip putting on make-up. I stare at the dark circles around my green eyes before choosing to ignore them. I dress in leggings and a black turtleneck sweater and pull on my favorite starry night blue cowboy boots. I trace the crescent moon outline on the boot. The night sky is bright, aware of the dark and hidden world below it. I throw my light brown hair into a messy bun, ruffle my bangs, and pull a piece of hair from each side to frame my face.

Our brunch is a standing reservation, and I plan to honor the tradition for my friend. I sent Emma a message telling her I was still going, deciding I would get mimosa drunk and look at pictures we've taken together. I will walk down memory lane before I have to join the real world again tomorrow.

Plus, I don't think I would want to eat otherwise.

I gather my things and lock up the front door. The walk to the restaurant is down the winding hill that leads to town. I live right on the outskirts of downtown in an old Victorian-style home with white paint chipping away and a bright red door that I painted last spring. The bushes could use a good trim. I bought this house after college with the money my parents had left me in their will. Between my inheritance and working minimum wage jobs the moments I could, I saved enough to live here on my own. It's not the most impressive house by any means, but I've been able to do renovations on it as I've been living in it. It's my piece of heaven in this gorgeous mountain town.

The table at The Roast is made and waiting. I'm sure the entire town has heard about Liddy by now but they still have our table set. I receive a lot of sad and apologetic looks as I head to the check-in counter. When I tell the waitress I'm here, she gives me a sympathetic smile that doesn't reach her eyes.

Maybe I should have stayed home.

"Rowan, we weren't sure if you'd be coming in today, but we have your table just in case." She stands there, just looking at me.

"Thank you," I offer back, hoping she will just show me to the table.

"Right this way."

I can tell she's uncomfortable, just like everyone else here. We make it to the table, and she removes the third set of dishes from the side opposite me.

Emma walks toward the table, her dark curls in a bun and a simple, long-sleeved black dress. I stand to give her a tight hug before I order our typical pitcher of mimosas, receiving yet another sideways glance. I'm being watched under a microscope. They want to see the grief unfold like I'm an animal at the zoo.

I glance up at the entrance each time I see movement, thinking Liddy would walk in anytime now. Emma follows the direction of my eyes and gives me a beaten smile.

"She's not coming, Rowan." She reaches across the table to

squeeze my hand.

"I know." I squeeze her hand back and notice the dark circles under her eyes conflicting with her olive skin. "How are you doing?"

"Not great, to be honest. This is all so sudden. I heard you were the one who found her? That must have been terrifying."

"It was; it still is. I can't get her out of my head. It was so bizarre, and I don't know how it happened. I went out with Travis, and I can't stop thinking what if I had just stayed home." My voice cracks, and I clear my throat while wiping the sweat from my palms down my legs.

"Travis? You can do so much better than that. There's something off with that guy." She tries to lighten the mood but it doesn't help.

"It was weird to say the least. I woke up on his couch Saturday morning-"

"Did he-"

"No, nothing happened. That's what's weird. He wasn't hungover, and I just got a bad feeling, so I ran out of there."

"I wouldn't mess around with him anymore," Emma states.

I nod my agreement, and the conversation dies when our pitcher is set on the table between us. She pours two champagne glasses to the top.

"To Liddy." She holds up her glass and I pick up mine, clinking it against hers and take a long sip.

"I'm going to say something, and please don't laugh in my face. It's been on my mind and I can't shake it. I think I need to say it out loud to hear how ridiculous it is…" I hold my breath and set the glass down.

"Of course."

"You know how I told you Liddy and I used to spend hours in the library looking up vampires? And you used to tell us all those stories."

Emma laughs, "With crazy Asta the librarian, of course." I brush off the laugh she gives me, my heart rate picking

up. I lower my voice, "When I found Liddy, there were two small incisions in her neck. I know you're going to tell me I'm crazy, but what else could that be?"

Something flashes in her eyes before she gives me a long empathetic look. "Rowan, there's no such thing as vampires, those were just stories. I think the grief is messing with your head."

"It feels like I'm missing something. There has to be something I'm not seeing, a reason for this." I let out a defeated breath.

"The thing you're missing is her murderer. Once they find who did this, you'll get that closure, I'm sure."

"You're probably right," I say to her, even though I don't feel it. I still feel there's more to the story that I'm missing.

The conversation turns lighter, and we recount our favorite moments with Liddy. Tears stream down our faces most of the brunch as we down glass after glass of mimosa until the pitcher empties.

The waitress returns to our table and I pay our check. "See you ladies next week." She gives us a forced smile.

We walk out onto the cobblestone road, dark clouds are moving in to hide the sun.

"Thank you for coming today. That was exactly what I

needed," Emma says and pulls me into a hug. "Are you sure you don't need a ride back home?"

"No, I'm okay. I could use some fresh air." She smiles and heads toward her car. I watch her drive away before I start walking through downtown.

I keep my head down looking at my boots, weaving through people making their way to lunch. I hear women gossiping about something Officer Perry told them. I bend down and pretend to adjust my boots so I can hear what they're saying.

"He said there was noise coming from the ranch. They're sending someone out there to check it. I think those boys are just partying. Harris is always stirring something up." Her friend laughs.

I stand and glance over my shoulder and our gaze meets. I give them a smile, trying to pretend I wasn't listening. Harris is always throwing parties that last until early morning; you can hear them all the way into town some nights. I wonder if they're trying to cheer Sylas up. I make a mental note to check on him. As close as we've gotten because of Liddy, we don't have a habit of texting each other, but it's strange he hasn't reached out.

The walk home gets the better of me. The cobblestone ends, and I start walking up the winding road lined with trees and fallen leaves. Walking uphill after drinking is not ideal, but I needed some time alone. We usually go to Liddy's after brunch since she lives downtown.

*Lived downtown.*

The way Emma brushed off my theory about vampires plays on repeat in my head. The rational part of me can't blame her;

vampires have been an urban legend our entire life, something made up to scare kids at summer camp. Still, I can't help but think what if? What if they're real and have been hiding in plain sight? What if a vampire killed my best friend? Pain squeezes tight at my ribs and my head starts to throb. I don't see the tree root in front of me before my boot catches, and I face plant into the damp leaves.

*Fuck.* I groan in pain.

I roll onto my back, spread my arms out wide, and just lay there. I watch the clouds pass by. There's not much traffic out today, and whoever sees me lying here hasn't bothered to stop. I lie here for a while taking in deep breaths of mountain air. I let the moisture from the forest floor soak into my clothes until I'm damp and cold.

My phone beeps, shaking me from the daydream I was in. I lift it above my face and see a message from Travis.

*I heard about Liddy, I'm so sorry. Do you need anything?*

Do I need anything? Fuck him. I close the message and shove my phone into my purse.

The buzz from the mimosas has worn off enough that I can make it back up the hill to my house.

Tomorrow, I go back to work at the news station. I can already feel their eyes on me, the pity covered as empathy and self-serving need for any details they could use for their front-page articles. I won't tell them a thing. I need to make a plan, though. I should be able to use the news database to search through past articles. I've had a weird feeling building in my gut after seeing Liddy. The details from my parents' deaths swirl in my mind and I start to wonder if they really died from the fire or if it was all a cover-up. There has to be someone who's reported on my parent's death. Maybe even find out what happened to the man at the fair.

No one can stop me from looking this time. I didn't have the tools to figure out what happened to my parents then, but I do now.

# Chapter Three

## SYLAS

My vision blurs and my eyelids feel heavy. I open them enough to see my brothers asleep before the weight crashes over me again.

*Liddy brushes my cheek with the back of her hand and smooths down my beard. I remember this day like it was yesterday.*

*"Tell me again how much you love me." Her smile lights up her face.*

*"This much." I stretch my arms out wide before scooping her up into my lap. Giggles bubble out of her, and I scratch my beard into the hollow of her neck. It only makes her laugh more.*

*"I can't stand being here when you guys are like this," Rowan chimes in from Liddy's kitchen.*

*"Would a group hug make you feel better?" Liddy laughs, but I know she's serious.*

*"Absolutely not." Rowan rolls her eyes and returns to cooking. Liddy stands from her spot on the couch to help her in the kitchen.*

*I look over my shoulder to watch them. I really do love that woman, but something deep in my gut tells me it's not what I'm meant to have. I push the feeling away knowing how incredible she* is. She has a whole life planned for us at the ranch—a whole world she has built up with me in the picture. Sometimes, she would tell me about our ten kids, 5 boys and 5 girls, who would all have a job on the ranch. I never saw myself having more than two, if I had any at all. Before Liddy, kids seemed like a reach.

Rowan interrupts my train of thought when she sets dinner on the couch between us. "Your favorite." She raises her eyebrows at me. "Creamy chicken with mashed potatoes and green beans."

"You make it best," I say to her letting my stare linger on her green eyes. She quickly turns away and grabs the TV remote. "Buffy again?" I don't mean to sound so defeated.

"Obviously!" Liddy hops onto the couch next to me with her plate.

"It would be such a shame if vampires were real and they were this ugly." Rowan laughs at her own joke, and Liddy hums her agreement.

I glance at Rowan eating peacefully on the couch, watching an episode I know she has seen at least three times. She hides behind her plate right before Buffy leaps into action, even though she knows it's coming every time. She sets her plate down and tucks her hair behind her ears, and a strand falls free.

I feel my hand reach out to tuck the missing piece behind her ear, but I can't move. My hands burn, and I scream out in pain. I force my eyes open enough to see my brothers still sleeping, but I can't tell where. My head feels heavy before it falls to my shoulders.

"Rowan," I call out, unsure if it leaves my mouth. "Rowan."

Harris turns up the speaker, blasting house music, making it impossible to have a conversation. His friends are dancing to the *beat in the living room, and on the couch next to them, couples are on top of each other, tongues down each other's throats.*

*"Does it really need to be this loud?" I shout into Harris' ear.*

*"It's a party. Loosen up, bro." He turns and dances away clearly ending the conversation.*

*Harris is taller and older than most of the people here. He's the oldest of the three of us but doesn't always act like it. I like to compare him to a Viking—all muscle, an unruly beard, and rowdy. That could also describe the cowboys out here. He does a lot of the ranch work, so I don't blame him for letting loose like this.*

*The music blasts against my building headache. I walk down the hall to retreat to my room, pushing people out of the way. The hall is filled with people holding red cups and whispering in each other's ears. A line forms outside the bathroom, and I quickly move past them. I spot Rowan on the other side of the hallway, talking to a guy I know is bad news. I move to go around them, but out of the corner of my eye, I see her shove at his chest.*

*"Get off me, Brandon!"*

*I turn to face them, and Brandon gives me a sideways look that tells me to mind my own business. I won't be doing that at all.*

*"Hey man, she told you to get off her." I get in his space.*

*"She came here with me tonight, so how about you go find your girlfriend, Sylas?" he chuckles and turns back to Rowan.*

*"Get out of my house. Now." I put my arm across Rowan's chest to move her out of the way, and this fucker just moves closer. He smells like cheap vodka and cigarettes. He reaches for her hand, but there's no way I'm letting her leave with him.*

*"I asked you nicely already. You're getting the fuck out." I grab the collar of his shirt in one hand and swing my other fist hard into*

*his jaw. He drops to the floor, and the crowd around him quickly backs away. Shouts of confusion fill my ears, but I ignore them. I pick up his limp body from the floor and drag him to the front, where he comes to, and I push him onto the porch.*

*"It'll be a lot worse next time. Don't come back," I spit at him, and he stumbles back before running to his car.*

*"Sylas, you good?" Harris says to me, but I brush him off with a wave and head to Rowan.*

*"Thanks. Is he gone?" Her face is etched with pain.*

*"Yeah, he's gone. What were you thinking, coming here with that piece of shit?"*

*"I had no idea he was going to try something like that."*

*"You weren't thinking." I rub my hand through my beard and let out a sigh. "I'll take you home. Liddy can help you get your car tomorrow."*

*We step out of the house into the damp summer air and walk toward my truck. I open the door for her and make sure she's in before rounding the front and starting the engine.*

*I look up from buckling my seatbelt and see the short denim shorts she decided to wear tonight. They barely cover her thighs, and her waist is left bare under a cutoff t-shirt. My stare lingers too long; she clears her throat, and I straighten, looking through the windshield now.*

*"Ready?"*

My head bobs from where it's laid against my shoulder. This time, I can't sit up, my eyelids too heavy to open. Pain wracks my muscles, and my vision spins behind the darkness in my mind.

"Rowan."

# Chapter Four

## ROWAN

*I TOSS AND TURN IN BED, TRYING TO GET THIS NIGHTMARE OUT OF MY HEAD. Someone rushes towards me, and I can't fight them off. I run as fast as I can out of town. My feet are pounding against the asphalt, pain shooting through my knees. I don't stop until I reach the Loughty Ranch. I can hear my heart beating in the dead silence. The full moon shines high above, reflecting off the wet grass and obscuring shadows around me. Muffled voices call my name, but I can't tell where they're coming from. I take slow steps along the fence line, inching closer to the direction of the voices. They repeat my name over and over while I move toward the sound.*

My alarm blares from the clock next to me, I swing my arm to hit the snooze button.

Monday comes quickly. A groan escapes me, and my head pounds like I was hit with a brick. Sunday's bad decision has come back to bite me in the ass. I don't feel completely ready to go to work. It has only been two days since I lost my lifeline. I don't have enough sick leave to take the day off, though, and I want to look into the old news articles at the station. Grief and determination are at war in my mind.

I dab concealer under my eyes to hide the dark circles tainting my face. I wash and blow dry my bangs before combing out the rest of my hair. Its waves sit past my shoulders. I wish the frizz would take it down a notch, but I never have gotten what I wished for.

Closing my eyes, I breathe in deep and slowly exhale. The window is rimmed with fog, and the peaks of the mountains are littered with snow while the terrain closer to us remains bright in fall colors.

I look down at my outfit: black jeans and my starry night boots, plus a black cowl neck sweater—good enough for work and the funeral I'm heading to afterward. I tug the neck of my sweater, trying to get a little breathing room. I grab my khaki coat and work bag and lock up the house. I didn't have coffee before leaving, so I'll have to suffer through the coffee in the office breakroom today.

I take my time driving into town, going in and out of focus, letting my mind wander. I'm not sure how much work will get done today; they probably don't even expect me to show up. I know my boss, Sam, would cover if I called out, but the higher-ups are such pompous assholes. They don't care about family emergencies. It's the one place in this cozy town that doesn't fit the "everyone is a family" charm.

The office is warm and bustling. The morning news was just completed, and everyone is taking a break before jumping into the dull afternoon work. I get sideways glances as I walk to my desk, some smiles only upturning halfway. The pain in their eyes is enough to know what everyone's thinking.

*What is she doing here?*

*What happened?*

I drop my bag at my desk in the sea of cubicles and move toward the breakroom near the back of the office. I need a large mug of coffee to get through the awkward conversations today.

Sam meets me as I pour my cup. Her silky red hair sweeps towards her ribs. Two small buns sit atop her head on either side, her signature look. She's effortless if ever it needed a definition. She hasn't aged a day since I started working here, and I've never seen bags under her eyes, despite how long her hours are.

"Hey, how are you doing? I didn't expect you to come in today. I kind of gave your work away to James and Sue," she says with a shrug. It's in my favor that she passed my work along. It will give me more time to dig around without looking incompetent.

"Yeah, I don't know. I guess I just needed normalcy today, but I can see I won't be getting that." I sigh, eyes searching the room beyond.

"Take it easy today. I'll slide work your way as it comes in." Her sweet smile puts me at ease, and her hand brushes my elbow.

The coffee burns my tongue as I take shallow sips from the mug. I'm mustering up the courage to walk back to my desk. I feel spacey and out of touch today. My vision is blurry on the edges, almost as if the events of the last 2 days never happened, and I'm having an off day. I need to get myself in check and stay focused on why I'm here—to get information.

I take a deep breath and straighten my spine. I lift my chin enough to fake confidence and walk out of the breakroom.

I pretend to be on a mission, on an assignment. I cool my expression and hastily walk past my desk and through the doors to the back storage room.

There are boxes of newspapers labeled by month and year. Anything that hasn't been transferred to the computers will be in these boxes. I never can find anything online about my parents' death, just their obituary and "tragic events in Georgetown."

It's almost an insult; they were so beloved here.

I set my coffee on the small table inside the room. I shift through the boxes, trying to find what I'm looking for. The boxes are all covered in dust and feel sticky on my hands. It makes me cough, and I have to wrap the neck of my sweater around my face to cover my mouth and nose. It has been 15 years since their death, so I have to search for what I need. It takes a few minutes, but I spot it—August 1990.

It only takes me a moment to drag the box from its spot on the shelf. It doesn't weigh much, and I can't decide whether to take it as a good or bad sign. This box doesn't seem to have as much dust as the rest. I wipe what remains of it away with my sleeve. A poor choice, considering I'm in black. I try to shake it off my sweater, but it stays.

After staring at the box wondering what I'll find, I open the lid. The cardboard scrapes as I toss it aside. The contents are worn but look untouched—except for one paper. I pull the newspaper from the box and read the headline.

*"Bodies drained of blood ruled as death by house fire"*

My body freezes, and my heart rate picks up. I shake my head to clear away the shock. I continue to read the article.

"*The bodies of Georgetown residents Robert and Laney Watson were found outside the steps of a vacation rental in Rose Creek. When I went to check the scene, their bodies seemed to have been drained of all blood and mangled at the neck. The police were called when other residents saw the cabin on fire. Police have ruled this death by a house fire. The case has been closed as fast as it opened. I had the chance to see the bodies up close; they looked pale and lifeless, their eyes were sunken in. I've asked for comments from the Rose Creek station as to why they've ruled this as fire and accidental. They've declined to comment at this time.*"

My hands shake, and the paper bows under my grip. This is outrageous. No one in their right mind would read this and think it's an acceptable ruling. They couldn't have died in a house fire without being in the house, and smoke inhalation isn't going to drain them of their blood. I remember the officers telling the Thomases they had been mauled by animals. Was that all a lie so they wouldn't have to show us their bodies?

The description of their bodies makes my stomach turn. Liddy only had two small punctures to her neck. She looked pale and weightless.

I want to know who else has been reading this paper. The edges where my hands hold it are worn. Voices grow louder outside the door. I have to leave before someone finds me; it's above my pay grade to be in here. I shove the paper under my arm and put the lid back on the box, moving it to the back of the shelf and fixing everything back in place.

I pick up my coffee and peek around the door before taking long strides back to my desk.

I take note of the name of the journalist in this article.

I might be able to contact her if she's still around. I slide the paper into my bag and start searching the journalist database for Marie Stellar. Marie saw the crime scene, and hopefully, she doesn't write me off like everyone else.

Her name comes up in my search, and there's a phone number for her line at the station she's at. I slouch down in my chair and dial the number. I glance around to see if anyone is looking and deem it safe.

The line rings twice before someone picks up.

"Hello?"

"Hi, is this Marie Stellar?" I try not to whisper, but it's coming out breathy.

"Yes... Who is this?"

"My name is Rowan Watson. I saw an article you did on my parents 15 years back. August 16, 1990. It was Robert and Laney Watson." The line goes silent for a long moment. "I know it's been a while since you did the piece, so I understand if you don't remember."

"Uh, yes. Yes, I wrote that article. Listen, that piece gave me a lot of negative backlash, and I won't speak on it. My deepest condolences," she whispers.

The dial tone hums in my ear, telling me she hung up.

I can feel the pain in my chest before my body recognizes the heartbreak, the breaking point I've hit. A guttural scream gets trapped in my throat. I choke. The phone falls out of my hand and I throw my hands over my head. My shoulders are shaking with silent sobs. This was the only lead I've had in years, and it was just another person telling me to give up.

Someone must have heard me, because Sam comes over

and places a hand on my back.

"Rowan, what's going on?" she says with knowing concern.

"God, sorry. This is so unprofessional." I wipe my eyes with the sleeve on my sweater.

Sam's eyes go to the dust littering my sleeve.

"Where did all that dust come from? Did you go into the storage room today?" Her eyebrows pinch together. Her concern turns to anger.

I'm going to throw up. If I tell her the truth, I'll get fired, but if I lie, she'll see right through it and fire me anyway. I go for the latter.

"No, I'm just a mess today. I'm sorry, I'll pull myself together. There won't be any more trouble today, I promise." I sniff and straighten myself.

"Okay, just let me know-" She pauses and looks down.

"Rowan, seriously? Is that a paper from the storage room you claim you didn't go into?" Her face is turning a light shade of red, and something flickers in her eyes. It's not a good look on her. I've seen her mad, and I don't want to be on the receiving end right now.

"Fuck," I mutter under my breath.

She pulls it out and inspects it. Her grip falls right to the worn patches, and she barely has to look at it to know what article this is.

"I get it. I get it, Rowan. But Jesus, you can't be doing this. And you lied to me." She takes a deep inhale. "You need to gather your things and head home."

"Are you firing me?" I look up at her through my lashes, trying not to show the wobble in my lower lip.

"I don't know yet. I need time to think and you need time to get yourself together. Take a few weeks off. I'll deal with upper management," she says sternly.

"Okay." I sound so weak. I hate that I'm just folding right now. Is it not my right to know? They were my parents.

I gather my things and stand to walk out. I look around the room, and everyone suddenly becomes very interested in their work. I know they're loving this drama. Workplace drama in the newsroom that doesn't pertain to themselves is like heroin to these people.

I walk shamefully through the sea of cubicles, ignoring the slighted looks, and walk straight out the doors. I slam my trunk closed and get into my car, putting my keys into the ignition. The cold bites at me, but I don't start it yet. I need time to think, and this is the best place to do it.

I try to think of a plan, but I'm just brought back to my childhood. I'm brought back to Liddy's parents, refusing to give me information on my parent's death. I tried to go to them with my questions, but they told me it was too late now, and the case had been closed, that there's no use in digging around for something I couldn't control. I didn't like this answer or understand why no one could give me the closure I so desperately needed.

I'm sure it was a lot, to take on a grieving child as they processed their own grief over losing friends. When you're a child, everything that happens to you or goes on around you shapes you in some way, and you place blame where blame shouldn't go. As I've grown older, I can see the distance that The Thomases had toward me was their way of grieving and handling the delicate situation. No one is perfect, and I'm sure this wasn't in the parenting book they read in the delivery room.

Growth and healing have a way of mending the soul back together and stitching the foggy pieces back into place. The memories flood back, and the feelings are another thing for me to overcome right now.

I grip the steering wheel and scream as loud as I can. I feel tears slowly falling down my cheeks. I reach my tongue out and grab the one falling past my mouth. The liquid is salty in my mouth.

*Okay, what are you going to do, Rowan? You have no one. You need to do something.*

*You need to do something.*

I turn my key to start the car and drive towards Liddy's house.

When I get to her street, I park my car down the block and walk the rest of the way. There's yellow tape around her front porch and covering the door. I still have the key to her back door, so I go through the gate that leads to the backyard.

The grass is slippery against my boots, and I almost trip going up the first step.

I unlock the back door and step inside, removing my boots so I don't track footprints inside. Everything is exactly how we left it, but the air in here feels thinner. I can feel my heartbeat in my throat and my skin growing warm.

I step lightly around the house, looking for any sign of something out of place. I left here in such a hurry after I found her, I didn't get the chance to look at anything.

I search her bedroom, the bathroom, and even the kitchen. Nothing is out of place. I glance in the dining room, and one of the chairs is barely pulled out.

I round on the chair, and my hand moves to cover my mouth.

I pick up Sylas' hat, and complete disbelief runs through me.

*No, it couldn't be you.*

I don't know him as well as Liddy did, but I trust her judgment more than I trust my own. Liddy was a good person, and she didn't settle. I know Sylas had a good head on his shoulders. How could he have done this? I still don't think I completely believe it was him.

I slide the hat onto my head and make my way back out the gate, leaving her key under the back mat. I have to confront him.

I turn into the cemetery and put my car in park. Sylas' hat still sits on my head. I take it off and set it on the passenger seat. I can see everyone arriving hand-in-hand, dressed in black. I take a deep breath in; I haven't been here since August, when I brought flowers to my parents' grave. I come every year on their anniversary date to celebrate their life instead of their death.

I stare out at the sea of graves and the people walking by holding flowers. I'm not ready to have another person to visit here.

My boots hit the gravel parking lot as I step out of the car. The crunch of the rocks under my feet is loud enough to cover the sounds of muffled chatter. The closer I get to the funeral, the more people I see huddled together. The whole town will be showing up for Liddy.

The talk quiets down, and Father Rice starts the eulogy before Liddy's parents stand to talk. A few others recount their memories of Liddy, but I don't have it in me to speak in front of everyone. After they say their piece, we're invited to the Thomas' house for the reception. I look around the crowd trying to find Sylas, but I don't see him. I walk towards the parking lot and look for his truck, but it's not there. He didn't come to her funeral. That only makes me think he's guilty, the one who took her life. I'd hoped I was wrong when I found his hat there, like it was a crazy coincidence and he just left it there one night. I guess I don't know him as well as I thought.

If he killed her, does that make him a vampire? Saying those words even in my head make me feel like I'm losing my mind.

# *Chapter Five*

## ROWAN

I slow to a stop at the gate of the Loughty Ranch, a large metal archway that is starting to rust. You usually can't get onto the ranch without a code, but the gate is hanging slightly open. I step closer and realize it has been forced open. My heart skips a beat thinking of who could have done this. Sucking in a breath, I take my chances and slide through the open gate. Doing this at 26 is vastly different from shenanigans like this as a teen. My rationality is screaming at me to turn the other way instead of itching to snoop around.

I'm almost through the gate when a sharp piece of metal snags on my sweater. I pull hard at the fabric, and it snaps free, but not before I trip over myself and fall on my ass. I brush the leaves from my clothing and replace Sylas' hat on my head and start toward the ranch.

The winding road that leads to the house is a surreal downhill slope. The sides of the driveway are lined with a wooden fence for the cattle. The ranch sits in the valley, green hills sprawling into the tree lines. It's an old-style Victorian farmhouse, painted a muted shade of mint and trimmed in white. It's a sight that makes me melt.

I try to remind myself why I'm here.

I finally make it to the front porch and knock. No one answers. I knock again and peek inside the window. I don't see anyone inside, so I try the door, and it opens.

"Is anyone here?" My voice echoes; it's dead quiet. I set Sylas' hat on the kitchen island and head around back to see if they're out working. Sylas and his brothers, Harris and Noah, all work on the ranch late into the evening.

I hear a sound come from the barn that sits behind the ranch house and walk toward it. I quickly notice the sound of chains banging against the ground. They get louder the closer I get.

The hinges of the barn door creak as I open it. There's blood splattered on the worn wooden floors. I see hay and debris kicked around like there was a fight. I hear a groan and chains smashing to the floor. I look up and see three sets of boots, three figures slumped to the ground and chained to the posts. My mouth falls open when I realize it's the Loughty brothers.

"Row-" Sylas groans my way.

I'm almost too stunned to process that he's speaking to me. There has been something new every day—things I never thought I'd witness, things I never thought could happen. Adrenaline races through my body like a speed train and my hands start to shake. I shift my eyes, scanning the three of them, and see blood staining their skin.

"What the fuck is going on?" I finally manage, running up to Sylas and inspecting him. His dark blond hair falls across his brows in a tangled mess. They look half-dead. Their bodies are sagging and pale.

"How long have you been here?"

He looks up at me, his brown eyes now a mesmerizing shade of bright gold.

"Three days," he coughs out.

Three days… "You've been here since Friday night?"

"Rowan, can you just get us out?" Harris yells out in pain.

"Yeah, yes. Let me think." My eyes search the chains wrapped around Sylas' hands. They don't look locked.

A painful groan comes out of Sylas. I look at his hands; they're chained around the beam, burns lining his large hands and scars wrapping around his wrists.

"The chains, they burn." His teeth show as he grits them, and I see a glimpse of sharp canines. The shiny silver metal of the chains moves with his pain, clashing with the barn floor.

I reach down and gently rub the pads of my fingers over the chain, only to feel cool metal. I grasp the chain in my hand, and it doesn't burn. Sylas cries out in pain as they shift on his wrists. I lift them carefully, and the burns quickly fade from his skin. I rub my eye with my free hand, wondering if this is real or delusion. The marks continue to fade the more I unwrap him.

I quickly untie the remaining chains from his body. He tries to get up on his own, but he's too weak, his legs shaking under the weight. I take his arm over my shoulder and lift him, using all my strength to keep him upright. He sags into me, his mouth hovering over my neck.

I feel a pinch and jerk my body back. There's a warm feeling moving down my neck, the sticky liquid flowing down my chest. I see Sylas' gaze, and I look down to see blood beaming against my skin. His tongue sweeps out to lick the blood from his lower lip.

"Did you just bite me?" I wipe my neck and look at the blood on my fingers. I put my hand back to my neck and feel two small incisions. "Wha- what is going on?" I try to step back, but I'm frozen in place, my legs rigid with panic.

He doesn't acknowledge me. He moves his mouth towards the flow of blood dripping down my breast. A warmth takes over my chest as he reaches his tongue out and licks the trail of blood back to my neck. His lips wrap around the incision, and he sucks hard. A small moan leaves my mouth, and I push him back, suddenly processing what's happening.

My eyes are wide as I take him in, his mouth covered in my blood. My breathing turns quick and shallow.

*Vampire.*

"Rowan-" he grunts out.

I take a step back, turning to run out. He steps toward me so fast now and grips my wrist.

"Let me go!" I tug my arm away, but it doesn't budge. I know he's strong, but this is different.

"I don't know what's going on with me. Please, I'm sorry." His golden eyes look through to my soul. "Where's Liddy? Is she with you?"

I take a slow step back, trying to put distance between us. "Liddy was murdered."

His jaw tightens, and stark red veins take over the whites of his eyes as they turn blood red. It's enough to tell me to watch out. I take another step back and then another, getting closer to the barn doors. I hear Harris and Noah begging me to untie them, but my focus is on Sylas. I don't know what he's capable of or who this version of him is. I've only seen vampires on TV and read folklore about these not-so-made-up beings. He could be stronger and faster than me, with a blood lust so strong that he bleeds me dry. My legs beg me to run, my head screaming at the instinct to flee. The man I knew has turned into a monster.

The anger I see on his face reads death. He sniffs, rubbing his beard, and starts for the side of the barn. While he's distracted, I look around the floor for anything to use as a weapon. I pick up a splintered piece of wood and back towards the barn entrance. If there's anything I've learned about vampires, it's that a stake through the heart can kill them. Sweat races down my spine at the thought of driving this through his chest, but I'll do what I must to survive. A vampire killed my best friend, and I'll be damned if they kill me too.

Sylas comes around the corner of the barn wielding an axe, and my body tenses. He strides toward me, and I lift the piece of wood in my unsteady hands. Our eyes meet under his furrowed brows, and at the last moment, he turns towards Harris, swinging at the chain until it breaks, the head of the axe detaching and narrowly missing me as I quickly duck out of the way.

Harris stands on unsteady legs and looks toward me. I don't take another moment to consider my actions as I turn and run from the barn. I need to put as much distance between us before they regain their strength and I have three vampires after me. I grip the wood tightly in my hand and run as fast as

I can toward my car. The sun has set, and darkness consumes the ranch. My knees ache from the impact, my boots sliding in the wet grass. Footsteps sound behind me, getting closer and closer. Sweat beads at my temples while the cold wind numbs my face. Whoever is chasing me sounds like they're right on my heels. My boot slips out from under me, and I land hard on my shoulder, rolling onto my back and gasping at the pain.

The edges of my vision turn dark, my eyes straining to adjust to the darkness. Long, dark hair hovers above me. I feel his body press into mine.

"Harris, plea-" My words are cut off as his teeth sink deep into my neck. My vision blurs, darkness wavering in and out of sight. I gasp for air and reach for him, but I'm too weak to move. I'm losing blood too fast. I try to hold on to the life that's slipping away from me.

My eyes shoot open, and I sit up, taking in a gasping breath. I'm in a bed that's not my own. The blankets are warm and inviting—a plush comforter and down pillows. The room is dark, and I can see the moon outside the window past long maroon curtains. The room is welcoming and has an old-school feel, vintage with a modern flair. The large brown dresser is littered with lit candles and a mirror.

I must be in the Loughty house. An uneasy feeling fills my gut as I remember how I ended up here. I touch my neck, prominent bite marks taking up space down its length. I gently trace the punctures, the area around them sore.

I slip out of bed, stepping lightly on my feet so they don't hear me. The floorboard creaks under my weight, and I freeze. There's no way they could have heard that, but I don't trust what I know to be true right now. I keep coming up wrong. When nothing comes of the sound, I continue my steps to the dresser mirror. I tilt my head and wince at the black and purple splotches covering my neck. The bites haven't healed at all. I need to get out of here before they get their hands on me again.

I step lightly towards the bedroom door and open it to peek out around the frame. I can hear them talking in the main room but can't make out what they're saying.

I breathe in and out. In and out. I straighten myself, suddenly aware of the blood crusted over my chest and in my hair. I walk into the main room towards the front door, and the three of them whip over to look at me. No one says anything for a moment. The tension is so thick, I can barely wade through it.

Harris gives me a sinister smile, and my blood goes cold.

I open my mouth to say something. I haven't decided what yet, but I'm cut off by Noah.

"Well, let me make you something to eat. Do you like eggs? Maybe you should get showered first," he says, way too chipper.

"Are we not talking about what happened tonight?" I'm so confused by this attempt to cover up the disaster of almost killing me.

"Tonight? You've been out for days," Noah calls over his shoulder.

"Wh- How many- What day is it?" My mind spins; has no one come to look for me? My heart drops into my stomach. I don't have anyone who would come looking for me.

"It's Thursday, so you've been out for almost four days." That's when I turn to see Sylas sulking in the far corner.

How could I have been asleep for that long? My hand runs across the bruises on my neck, and I wonder what the hell they did to me. They could have left me at the front steps of the hospital, but they kept me here. I can only begin to wonder why.

"Get showered, Rowan. You stink of blood, and I don't want us snapping to get a taste of you again," Harris says with dead certainty.

"There's some of Liddy's clothes in the room you slept in," Sylas says, looking away from me. I nod in acknowledgment. My palms sweat, and I slowly walk down the hall, searching for the bathroom. I'll play it safe for now until I can get out of here.

The bathroom is large enough to have a standing shower and a separate bathtub. The tile is cold on my feet, but the steam billowing out of the shower begs to change that for me. I step in, and the warm water stings my skin until it's a soothing temperature. My flesh turns bright pink as I scrub away the blood. I lean my head back and let the water wash over my face.

A noise comes from outside the door, and I wipe the glass shower door clear of fog. I don't see anyone at the door but decide it's time to get out. I reach for the faucet knob, but I'm suddenly jerked back by my hair. My back slams into something hard, and a hand wraps around my mouth.

"Hello, Rowan. So nice to see you again." Hot breath on my neck makes my skin crawl.

The man tilts my head back, allowing me to see his face.

My eyes go wide, pleading. I'm panting into his hand. I knew there was something off about Travis.

"I should have turned you when I had you passed out on my couch. I knew a whore like you would come straight home to me. Such a weak girl; you ran off like I'd done something to you, but I could have made it so much worse." He presses a sharp knife into my chest. In the mirror, I see him admiring the bites along the curve of my neck. "I don't want you dead, Rowan. I just wanted you alone. I can give you a *real* life, one to live with me. You'll thank me later."

He licks the side of my neck, and I struggle against his hand, trying to break myself free from his grip.

"Now, don't scream when I remove my hand." He says it as if I'm going to listen.

He removes his hand and slashes across his palm with the small knife.

I scream as loud as I can and turn to run out of the bathroom, still naked and wet. My feet begin to slip, but Travis catches me and shoves his bloody palm into my mouth.

His blood spills onto my tongue, and the sharp bite of iron makes me gag. I'm trying to breathe, trying not to let his blood go down my throat, but I gasp in breath after breath, drinking down his blood. I struggle against his body, making the blood smear across my face. The smell of iron clouds my senses.

The door to the bathroom shatters open, and Sylas stands swallowing the doorway. I see him take in the scene before him and rush Travis. Travis loses his grip on me, and I run out of the bathroom. I turn back to look at them, only to see Sylas stab a wooden stake into Travis' chest. Blood bubbles out of his mouth and his arms drop, limp.

Sylas looks at me, showing his teeth. "Get cleaned up."

I turn to grab a towel and scream out in pain before dropping to my knees. My hand flies to my throat as I gasp for the air rushing from my lungs. Burning pain shoots through my body, filling my lungs and veins with fire.

Sylas mutters obscenities behind me, and I try to focus on his words—try to ground myself in the familiar. I reach up to grip the counter tightly, gaining the ability to use my limbs again.

The blood on my face smells inviting, and I'm hungry. I wipe it from my face with a single finger and suck it into my mouth. I close my eyes and let out a blissful moan, humming as I lick more from my lips.

My body starts to flow with cool electricity. I can breathe deeper now, can smell the blood pumping out of Travis's dying body. I can smell the heat coming from Sylas. I can hear Noah and Harris behind me.

I open my eyes to see Sylas' gaze still trained on me. He's rigid, and his mouth parts when he looks into my eyes. I turn to look in the mirror, the blood a stark red against my pale skin. I meet my own eyes and see gold staring back at me.

# Chapter Six

## ROWAN

I'm finally able to dress myself in some of Liddy's old clothes. I move the curtains to peer out the window; the sun is starting to come up now over the hills. The frost on the trees reflects brightly into my eyes, stinging them slightly. I feel new, whole and untouchable. My brain is rewired and my muscles are stronger. The feeling I once knew as anguish deepens, and the lust for revenge runs through my veins.

My head begins to clear up, the thoughts running rampant and curiosity taking hold. I don't understand how I was turned—was it just from drinking vampire blood, or was it because I was bitten? Travis was the one who forced this on me, but Sylas and Harris are just as guilty. As if I already didn't know what to do with my life, the confusion lingers stronger than ever.

I don't know who I am now.

The reality of losing Liddy only days ago hits me like a bus, and cries start bubbling out of me. I can't believe I have to do this alone. She would have known what to do in this situation, made smarter choices.

That thought starts a fire inside me. I've turned into the same monster that killed my best friend—the same monster I dreamed of becoming when I thought it wasn't possible.

I think back to the times I spent in the library combing through all the vampire folklore I could find and reading endlessly about the paranormal world. The thought of being immortal drew me in so heavily. I wanted endless time to become who I wanted to be and the strength that came with it. To be unstoppable, untouchable, to give me all the time in the world to find where I belong. I've been given that blessing now, but it feels like a curse—to become the one thing that took away so many people I love.

I step away from the window and wipe at the tears lining my eyes. I will honor my parents and best friend by doing the exact thing this body was made for—killing anyone who had a hand in their murder.

A new sense of hunger fills my gut as I realize I need to eat.

Muffled sounds come from the main room, and then the sound of the front door shutting follows. I move to the window and look out to see the sheriff walking back to his car and taking off. How Harris hid what he was is beyond me. I'm just glad he's gone. Thoughts of how he might taste flit through my mind.

I leave the room and walk down the hallway toward the kitchen. The hallway is painted a deep shade of gray, and family photos coated in dust line the walls. There are photos of the boys with their mom; Liddy told me she took off when they were still young. I understand what it's like to lose a parent but not how it feels to be abandoned by one. I let my eyes wander over the other frames until I step into the kitchen. Travis' body has been moved to the large, worn, oak table, his arms hanging limply off the edge. I look up to see Harris leaning over the body with his teeth deep in Travis' neck. His hair is tied in a bun, and a black t-shirt stretches over his large arms. I walk around the table, inspecting the body and watching Harris drain the blood from him. Knowing we're the same creature now eases me around him, but not enough to keep my guard down. My body begs me to bite into the body laid out in front of me.

"Can we drink vampire blood?" I ask, never taking my eyes off where his mouth meets Travis' neck. My hands fidget at my sides.

"It doesn't taste as good as you did, but I'm not dead yet. I think it's as good as any."

His comment makes my skin crawl.

He raises his head and nods—inky red blood stains his dark mustache and long beard, a silent offer for me to drink from the lifeless body on the table.

The smell makes me feel feral, and my pulse speeds up thinking about taking a drink, but I don't accept the offer.

"Tell me what's going on."

He lifts his head and wipes the blood from his mouth. "I– all I know is that I'm starving and my feelings... I can't control them. I know it's only been over a week but–" He trails off.

"Is that why you attacked me?" I grit my teeth, reliving the moment of being chased down. The anger simmers just below my skin, ready to tear him apart.

He takes a step back. "Rowan, I wouldn't have done that if

I had any control. I was so hungry, it's all I could think about."

I look at the plea in his eyes and back down at the pale body in front of him. I lick my lips, thinking of how he might taste.

"You don't touch me again."

"I won't, I swear." He extends his hand, and I shake it, our skin cool to the touch, before my eyes dart back to Travis.

I lift one of his arms and sink my teeth into a fleshy wrist for the first time. The liquid warms over my tongue, it's euphoric. Life is being pumped into my veins. My vision is growing sharper the more I drink. I can feel the same buzz under my skin as when I turned.

Blood gives us life.

Blood gives us power.

I smile with my mouth still on Travis' wrists. Harris returns a devilish grin and finishes his meal.

I hear Sylas' boots before I see him enter the room. "Are you guys done eye-fucking? We need to figure out what to do with the body." He grits out.

My spine straightens, and I wipe the blood from my lips. "B-Burn it." I grip the edge of the table. "We need to burn it." Saying it out loud makes me nauseous.

Sylas' brows knit together. "How would you know that?"

"Asta, from the library. I would go there to read about vampires, and she would tell me these pieces of information. I thought she was crazy or messing with me but…" My eyes shift around the room. "She said you have to burn them to kill its soul or something." I shift on my feet.

"Fuck it, it's worth a try," Harris says.

"As long as it gets this rotting corpse off my damned kitchen table." Sylas lets out a breath.

Harris looks between us, wiping the blood from his facial hair onto his t-shirt. "I'll take him out back." He lifts the body over his shoulder like it's nothing. The hollow form is draping over his lean back.

"You're going to want a hat." Sylas tosses me a black Stetson.

I settle the hat onto my head. It's a perfect fit. "I know I look great, but why do I need to wear this?"

"Sun," he said pointedly, "It doesn't kill us, but it will burn your eyes if you're exposed too long. Learned the hard way." He leaves it at that and follows Harris outside.

We step off the back porch, and the body makes a thud as he tosses it onto a pile of wood, ready for a bonfire.

"We'll light it tonight. I don't want anyone getting suspicious and coming over here during the day." Sylas is all business. He could use the stick in his ass being yanked out.

My leg bounces, and I start to feel restless. I feel renewed and strong after eating, my body pulsing with energy. I rub my neck at the base and blow out a breath. I still have so many questions to ask, so much on my mind, looking for answers they probably don't have either. I have to remind myself that they are going through this for the first time just as much as I am. I try to lighten the mood and remind myself of the perks of being a vampire. If there's one thing I need to know before casting my energy on finding these killers, it's what my body is capable of.

"Should we see what these bodies can do?" I turn up the

corner of my mouth, biting my bottom lip. I do my best to sound confident. "We're supposed to be faster and stronger than ever. I'd like to believe there's more to this than killing."

Before they can respond to me, Noah rides up on the back of a chestnut mare. I cross my arms and lace my face with a big grin. "Want to see if I can run faster than you on horseback?" I challenge.

Noah looks up from underneath his hat. His short-cropped hair is barely visible underneath his Stetson. His clean-shaven face makes him look so much younger than he is. "You're on, vamp girl!"

I give him a smirk and race off. He's fast, and it takes me a minute to get in tune with my legs. The muscles stretch and move fluidly. I would have been out of breath by now, but the air smoothly fills my lungs naturally. All that time I spent obsessing over a fantasy is paying off. My calves burn with the desire to move, and I pick up speed. I direct all my power into putting my feet on the ground—I catch up to him fast.

I can't think of a time I've felt freer. The wind whips my hair back, and I brush my bangs from my face. The air isn't as cold as a vampire, but it nips my nose. I gain on Noah and stick my tongue out at him as I run past.

He lets out a playful laugh before easing up and telling me to hop on. I slow down and walk to his mare. I let her smell my hand before petting her nose slowly. Her silky coat shines through the sun peeking out above the trees.

My boot grips the top of the stirrup, and I swing my body over the saddle, placing myself in front of Noah. His arms wrap around me, holding the reins at my side. He starts us into a slow walk towards the tree line at the edge of the fields that move into the mountains.

"I'm scared, Rowan." Noah lets out a sigh.

"Me too." I can't quite put it into words how I feel right now, so I give Noah room to speak. "What is it like for you?"

"I can feel everything. The blood pulsing through your veins, every bad thought I've ever had has been rushing toward me. Sitting in that barn was torture. I would have ended it all there if I could have."

I turn to look at him, but his gaze is cast outward. Hearing him say that burns something inside me. Noah has always been the cheery cowboy, the one who did no wrong. He's gentle and kind. For him to lose that because of these monsters would be a tragedy. "I thought losing Liddy was hard enough as a human. This...this feeling is worse. And Harris, he really scared me. I never want to feel like that again."

"He fucked up. I don't want to defend him, but that craving is intense after being trapped for days..." He pauses for a moment. "I got up this morning to move the cattle, and it was like I could see the blood pulsing in their necks. I wanted to sink my teeth in there so bad, Rowan."

"But you didn't?"

"They're all I have, I couldn't do it. I caught a rabbit running off into the pasture. It was disgusting, almost made me gag, but it helped."

I take in the view before me, drinking in the scenery before responding. "All I can think about is killing everyone responsible." It slips off my tongue with more of an edge than I anticipated.

He smiles and looks down at me. I can feel him pull the reins tight to stop our movement. His hands fall to his thighs, and he wipes them across the fabric. "All I thought I had in life was the ranch. The cattle have been my life since our dad passed, and I always knew this is what I would take over. Sylas and Harris don't need this. I doubt they want it. They've stuck around for me, though. This…This could be a new start. I want to get out there and find the fucker who did this to us and then live my life right here." He holds his chin high with pride, practically beaming.

"I knew I always liked you, Noah." I tip my head back to meet his chest. Noah has always been like a brother to me. We don't see each other much, but we always connect naturally.

He chuckles and straightens on the saddle. "I should get the cattle back in before tonight. Are you okay to run back? Put your new shiny strength to the test." He winks.

My nose wrinkles, and I wink back as I jump from the saddle and race back towards the house. We had made it quite a ways away from the ranch house, but the run frees my mind. I want to use every ounce of my new power to destroy what almost destroyed me. I have to keep my wits and strength up.

I make it back inside, and I can feel I need to eat again. My hunger isn't in my stomach like it should be, and I wonder when I last ate regular, human food—or if I can. I stroll into the kitchen and find a loaf of bread and put a slice in the toaster. This mundane task that used to feel normal is suddenly entirely strange. The toast pops out, and I take a slow bite. It almost satiates my hunger, but it doesn't stop the need inside me. I prefer blood.

The Loughty boys make their way back inside. They all stop and watch me eat my slice of toast.

"Hell yeah! We can still eat food, brothers." Noah jumps around me, patting my shoulder as he goes around to the fridge. He gets everything out to make a sandwich, but no one else seems interested enough in this.

Sylas clears his throat. "We all decided that you should stay here. For now, at least. Until we can control our cravings, figure this whole thing out."

"Oh, we decided? I don't remember being asked about this." I cross my arms and look him dead in the eyes. "I need some time on my own. This is all too much, and I need time to come to terms with this." He rolls his eyes.

"Don't you think-" Harris starts, but I glare in his direction.

"I'll drive you home, then." He motions for the door and we leave.

# Chapter Seven

## ROWAN

SYLAS SLIDES INTO THE DRIVER'S SEAT OF MY CAR AND STARTS THE ENGINE. He lets the car idle for a moment before putting it in gear and driving toward town.

"I don't think this is a good idea...you being on your own right now." He keeps his eyes fixed to the road. "I'm afraid you'll do something you'll regret. I mean, I almost ripped out Harris' throat this morning. He has always such a smart ass and I'm starving." His jaw clenches.

"I'm a big girl. I think I'll manage." I pull my sleeves over my hands as my throat starts to burn, knowing he could be right. "I just don't know who I am right now. This change that was forced on me—that you forced on me...I know it was Travis' blood that did the trick, but you bit me..."

He cuts a glance at me. "I'm sorry. I didn't mean to—at least, I don't think I meant to." He takes a hand off the wheel to rub his hand across his mouth. "All I could think about was eating, and you were right there. I could smell the blood and fear on you."

I remain quiet as I look out the window at the passing trees and winding road. I was terrified of them, and it still stings deeply.

Sylas lets out a sigh. "You can't go back to work, you know. There's no way you'd be able to control yourself."

"Well, I think I'm fired, so no use fearing that." I look down at my boots.

He looks toward me, waiting for an explanation.

"I was digging around somewhere I shouldn't be. I went through the old newspapers and found the one from when my parents died. I shouldn't have been in there, but I wanted answers."

Sylas just nods seemingly unimpressed. He clears his throat and tilts his chin up. "So what did you find in that paper that got you fired?"

I let out a sigh. "Really, it was nothing. I did get a weird feeling from the journalist who wrote it, though. She wrote that my parents died in a house fire, but they were found bloodless outside their cabin. I called her to see if she remembered anything, and she practically hung up on me." The pain of recalling the events starts to sting in my eyes.

"You don't think it was vampires, do you?"

"I'm starting to think it was. There has to be more of them out there. I think I saw one the night of the carnival, but I didn't get a good look at him."

"All I feel is rage when I think about that night." Sylas is quiet for a moment. "Could you tell me what happened to Liddy?"

"Yeah," I say quietly and take in a deep breath, not entirely ready to recall the morning I found her. "S-she was murdered."

My breathing is shaky. "I left her that night you told us to stay in. I went out with Travis, and when I got back the next morning…" I pull in deep breaths to steady myself. "She had bite marks on her neck. I didn't know what they were at the time."

Tears start to roll down his cheeks, and the grip he holds on the steering wheel forces his knuckles white.

"I went back to her house and found your hat. For a moment, I thought you did it, and when you didn't show up to the funeral… I know now it couldn't have been you." I wipe the tears falling off my chin.

The rest of the drive to my house is silent. Beyond silent. We don't say a word to each other, and he keeps looking over at me like I'll combust at any moment. His jaw flexes, and I can see the tears in his eyes begging to fall. He should blame me for her death; he wouldn't be wrong. I feel responsible for it.

We pull up to my house, and I can't help but notice how dingy it looks compared to the ranch house. I could have done much more to make this place feel like home. The bushes are overgrown and the paint is peeling off the side. I didn't even give the front door a proper coat of paint. It looks sloppy and rushed.

"You're sure about this?" He cuts the engine and turns to me.

I nod. "I'm sure. How are you getting back to the ranch?"

"I need to clear my head. I'll walk." He steps out of my car and rounds the front to hand me the keys. "Be safe, Rowan. I'm serious."

"At least I can fight back this time," My smile is pathetic, and the attempt at a joke only hurts more.

Sylas jogs off, leaving me to walk inside my house for the first time in a few days. Grief instantly fills my chest as I step inside and feel no instant comfort in coming home. I slip off my hat and boots and set my things on the entry table. I don't know what I'm supposed to do here anymore, as if stepping inside my home put life on pause.

There was always one thing that could clear my head: deep cleaning. I turn on the radio that sits on my kitchen counter and start cleaning out the fridge of everything that has gone bad. Most of the food gets thrown out after discovering I don't have the stomach for a good portion of it. The broccoli made my stomach roll and the hummus made me gag. The only things remaining in my fridge are bacon and a loaf of bread.

I make quick work of vacuuming and mopping the floors throughout my home and then clean off the counter in my bathroom. It's littered with makeup and hair ties because although I enjoy cleaning, picking up after getting ready falls last on my to-do list. I turn to do a quality check on my work, my eyes fixed on the toilet, something I realized I haven't needed in a while, and the desire to use it is gone. The question lingers in my mind as I realize there's still so much I don't know about myself.

I would usually be tired by now—my legs aching and sweat building up in undesirable places. I wipe at my forehead, my hands feel the cool skin, and there's not a bead of sweat on me. I continue with my normal routine, trying to get any sense of relief from being back home. I walk out to the living room and light the candles on my mantle before sitting on my couch, suffocating in pillows and turning on the TV.

It turns to the last watched channel: Buffy reruns playing all night. I clench the remote in my hand hard enough that the plastic cracks under my grip. My body starts shaking before I feel the tears run down my face. The hole in my heart cracks wide open, and I scream as loud as I can, not holding back anything this time. The grief consumes me, and I can't stand to look at Buffy's face, as it only reminds me of Liddy. I turn the TV off and lose hope of ever having a normal life.

I pull out the drawer of a deep walnut side table nestled next to the couch that Liddy thrifted for me and grab my notebook and pen. I avoid looking at any of the pages I've written on, not wanting to see my past thoughts and start fresh on a new page.

*Dear Liddy,*

*I don't think I can do this without you. You always knew what to do, always so in control and calm. If anyone could turn into a vampire and make it look easy, it would be you. I don't know why they couldn't have killed me instead. Life felt like paradise when you were around, and now, it feels like hell.*

*I wake up in the morning and hope it was all a nightmare, but you're still gone each time the sun rises. I would do anything to have you back, anything to have your help wadding through this hell.*

*I miss you so much.*

*I love you forever,*

*Rowan*

Tears drop on the page and smudge the ink. I can't handle the weight of the pain sitting in my chest. I rip the page out of the notebook and fold it in half. The fire burns bright over the candles as I step towards them and hold the paper out. It catches quickly, the ashes falling over my hand.

"I will find who did this to you," I whisper into the flames.

A cool gust flies past me, making my hair fly forward as a small gasp leaves my mouth. Suddenly, the candles are out, and the room goes dark. All I can see is the smoke dancing above them. Chills line my arm, and I cling to the mantle to steady my shock. I look around the room and see nothing through the darkness. I feel my way back to the side table and reach for the lamp, pulling the string to turn it on. The room lights up, and I quickly inspect the other rooms in the house—the storage closet, kitchen, and bedrooms—only to find there's no one here. I quickly walk back to the living room and search the windows to check if they're closed. I don't know how the wind could have blown in here with them shut.

A loud knock at the front door makes me jump, my hand flying to cover my chest. I take a few breaths to steady myself. With my hands shaking, I open the door.

"Emma! Hi." My voice comes out breathy. I can smell the iron in her blood immediately, and my body goes rigid.

"Hey, I wanted to check on you. Can I come in?" Her smile reads concern.

"Always." She squeezes me tightly, and I bite my lip hard, resisting the urge to taste her before she turns and walks to the couch. Emma used to believe in vampires, so I'm worried she'll be able to tell what I am right away, worried I won't be able to keep my hunger at bay. Maybe she'd be open-minded about it if I confide in her. I need someone on my side, someone who knows more about this than myself. I sit next to her and decide not to lead with it—not when I can see the blood pulsing through her veins. I swallow hard and hold my hands in my lap.

"You ran off after the funeral. I've been worried about how you're taking this." She reaches for my hand, but I pull away. I don't want her to feel how cold my skin is. If she touched me, I don't think I'd be able to let her leave alive.

"I didn't see Sylas there, so I wanted to make sure he knew and see if he was okay." I feel like I threw him under the bus with that statement, but I want to be as honest as I can while holding so many secrets. A few white lies won't kill her.

"Well, I'm glad someone went to check on him." She looks into my eyes, and I don't remember their change in color until it's too late to look away. "Your eyes are so much lighter than normal... They look gold."

I laugh it off. "I'm sure it's just the lighting in here." Emma doesn't return the sentiment. Instead, he studies me harder, and I try to change the subject. "How are you doing? It's been almost a week now and I still can't wrap my head around it."

"It's been hard but..." Her brows scrunch together. "Rowan, you really look different." Her hands reach toward my face and cup my cheeks before pulling them away quickly. "You're freezing."

She stands from the couch and backs away.

"Emma, please," I say.

"Tell me the truth right now, Rowan." Her face is lined in terror, and I can smell her fear.

I open my mouth to tell her another lie, but her eyes go wide at the sight of the sharp canines extending below my lip. "I-I'm a vampire." I open my mouth just enough to prove what she saw to be true. Tears line my eyes, begging to fall, and I wipe them away.

"This isn't real, you can't be real." She tries to back out of the room towards the front door with a hand clenched at her side and the other searching for her keys. "Is this why you brought it up at brunch? Did you kill her?"

"No, of course not. Please, don't leave," I beg as I stand from my seat. "I didn't want this. I don't know what to do."

"I'm sorry, I can't." She turns and runs to the door, her hand reaching toward the handle as I move fast to grab her. She twists the door handle, and before she can pull it open, I sink my teeth deep into her neck. Her screams dissipate into small whimpers as her knees begin to buckle. The sweet taste of her blood coats my tongue in thick waves, drops of poison leaking from my fangs and mingling with the taste of her. My body hums with pleasure, and my senses heighten immeasurably. She tastes so much better than Travis—fresh and addictive.

Her body slumps to the floor with a loud thud that makes me break the bite I have on her. My tongue sweeps out to clean the corners of my mouth before I use my hand to wipe off the rest. My muscles ease, and the thoughts in my head buzz with enjoyment.

I look at the ground just as the high begins to wear off and nausea fills my stomach when I see Emma's eyes wide open in terror. Her arms are limp at her sides, clothes disheveled. I watch her closely to see if there's a rise and fall in her chest— she's not breathing.

"Oh god, Emma, what have I done?" I panic and my hands search her body for any sign of life. I can't believe I killed the only other friend I had.

"Fuck, fuck, fuck..." I lift her from the floor, and my breathing becomes quick and uneven. "I can fix this, right?" I start to run down the hall towards the guest room, where I lay her on the bed. Her eyes stare at me, and I cover my mouth to keep in the bile rising in my throat. I use my other hand to carefully lower her lids.

I pace the room, wracking my mind with what I can do. I don't know anything about this, if I can even save her. My eyes are flooded with tears and my hands shake uncontrollably.

Maybe if I can turn her, she'll wake up. Maybe if I can feed her my blood I won't have to lose another friend. Before thinking about it any further, I bite down hard on my hand and shove it into her mouth. I squeeze hard on the bite begging that it's enough blood. Once the wound on my hand heals, I remove it from her mouth and sit on the bed next to her. Clasping her face in my hands, I let my eyes take her in.

The reality of what I've done comes crashing down around me. What if she doesn't want to be a vampire? She didn't even want to be around me? What made me think she would want this? I was stuck in my own selfish feelings, my own guilt about killing her.

I rest my head on her shoulder and cry. I cry until there's nothing left to fall from my eyes and even then I don't leave her side. My eyes fall shut, and I let the darkness sweep over me, consuming me and my shame. I lay with this guilt until my mind drifts and I start to fall asleep.

Movement stirs next to me, and I let my eyes flutter open.

"Emma," I whisper out in a groggy tone.

She doesn't say a word and sits up in the bed before hovering over me. Her hands come up to wrap around my throat with a tight squeeze.

# Chapter Eight

## SYLAS

I JOG THROUGH THE WOODS INSTEAD OF TAKING THE WINDING ROAD BACK TO THE RANCH. There's a narrow secluded path that leaves Georgetown and typically doesn't get a lot of visitors, especially at this time of night. The air is cool, my breath lingering in front of me, but I don't feel the chill against my skin. Hunger is the only thought in my mind. Noah set a house rule that we're not allowed to eat his cattle, and I accept that. They mean a lot to him.

I grew up hunting with my dad, but that was with rifle—hunting with my bare hands is foreign to me. After losing a few rabbits, I start taking a different approach. I take easy steps, careful not to stir up any leaves, stepping over fallen branches. The moon is shining high above giving me enough light through the trees to see every small movement. My vision has never been sharper—like night vision without the goggles. Tall trees line the side of the path, and I crouch behind one of them, waiting out a small deer in the distance. Its eyes glow in the moonlight, and I see its ears twitching toward forest sounds. Inching closer, I steady my breathing and set it in my sights.

Another animal in the distance spooks the deer, and it takes off. I break away from the trees that gave me coverage and speed through the woods, dodging broken limbs and fallen trunks. My legs move smoothly through the air, and I pick up speed with ease. Over the sounds of my feet moving along the forest floor, I can hear the footfalls of the deer slowing down. The chase is easy. Reaching my arms out, I jump to grab the deer and bite down on its neck as we roll on the damp ground.

Animal blood doesn't have the same sweet, intoxicating taste that human blood does, but it satisfies me enough to take the edge off my rage. I've never felt as lost as I do now. Liddy guided me in the right direction and gave me something to hold onto. I didn't need to think of my future when I was with her, because she had everything all planned out. Maybe she was doing me a disservice. Now, I don't have anything but my brothers and the ranch our dad left to us. I was setting myself up for failure, letting someone else guide me—letting myself be ignorant to choices I should have made.

I walk in the silence of the woods around me, giving me time to think before dealing with my brothers. Rowan holds us responsible for how she turned, and I don't blame her—we couldn't protect her for one goddamn day. She's better off on her own.

The weight of the last few days crushes against my chest, and a painful laugh leaves my mouth. "Fuck!" I kick a fallen log as hard as I can, and I watch as it flies across a clearing and slams into a tree with a crack. No amount of physical strength could outweigh the consequences of becoming an animal.

"You look like shit," Harris says as I walk into the house.

I give him a glare that tells him not to push me.

"You couldn't get her to stay here, then?" Noah chimes in with less attitude.

"No, and why should she? We almost killed her, and we're just as responsible for her turning into *this* as Travis is." I don't bother hearing their reply and stalk to the bathroom to wash off. The cracked door lies in the hallway, leaving the room open.

Any sense of control over myself is lost. I'm grasping at reality, trying to piece together the unknown. The pained gold reflection of my eyes in the mirror only solidifies my pain. I open the bathroom cabinet and reach for my beard trimmer. I feel the buzz in my hand and start cleaning up the lines of my beard—removing the extra length I've grown over the past month. I consider shaving my head, but I'm not ready to lose the way Liddy's hands felt combing through my hair.

The knob on the faucet squeaks as I twist it and water starts spraying out. I lose myself in the warmth and distance myself from the body that now feels so foreign. I will be making my own choices now—deciding where I fit in, choosing how I live this possibly immortal life. I never did believe in vampires; the thought of them was outlandish, childish even. All I know about them is what I've seen watching Buffy with Liddy and Rowan, and even they got it wrong. I don't combust in the sunlight and my face isn't grotesquely ugly, but I'm fast and strong—my body is rewired to live off blood. A true demon.

I towel off as I walk past the shattered door to my room. I

pause before I reach my door and grab the handle of the room Rowan slept in. Thinking better of it, I remove my grip and continue to my room. It would be a lie to say I'm not worried about her, and I continue to question if I'm doing the right thing by leaving her alone.

My room is a mirror of hers—dark wooden furniture and long drapes that cover the window. I don't have many sentimental things aside from a few photographs of my parents and my very first Stetson. I thought I would one day give it to my child when Liddy and I became a family—another one of her dreams for us. I didn't put much thought into kids before her, it's what my family did. We had children and raised them to work on the ranch. My father was an outlier. He moved us to the Carolinas shortly after I was born to start a ranch of his own, a place he could run without anyone else's say. I only hope to be as strong as him in that regard.

My head hits the pillow, and nightmares follow me through the night: how weak I was against the men who attacked us, knocking me out with a single punch thrown and waking up in excruciating pain. Flashbacks of Harris attacking Rowan quickly follow. My heart leaps each time I see him bite down on her flesh. The feeling digs deeper, hurts worse, each time I live through it in my mind. I see the fear in her face as I lick the blood from her chest.

These nightmares follow me each night.

"It has been two weeks, man. Have you gotten any sleep?" Noah asks as I sit at the kitchen table.

I grip the mug of coffee in my hands and look down at the table. "Obviously not."

Noah snorts. "Well don't take it out on me."

"Sorry," I say with an empty promise. I haven't been a pleasure to be around the last few weeks, and they've made sure I know.

"You should just go see her, see if she's doing okay."

"She-"

"Yeah, she's better off without you? Keep telling yourself that, brother. But I think you'd sleep better knowing she's okay." Noah raises his brows at me.

I scowl and take a sip of my coffee, ignoring him. If she wanted our help, she would be here; it's obvious she's doing fine on her own. I stop my mind from wandering to a darker place. The nightmares haven't stopped, but at least the leash on my cravings has been pulled tight. It slips when I can't control my anger, but I'm not jumping to gut Harris any more than usual.

I keep busy, taking care of the cattle now that I know to eat before coming out here. My work is half-assed; I clean the stalls to the bare minimum and move the cows into the closer pasture to get ready for winter. These mundane tasks keep my anger in check, being able to work without thinking too hard. Rowan fills my head as I ride my mare and rake straw, wondering if it's too late to see how she's doing, but that's all it will be—wondering.

Once the sun sets, I make my way down the secluded forest path into town. The moon doesn't give much light tonight, but it's not a problem for my adjusting eyes. It's freeing not having to hide what I am in the darkness, no hats or holding my shit together. At night, I can hunt—in tune with my desires for blood.

I set my sights on a coyote deep in the trees, hiding in the brush. Over the last few weeks of hunting, I've learned how to move quietly—near silent. My steps are quick and weightless, and I make it closer to my next meal in moments. The coyote lifts its head before dipping it back down to inspect something before him. I crouch, stalking closer to my prey until I'm only a few feet away. A branch snaps under my weight. I was so excited about a large meal that I stopped paying attention to the ground below me. The coyote startles and lifts its head in my direction, and that's when its bright yellow eyes meet mine. This is when I realize the coyote I've been stalking is truly a wolf. I make no sudden moves, the animal appearing to be studying me, staring into my eyes with a humanlike feeling. It turns and walks away with ease—I don't go after it.

After drinking my way through a few rabbits, I trudge home with my head hanging low. I slide my hands into the pockets of my jeans and let my hand linger over the phone in my pocket. She hasn't reached out, not a single text to let me know she's alive. Is she really doing okay, or was I just too big of an asshole for her to reach out? I don't need to think that one over. I know I was an asshole toward her, made her feel unwelcome and cold. I don't know any other way to grieve.

My fingers slide against the cold screen of my phone, my hand itching to lift it from my pockets. I give in and let my fingers trail over the buttons to check in with her.

You alive?

It's the best I can think of, just to let me know she's okay without intruding. I remind myself of her words—she needs time, space. I take my time getting back to the barn, gripping my phone in my hand, giving her time to reply, giving myself time to come to terms with whatever comes of this before I'm back inside. Only a minute passes before the screen lights with a notification.

Yes.

A relieved sigh leaves my mouth; that was all I needed. Tension starts to ease in my shoulders as I slide the phone back into my pocket and go home.

# Chapter Nine

## ROWAN

"I STILL CAN'T BELIEVE YOU TRIED TO KILL ME IN MY SLEEP," I SAY TO EMMA.

"It's been weeks since that happened; not to mention, you turned me into a vampire!" Emma shrieks at me from across the table.

"Would you rather be dead?" I say flatly.

"I would have rather you never attacked me in the first place." Her eyes meet mine with a dead stare.

"...Fair."

We sit at the kitchen table with freshly killed rabbits on plates in front of us. The dining room is small and inviting, with warm tones and a buffet along the back wall decorated for the season.

"Why are we eating them like this again?" I raise my brows, and my mouth turns downward. "We could just drain them and leave them for other animals to pick at...outside."

"I'm trying to cope. This feels like we're having dinner together in a more human way. You know, what I once was?"

"Oh, give it a rest." I pick up the rabbit set before me and drain it of its blood quickly. It's not the biggest meal we could have caught, but Emma screams each time we set out to catch something. I try to convince her this is better than feeding on humans and will draw less attention, but this human part of her remains—standing against animal cruelty has been a passion of hers for as long as I've known her.

We've been hiding out in my house for the last two weeks, only hunting at night and trying to take on all these new changes together. We fought for the first few days after I turned her, and she's not wrong: I wish it hadn't happened this way. Selfishly, I'm glad I'm not alone with my feelings right now. Having her to lean on and distract me has helped my emotions stay at bay. I have someone to confide in. I told her everything that happened the weekend of the fair, and she finally believed me about Liddy. My hands clench around the animal, and my anger starts to surface at the memory.

"I think we've been hiding long enough." I put the rabbit down on my plate in a swift motion. "We should go into town tomorrow, something small. I want to go to the library and see if we can dig up any of those old books we used to read."

"The ones on vampires?" Emma looks up from her plate with blood dripping down the side of her mouth.

I nod. "It's been a while since I've read them, and now seems like the time to take it seriously." I clasp my hands together tightly. "I still want to find who killed her."

Emma's face softens as she wipes her mouth clean with a napkin. "Of course. I'll go with you."

I smile softly at her. The doorbell rings, shaking me from my thoughts, and my gaze flicks toward the door.

"Pizza's here." Emma stands from the table to grab it.

"You ordered a pizza?" The judgment slides off my tongue before I can rein it in.

"Just like old times," she says to me over her shoulder, and I shake my head.

Shortly after the door opens, there's a heated exchange of words coming from the two of them about how much change she should have gotten back.

"I gave you a fifty for a twenty-dollar pizza. Give me my change." Her voice lowers, telling me she's about to lose it. I jump from the table and step around the corner to act as a martyr, but it's too late. She grabs the pizza with fast movements, and before the man can turn away, she bites down on his neck.

He collapses as she removes her grip on him, the poison in her fangs settling into his body quickly. She looks at me in horror. "Oh, fuck." Her eyes widen.

"Get him inside before someone sees. We're lucky it's late." We each grab one of his arms and haul him to my back porch, leaving a trail of dirt from his shoes through the house. It's there we indulge in his blood—fatty and warm—before ditching his body deep in the woods, along with the bike he rode over here on.

"We should probably go to the library at night..." Emma says with a look of guilt.

"We're definitely going after it closes." I let out a breath and lock the front door.

The desire to kill anyone who crosses our path has been strong the last few weeks, but I can feel the need damper with each passing day, only needing to feed to keep my strength up and the rage at bay. I can tell this isn't the case for Emma. The only person I've killed is her, and I can't begin to imagine how she feels or what she might be thinking—how I've turned her into a monster, a killer.

I wake up to Emma's arm draped over me, and I carefully slide it off. Wrapping my robe around myself, I head to the kitchen to start a pot of coffee. It's not a necessity, but I've gotten into such a routine of having a cup each morning, I just can't stop. I suppose there's a desire deep inside me to keep some of the humanity I once had. Steam billows from the mug, and I inhale deeply to take it in. My gaze flicks to the kitchen island, where an empty pizza box sits—bloodied hand prints line the front. Saying we have our cravings under complete control is a lie I've been telling myself all night.

I move to the living room, settle into the couch, and turn on the news. I haven't been keeping up with it like I should have. We've only killed one person; it's not like we've littered the town with corpses. The weather report ends, and colors flash across the screen as the news reporter starts sharing a recent discovery.

*Reports are showing several dead animals in the areas just outside of town. Officials say this could be sign of a coyote pack. Please keep vigilant, keep your pets inside, and stay safe.*

There's a pause in my movements before I start hysterically laughing.

"What's going on?" Emma rubs her eyes and walks down

the hall.

"I'm worried we'll be found out, and they blame it on fucking coyotes." My belly starts to ache as I hunch over, unable to control my amusement.

"We need to talk about this." She sets her mug down and walks toward the couch.

"We'll get better at this. We won't have to hide in the shadows forever," I assure her, but I don't know that for certain.

"No, Rowan. You did this to me, you made me like this." Her eyes glaze with tears as her hands press into her chest. "I killed someone! And now you're laughing because we didn't get caught?"

"I-"

"No. This isn't about you right now. This isn't a childish disagreement you can brush off as if it never happened." Her body starts to shake, and I take her hands in mine.

"I'm so sorry, Emma. I'm sorry my control slipped with you. I'm doing better with it, and I know you will get there too."

"You still don't get it." She removes her hands from my grasp.

I haven't been a vampire for long, I know how she must feel. Her world is turning upside down because of me. Everything she worked for is ruined because of me. I'm leaving devastation in my wake.

"I was so selfish in turning you… I didn't want you to leave. I wanted someone on my side. I thought you'd understand once you knew, and it crushed me when you started to run. I panicked, and I did the only thing I knew how. I didn't want to be alone." The guilt slowly starts crushing me under its weight.

"You destroyed the life I had planned so you wouldn't be alone?" She scoffs.

"No, that's not-"

"I'll go to the library with you tonight, but after that, I'm leaving."

"I don't think that's a good idea. You just killed the pizza guy." My brows furrow together.

She scowls at me. "I will deal with it alone. I've been trapped here long enough with you. It's not helping anyone."

I give her a nod and walk to my room to give her space. The sun is shining brightly through the windows, but cold air seeps through the cracks. I tug and wiggle tight jeans over my legs and slip a heavy gray sweater over my head before grabbing clothes for Emma. I leave them in a pile on the guest bed. The blankets are still half off the bed from the night I turned her. The pillows are thrown around the room from when she rightfully tried to choke me.

I force myself to remove my gaze from the room and move back to my bed, waiting for darkness to fall. I do feel guilty for turning Emma; it *is* my fault in the end. Still, I can't help feeling glad she's here with me—that I'm not alone. She said she's leaving after this, and I can only hope it's not true.

"Are you nervous?" I turn to Emma and hand her a baseball cap.

"Of course. You've had me holed up here for weeks. I had to tell my boss I'm out of town, so we better not get caught," she says with dead certainty. "I don't want to kill anyone else. I can't have that on my conscience."

"It's just the library. Nothing should set us off there this late at night." I reach out and smooth a stray curl on her head. "Then, we'll come right back."

"What are you hoping to find?" She studies my eyes.

"Confirmation that I'm not crazy, mostly…" I whisper. "Asta always gave me some information here and there, and it's all been true. Everything I used to read in those books has been true…except for combusting into flames when the sun touches you, thank God."

I look closely at Emma, and questions linger in her eyes, but she doesn't say anything.

"I believe my parents were killed by vampires too," I finally admit to her.

Her mouth hangs open in disbelief. "I'm not saying you're wrong, but why do you think that?"

"Nothing of their story makes sense. The lines blur between the truth and what this journalist saw," I say, and she lets out a sigh.

"What made you stop believing? I was surprised at brunch how quickly you wrote me off when you were the only one who told us tales of bloodsuckers and magic."

She worries her lip under a gentle bite. "My grandparents told me those stories of witches and vampires. How they found a small town tucked between mountains to live freely as what they truly were." A sigh leaves her mouth. "That summer after my grandma passed, my grandpa moved back to Stanton, and I stopped believing. There was no one left to keep the stories alive for me."

"I'm sorry." I squeeze her shoulder.

"No use in dwelling on it. We should get going." She rests her hand on mine before pulling away.

I pick up two pairs of sunglasses from the entryway table and signal for her to try them on. "Is this too much?" I turn to her before looking in the mirror.

Emma starts cackling. "We look like vigilantes."

"Okay, hard pass then," I laugh, chucking the sunglasses back onto the small table.

We pull into a parking lot across the street from the library, and I readjust my hat before stepping out of the car. It's after ten pm on Wednesday, and the parking lot is empty, most of the town at home right now. I steady my breathing—something I forget how to do sometimes—and notice how rigid Emma looks.

"We can do this." I lace my fingers through hers and check the code panel next to the door.

"Asta gave me the code one summer when I was in middle school since I practically lived here. Let's hope it still works."

I type in the code *6-3-1-0* and hear a silent beep before the door unlocks.

We step into the quiet room. It feels eerie without the squeaky wheels of carts sounding in the distance, but the smell of old books fills me with a sense of calm. The moonlight shines into the room, giving off enough glow to make our way through, but we would be fine without it. At the front desk, I don't see any sign of librarians working late—not even Asta, who would be here until late hours of the night. We head to the back section of the library first, a small corner closed off by tall shelves. The space is filled with history books and folklore. I used to think how odd it was that they were organized together, but it doesn't feel so strange now.

There's a small table in the center of the room, where I place my bag on one of the chairs. I walk to the shelves I know house what I'm looking for and let my fingers drift along the spines. Once I find a few books on vampire folklore, I bring them to the table for us to comb through.

The silence is so loud, I'm afraid my thoughts can be heard. My fingers skim page after page, sorting out the frivolous details with real facts and information we already know—how to be turned, how to kill a vampire, and-

"Turning off their emotions, vampires can regulate how they feel and behave. In most cases, this turns them into savage killers," I whisper.

"Like a switch on the back of our heads?" Emma questions.

"I'm sure it's more complicated than that, but there's no how-to guide."

She chokes down a laugh, trying to stay silent. "I swear, this is some twisted nightmare." She looks back down at her book. "Oh, here: many of the first vampires to date have been around since the early 18th century, blah blah blah, and could still be alive today."

"So, these people we're trying to track down could be centuries old." I let out a defeated sigh and close the book.

"You're not usually one to give up so quickly." She lays her hand on my arm, her eyes soft with empathy.

"We already know most of this stuff, and it doesn't feel like

we're getting any closer. My head is spinning."

"Ladies," a gentle voice snaps us from our daze. Emma grips my shoulder tight to stop herself from jumping for the woman.

"Asta." I turn toward her and her eyes widen for barely a moment before she straightens her spine. "I didn't think anyone was here."

"I see you're back for more vampires." Her smile is easy. "I'm so sorry for your loss, girls. Liddy was such a light."

"Thank you. It's been hard," I confess.

"I know you'll find a way to celebrate her life one day." She places a hand on my shoulder, and I hold back my tears the best I can.

"Asta," Emma breaks the moment. "We came in hoping to find out more about vampires. We're doing…research." She stumbles at her words at the end, trying not to draw up any suspicion.

"You know I would love nothing more than to tell you what I know." She smiles.

She seats herself in the chair across from me and studies our faces for a few moments before clasping my hands in hers. I look down at our hands, knowing how cold my skin must be. She doesn't shudder or pull away but gives them a gentle squeeze, telling me she knows.

Where I'd usually have the urge to feed, there's a calmness instead. Maybe it's because she's so familiar. My love and appreciation for her overpower the urge to bite her neck, even though I can smell her sweet blood and hear her heart pounding.

"The first vampires were created centuries ago, but they didn't settle into Georgetown until about 300 years ago, when their queen wandered here in search of a quiet town to inhabit. Slowly, she started taking over, ensuring she could control how people saw them and would never find out what she was. Legend has it, the portal to hell where she rules is easier to reach from our very town." Asta pauses, and chills go up my arm. I look at Emma, and her face is ghostly pale.

"This queen—she's a monster?" I ask.

Asta nods. "Like the devil himself."

This runs much deeper than I could have imagined. This is more than just bloodlust and power—a devil is working in disguise here.

"But...what does she want exactly?" Emma manages to ask.

"That, I don't know, dear. I've never seen her with my own eyes, but I've got a sense of when her kind is around. These stories have been passed around my family. My grandfather would warn me of such animals—and tell me what to look for. The ones bearing red eyes that glow like molten lava are the ones to stay away from, the queen's followers—evil runs through them. I'm sure they've found a way to hide it by now, but the ones who bear golden eyes... Well, let's just say they're not so bad. Most people think we're crazy. I've heard it all, but I believed him all my life until I finally met one—golden eyes, luckily. This was such a long time ago, and I'm not sure where she ended up, but we were dear friends." She dips her head and smiles at the table.

"Where you scared?" I ask. "When you met her?"

"Terrified," she chuckles. "But I trusted everything my grandfather taught me about them, and even then, I could sense the pure heart in her, just as I've seen in you since you were a little girl."

"Thank you for telling us all this. It's very helpful for our project," Emma bites her lip, and I nudge her with my elbow before she closes her mouth to hide her fangs.

"No need to hide it from me, girls. I noticed the moment I saw you. It's okay."

"I'm sorry, I didn't think-" She cuts me off.

"No need. Your secret is safe here." She stands from the table. "There's something I'd like you to have: my grandfather's journal. He used to write everything he heard about them, all his encounters and sketches." She walks toward the front desk, and we follow her.

Asta pulls a leather-bound journal from her bag and places it on the counter. "Keep it safe, please. I'm sure this will help you in your research. There's one more thing I want to warn you about, something you'll find out for yourselves one day. The older vampires, they are much stronger."

I nod trying to shake off the initial terror of her words. "Thank you so much," I say with genuine appreciation.

"Be careful. If you ever need anything, you know where I am." Her smile is lined with worry.

"I know I already said I'm leaving, but I think I should go stay with my family in Stanton for a while," Emma says as we step outside the library. "It doesn't feel safe here anymore after hearing what Asta said. I'm still mad at you but…you could come with me."

I stop in front of my car and turn to her, "You know I don't love this idea, but you haven't seen your grandfather in years. As long as you'll tell me if you're in trouble or if you can't control your hunger like you might think you can. I need to stay here, though. As terrifying as this is, I can't shake the feeling that I'm missing something. I need to do this for Liddy." I shift on my feet and grasp the journal tightly under my arm.

"You promise to come see me if anything goes wrong?" Tears build in her eyes.

"I promise." I pull her into a long hug, not wanting to let go. "At least let me drive you home to pack."

"Obviously." She chuckles.

# Chapter Ten

## ROWAN

THE TV FLICKERS ON AS I LEAN BACK ON THE SOFA. The only reason I watch the news anymore is to see if I need to run or hide. It's radio silent on any matter that would concern me until the news anchor starts reporting on a coyote pack that has made its home here. All I can hope is that they made their way here to take care of the body we ditched in the woods.

There's an empty pit in my heart that shows no signs of closing. Turning into a vampire has been hard, and nothing feels whole without my best friend. The loneliness creeps up on me and takes over a little more of my soul each day. I start to wonder how the Loughty brothers are doing—if they're okay, if they've been able to control their bloodlust, if he's thinking about me. It's been a month since I've seen Sylas, and I have to admit, I miss him. I don't feel any closer to getting justice either, and I'm starting to think I could use his help.

I open my phone to look at our short text thread, weighing the decision to text him. He's the only other person who would understand the weight in my heart right now.

I miss her.

A beat later his message pops up.

I miss her too.

You okay?

I let out a ragged breath before replying with a lie.

I'm okay.

The sun starts its descent into night earlier these days, and I curl up on the couch with the journal Asta gave me. Her grandfather wrote meticulous notes on everything he saw and heard. There are sketches of strange men in gothic disguises with glowing red eyes; my breath catches every time I see one. This same set of eyes plays back in my memory like a film reel, the same eyes I thought were a hallucination at the fair. I scan the pages for any information about them, but there's only one line of text written, *the queen's henchmen*. This must be the army she was talking about. A cool breeze brushes against my arm, and I pull a blanket around me. I haven't been cold like this since turning, but the chill quickly fades.

The more information I gather, the more confused I become. If they've been hiding all these years, why come out and make a spectacle at the carnival? This is all much bigger than me—much bigger than I can process. All I want is to avenge the people I love, but the odds against me keep stacking higher.

I slide the book from my lap and stand to put on my boots. I need to take the edge off this frustration, and there's only one way I know how—hunting. I slide open the back door and step off the patio into the cool fall air. I take in deep breaths; hunting was never something I did in my childhood, and I start to wonder if it'll get harder during the winter months and what I'll have to resort to. I shake the worry from my mind and set out into the woods.

I take gentle steps on the covered ground, barely making a sound as I move deeper into the darkness. I pause to listen for any movement. Having enhanced senses has made hunting unfair for my prey. I hear small steps to my left and dip behind a bush to scan the area around me. A small deer takes easy steps into view before two larger ones come up behind it. I set my sights on the larger one closest to me and start the chase.

It's over quickly, and I stand to wipe my mouth with the back of my hand. Calmness sweeps over me, and I take a second to enjoy the animal's blood that satiated my hunger. I take the walk back slowly to enjoy the woods around me before stepping back inside my home. I wash my hands in the kitchen sink and let my eyes glaze over all the things I'll probably never use in here again—expensive pots and tools I worked so hard to get, all seemingly meaningless now.

There's a harsh knock on the door, and I quickly make my way over without thinking twice about who's behind it. I pull open the door, and I'm met with striking red eyes.

"Hello," the man says, pushing himself inside.

He towers over me and removes the dark hood of his jacket to show short-cropped hair and a sharp jaw. His smile widens to reveal razor-sharp teeth that make my body go rigid.

"Wh-who are you?" I stumble over my words, unable to find confidence.

"Saul Huntsman, a pleasure to meet you." His hand reaches toward me and his grin turns vile.

With hesitation, I clasp his calloused hand to shake it. No other words leave my mouth. I'm unable to find the questions I want to ask.

"I can smell the fear on you, little one."

"What do you want? I don't know you." I shift my feet to steady my balance.

"I wanted to come meet the fresh vampire in town." His tongue swipes his lower lip. "Rumor has it, the queen wants your head."

"Who? No, I think you're mistaken." My muscles tighten, and my chest rises faster.

"Rowan Watson." He pauses his words to look me over. "Bringing your head to her would get me into the inner circle… I've been here at the bottom far too long, and I'm ready to get a taste of power."

His words slam into me, and the realization that he's here to kill me sets my feet into motion. I turn and run through the living room into the kitchen. I frantically move for the jar of utensils, reaching my fingers to grab the wooden spoon. He grips the back of my hair and pulls down hard, but not before my hand wraps around the smooth handle. I grab for the counter trying to pull myself back up, my boots slipping from under me.

"You're putting up quite the fight, little one," he grunts and grips my hair harder.

A loud groan of pain leaves my mouth as he pulls me up. I struggle to get to my feet, gripping the spoon as hard as I can. My hands swing around, trying to push him off me, but he pulls harder and turns me to face him. His sharp teeth are clenched and start to widen as he comes down on me fast. As hard as I can, I swing my arm and plunge the dull end of the wooden spoon into his chest. It misses his heart by an inch.

He recoils, and his hands fall from my hair to cover the leaking wound. I take a quick breath trying to figure out if my body wants to run or fight. He starts toward me, and that's all I needed to make up my mind. I pull the spoon from his chest and plunge it straight into his heart before he can take another step forward. His body falls to the ground, and the color of his skin slowly fades to a sickly purple.

My back slides down the cabinets behind me, and I pull my knees into my chest. I let the tears fall freely now. The aftershock of being attacked and almost killed, the confusion of not knowing what's going on around me...It takes over me, and I let it.

"Fuck, what am I supposed to do?" I sob into my sleeves. If I leave him in the woods, I'm afraid more of them will come after me, and I can't just leave him here. I lay on the kitchen floor and cry until my eyes close and I lose track of time, stewing in my agony.

I sit up and look at the clock on the stove that reads four am. "Oh God, it's morning." I can't believe I laid here so long." The man is still slumped dead on the floor in front of me.

The only thing I can think to do is go to the ranch, but I can't leave the body here like this. I look through the front blinds to make sure no one is outside before backing my car into the driveway and popping the trunk. I jog back into the kitchen and grab Saul by both wrists and drag him through the house. His body is still heavy, full of blood I didn't dare drink. His head thumps against the front steps as I pull him down. I stop once we reach the trunk to look around the street and listen to anyone who might be around. When I only hear the sounds of morning birds chirping, I lift his body into the trunk, shifting his limbs to fit in the small space before I slam it shut. I jump into the driver's seat and take off for the ranch.

# Chapter Eleven

## ROWAN

I walk to the worn metal gate to the ranch, noticing they still haven't fixed the lock, and swing the doors open to drive to the house. As I come up the hill, I can see all three of the brother's trucks parked in the glistening grass, and the sun starts to peek out from behind the mountains. Thankful they're home, I cut the engine and rush through the door without knocking. It's dark and quiet inside and, realizing it's still too early for them to be up, I lay on the couch in the main room to rest my eyes.

"Rowan? Are you okay?" Noah's voice wakes me.

"Oh, I'm so glad to see you," I stand to hug him.

"What's going on?" He breaks the hug and clasps my arms to look me over. He spots the blood on my sleeves.

"Everything was fine until this man showed up. He said he needed to bring my head to the queen."

"The queen?" he says in confusion.

"I have so much to tell you but later. I-I killed him, and he's in my trunk."

His eyes widen. "Okay, yeah." His voice is unsure. "I'll

wake up my brothers and we'll figure this out."

"Yeah, yeah, that's good. Thank you." I let out a heavy sigh.

Sylas groans and walks down the hallway, his hair disheveled from sleep. "Rowan," his voice scratches. "Are you hurt?" He grabs my arms and inspects my sleeves.

"No, I'm okay." I look into his eyes, and he quickly looks away.

"Why am I awake then? What's going on?" He groans and flops onto the large leather couch.

I sit next to him and start telling him everything about the last month. He listens with eyes fixed on me in disbelief.

"You turned Emma?"

"I couldn't control it. I jumped at her and immediately started panicking. She was mad at me for a few weeks; she might still be," I confess.

"We've been keeping to ourselves here, just trying to figure things out, trying to go back to normal, but it's nowhere near normal." he chuckles.

"No, it's not. I still haven't gotten over how weird this is. I would like to say I was the only one who knew vampires were real." I give him a boisterous smile.

"Bullshit, Row. You just liked the idea of them. You were scared shitless."

I let out a small laugh and lean my head back against the couch. "So, you guys are doing okay?"

"We're fine. Hunting is getting easier, but I don't think animal blood is doing it for me anymore." He mimics my position and leans his head back.

"What do you mean?"

"It takes the edge off, sure, but it doesn't relieve the rage inside me."

I eye him, wondering if he's really getting used to being a vampire—wondering if he's still grieving. Harris walks into the room and starts ordering us around.

"Alright, let's get this fucker out of your car. We'll do what we did with Travis. That means you two need to go get me some firewood." He looks between Sylas and me.

"Nice to see you too," I grumble, but I'm thankful for their help.

"Let's get to work!" He claps loudly.

Sylas turns to me, "We already have some logs out back. Just need to chop them." He slaps his hands on his thighs and gets up. I follow suit.

I slip my hat onto my head as we step off the back porch. The grass crunches under my boots, and we walk toward the barn. The inside of the barn is meticulously clean, the splintered wood cleaned up and the hay fresh.

"Been busy in here, huh?"

Sylas hands me an axe. "It's the only thing that keeps me occupied."

I nod silently and follow him to the pile of logs. It doesn't seem like he's doing as well as I initially thought, and I start to feel guilty for leaving them.

"Are you doing okay? I know it has to be hard-"

"Just swing the axe hard onto the middle of the log, and it should break," he interrupts. He lifts the axe over his head and swings down hard, wood flying to the side in many smaller pieces.

"Got it." I give him a small smile and get to work chopping wood. Being much stronger means I don't have to embarrass myself—I chop many logs in the span of a few minutes until Sylas says it's enough.

We carry the logs to the firepit in silence. I step around him with caution, not knowing where his head is at. I know how hard it must be for him—the things I did while grieving weren't short of horrible.

We arrange the logs for the fire, and Harris slings the body on top of the pile.

Harris dusts off his hands on his jeans. "We'll light it tonight. You should stay this time, Rowan."

I look to Sylas. "Is that okay with you?"

He gives a stern nod. "As long as no one else ends up dead. There are a lot of dead bodies where you're concerned."

I turn to glare at him. "Real nice, Sylas."

"Dude, come on," Noah chimes in. "You're staying here. He'll get over it."

I smile at Noah. "Thanks, I'll stay. I left in such a hurry. I'll need to grab some things from my house first. I'll be back before the bonfire."

"I'm coming with you," Sylas says. "We'll take my truck."

"I can go on my own. I don't want to be stuck with your grumpy ass. I swear, turning into a vampire hasn't done you any favors."

"Non-negotiable. Ready?" He hikes his thumb over his shoulder and heads for the truck.

I turn to Noah and lower my voice, "Save me, please."

"I heard that," Sylas calls out.

Damned vampires. I shift my hat and let out a groan.

My body sways side to side, and I hold the door handle to steady myself as Sylas flies down the empty mountain roads. I can't tell if he's being carefree or reckless. My grip tightens, and I watch his face—he's concentrated on the road ahead of us, so I take that as a good sign. I don't know how the impact of an accident would injure me, but I'd rather not find out. A breath escapes my lips as we pull into my driveway safely.

"I'll just be a minute," I say to him, but he cuts the engine and gets out of the truck. I narrow my eyes at him. "Do I need an escort?"

"You might. I don't want you running off, but more importantly, there might be another one of them waiting inside for you." He tips his hat toward the front door.

I weigh what he says and let him follow me inside. I step through the door and see dirt and blood on the floors, I left in too much of a hurry to clean this up. My eyes land on the kitchen and the mess of utensils scattered on the counter. Now this looks like a crime scene. Sylas comes inside right behind me and checks around the rooms, looking for any threats himself.

I rub the back of my neck and let out a sigh of defeat. I think I could take on another fight in my current state, but I don't want to play with uncertainty.

He settles into the couch, unwrapping a lollipop left out from Halloween. I haven't seen him eat at all today. It doesn't mean he hasn't, but I'll bet he's hungry. I move to stand over him on the couch.

"Have you eaten? You look like you could use something."

All he does is wave the lollipop at me. I give him a sneer.

"You know, you'd probably loosen up if you drank some blood." My grin widens. I bite my wrist and hold it out for him. "Come on, try it."

When he doesn't move, I take the stick of the lollipop from his mouth and pull it out. I wipe my wrist across his lips. I feel his tongue sweep over the incisions. The warmth makes my heart pick up, and a heat forms lower in my belly. It ends almost as fast as it started. He stands up and grabs my throat in one quick movement. My back slams into the wall beside the couch.

His head dips low, and I can feel his short beard tickle my neck and his hot breath against my ear. "If you ever do that again, Rowan, I'll rip your throat out with my teeth. Now, get your shit. I'll be in the truck." Humiliation strikes me in the chest.

In this moment, I realize I don't actually know how he's doing. I haven't asked him about Liddy or how he's feeling about losing her. I assumed during the last month he'd had time to come to terms with this, but now, I see how wrong I am. I chew my lip, feeling increasingly guilty about my actions today and lack of empathy. It's unlike me to leave feelings unnoticed. It's as if turning me into a vampire has made me lose that about myself.

The truck horn blares, jolting me out of the thought. I hurry to grab my things, I don't take much. All I need are some clothes and my bathroom items. There's not a lot of value in what I own here. Before I run out of the door, I grab the journal Asta gave me and tuck it into my bag.

I lock the door and take a step back on the porch, admiring

the home I could have put more love into. I may never be back here, and that scares me the most right now. I put my hat on, and we head back to the ranch.

We arrive just as the sun starts to set early in the day. The view of the sunset here is incredible. The reds and oranges mix into pink, and starbursts of color wrap around the fall-colored tree line. It feels like a completely different place. I can breathe better, and it doesn't carry the burden of the real life I just left at home.

That is, until I see Saul still stacked on top of the bonfire.

Harris is getting the kindling ready, and I run back to the truck to get my bags. I pull a loose sweatshirt out of my suitcase and wrap myself in it, suddenly feeling the need to cover myself.

Metal chairs circle the open pit. I brush the leaves off one to sit and wrap my arms tightly around myself. The boys are working to get everything set for tonight, and I'm enjoying the eye candy.

When Liddy started dating Sylas, I met them all at the ranch for dinner. She never told me he had good-looking brothers. She warned me not to get involved with them, telling me not to ruin this for her with my inability to commit. She didn't want tension to build between us, and I wanted to be there for her. It seemed like Sylas was a catch, and up until now, I did think that. There's no doubt he has been reliable, but I can't shake the feeling that he's not being honest about how he feels. I can't help but wonder if he blames me for her death.

I need to apologize after tonight and settle the score between us. We're both in this for Liddy. We both have high stakes here, and we could use a little camaraderie. I need to get my head back on my shoulders and dig deep for that person I used to be. I'm loyal to my core. I don't want this to get worse and be left alone to figure out this new fight by myself. I'm terrified I've messed things up.

# *Chapter Twelve*

## ROWAN

THE SPARK OF THE BONFIRE LIGHTING ALMOST SHOT ME OUT OF MY SEAT. Noises around me have become clearer but also louder, and this one caught me off guard. I pick up my chair and scoot back. The fire is warm and building higher. The smell of Saul's body is pungent, and I have to cover my face with my sweatshirt. The boys come to stand behind me, mimicking my sour face.

"Rowan," Noah says, and I look to him. "Want to tell us about this whole situation now?" He waves his finger at the burning body.

I lead with Saul coming to see me, skipping over the Emma conversation I already had with Sylas. Harris grits his teeth, and Sylas clenches his jaw before running a hand through his beard. I tell them everything I found out in the library, how there are more of them, how long they've been around.

"Jesus..." Noah says at the end of it.

"Well shit, you got more done in the last month than we did. Hell, Sylas here keeps cleaning the already clean barn," Harris says before Sylas jabs him with an elbow.

I let out a forced laugh. There's a subtle sound in the distance that draws our attention.

Beyond the fire in the field, I see what looks like a figure. There are three shadows in the flames, and they are growing closer. I squint to make sure I'm seeing this right. I look up at the boys and see their eyes trained on the shadows. I'm not imagining this.

"Rowan, get up, stand behind me." Sylas grabs my shoulder and moves me. Harris picks up a thin log that strays from the pile.

They stand much taller than I do, and it takes me standing on my tippy toes to see beyond them. The figures are considerably closer and coming into plain view.

Three hooded figures are dressed in the same dark sweatshirt as Saul. Smoke billows around us, and I try not to cover my face this time as they close the distance between us. The sun is replaced by the moon high above, our only light, save for the fire dancing next to us. They look like shadows, but their pale smiles and razor-sharp teeth give them away.

*Vampires.*

My hand goes to Sylas' back.

There's a large black blur of movement, and the three men come into view only steps away from us. I clench the back of Sylas' t-shirt, bracing myself for the worst.

Harris speaks up first. "Who are you? What are you doing on private property?"

The men give a soul-shaking grin that reaches from ear to ear. "We can smell it. You burn one of ours." Their gaze goes to the fire. Saul's body is decaying, and flames shoot through the holes being made in his thin flesh.

"You were given this new life, and this is how you return the favor? We thought the three of you would make such good followers—gallant fighters—but it seems we were wrong."

New life? They consider turning our lives upside down and killing one of *our own* a favor. My grip tightens, and there's rage coiling around me. Sylas senses the anger, or maybe he can just feel the grip I have on him, because he reaches his hand behind me and places it over mine.

"Oh, and who is that behind you? She smells fresh too." The men remove their hoods, revealing buzzed hair. Their skin is sickly pale, and dirt lines their features. Their eyes are golden but bloodshot in red so vivid, they look like animals. They are dressed in tight pants with chains attached to their belts and their hands hide under leather gloves.

Harris snarls at the men and puts a protective grip on my free arm. "Who are you?"

"We are the henchmen. We were sent to see what happened to this one. Tell me, why shouldn't we seal your fate the same way you did our dear Saul?"

"He was preying on an innocent woman. He threatened her, tried to rip her head off. We won't stand idly by and let you terrorize this town." Sylas takes a step forward, and I lose my grip on him.

"He just wanted a taste of our power, boy," his voice booms and echoes. "You were given this immortal life, and now you must follow our orders." The two men flanking the head demon move to surround us.

"Your orders?" I whisper, swiveling my head to keep an eye

on each of the men.

The henchmen start gathering the chain from their belts. The one in the middle begins pacing, swinging the chains in swift loops. They look like the silver chains that held the brothers in place. The leather gloves these men are wearing stop their skin from burning. "You see, we're here on orders from The Vampire Queen herself, the Devil in Disguise. We, the henchmen, do her bidding. We create only the strongest Vampires. Only the ones we see fit to follow get turned. The rest shall die—our dinner, if you will." He wraps the chains tightly around his hands.

I push past Sylas. Harris quickly grabs my arm, but I shove him away and stand front and center, looking the head of the group straight in the eyes. He shows his blackened teeth that come to a point and swipes his tongue across them. The vile gesture makes my stomach turn. Before I can think any further, I open my mouth. "What do you do with the ones you turn?"

"Become one of us, of course."

My lips turn downward, and my brows knit together in anger. I ball my fists at my side, my nails digging deep into the skin on my palms, and take a step back.

"I'll make you a deal." He starts pacing and clasps his hands together. "The girl comes with me, and the three of you can stay unharmed."

"Fuck you, I'm not going anywhere. Not with you monsters."

"Ah, but what a mistake you're making." He steps forward, and I feel the boys at my back instantly.

"It doesn't matter what you say. I'm not turning into this

disgusting devil you are."

"Girl, I think that's enough talk for tonight," he spits out. The chain he had wrapped around his fist comes flying toward me. I don't have enough time to duck before it hits me across the face. I gasp and grab ahold of my cheek, moving my jaw back into place. The flesh is burning, and I feel it healing underneath my hand.

The Loughty brothers each take a fighting position against the demons. They are dancing a dangerous game. Each henchman throws out a chain of silver, and I watch them dodge them with ease.

Harris grabs the chain flying toward him and screams while pulling it towards him, the henchman at the end of the chain getting closer to him. Harris's hands drip with blood as he wraps the chain around the demon tight enough to strangle him. Harris opens his mouth and closes his teeth around that man's throat. A guttural noise comes from both of them as he rips out the demon's throat. He spits it out and throws him into the still-burning fire. His body thrashes for a moment before being torn apart by the flames.

"Such a big mistake," another henchman says, chains wrapped tightly around his hands, ready to swing.

I try to get up before it hits me. I'm on my hands and knees when the chain hits my thigh and wraps around my leg. I scream, scratching my hands into the dirt, but I'm being pulled away. The metal doesn't burn through my jeans, but it tightens and suffocates the muscles.

The henchman pulls me towards himself. I feel the tug of the chain and the dirt on my stomach where my sweatshirt is being pulled up. Harris is on his knees, gasping, taking in the damage to his hands. His hands are taking too long to heal. Noah and Sylas run to grab me, but the henchman is faster. He picks up speed, and the dirt scrapes against my skin and burns my stomach. My nails fill with dirt and splinter under tension. Panicking is making my throat tighten, and I try to kick myself free of the grip he has on me.

I see a shadow gaining on Noah. "Watch out!" I manage to scream out, but Noah is slammed to the ground before he has time to react. The chains start to bind him, his arms burnt and cut. I see a tinge of steam coming off him. My eyes fill with tears as I thrash harder. I hear a dark chuckle behind me.

Sylas is almost to me but turns to see his brother in the struggle. I'm panting, "Go, go. Help him." My eyes plead, seeing the war going on in his head. The henchman lifts me by the back of my hair, gathering a fistful, my feet struggling to stay on the ground. They are much stronger than us. His skin is leathery and scarred. His breath smells rancid when he turns my head to face him. My bottom lip starts to shake on its own accord. I try to harden my features, but my body turns against me.

"I can smell your fear, girl. This is why you must die. I hear our queen wants your head. You're not fit to rule over mortals, so immortality won't be your path. A shame, really; you're such a pretty thing." He sweeps my bangs aside with his long fingernails. His grip tightens in my hair, and his other hand disappears behind him. When his hand comes back up, he's gripping a wooden stake. He reaches beyond his head and starts to swing downward.

The stake plunges into my chest and nearly hits my heart. The scream that comes out of me would have woken an entire neighborhood. Out here, though, no one can hear me. I gasp out, trying to find my feet and comprehend what happened.

I can feel blood spilling from my mouth. My eyes widen and tears stream out. The henchman smiles, and his slimy tongue devours the blood leaving my body.

This is not how I thought I'd die. The last few months have been a whirlwind of grief and finding new meaning in my life. I thought I could avenge Liddy and my parents. I thought I could move past this life-altering trajectory and find my place. I wanted to do right and fix what I wronged.

My arms become weak, and they drop to my sides. I can't feel much of anything anymore. The wooden stake is rubbing against my heart, causing splintering pain that ebbs and flows. I can't hang on to life for much longer.

Shadows are moving around me in a fight, but I can't tell who is there. I can't tell who made it out of this fight. Who's winning? My body is jerked free of his grasp, and I feel the wind through my hair. It offers relief before I close my eyes.

I don't open them again.

# Chapter Thirteen

## SYLAS

I RUSH ROWAN INSIDE WITHOUT A SECOND THOUGHT. There's a wooden stake lodged in her chest, but she didn't die on impact. I think it missed her heart, but she's losing a lot of blood.

I lay her in my bed since it's the closest room off the back porch. Instinct has taken over my brain, and I'm just going through the movements.

*Keep her alive, keep her alive.* I hear those words in Liddy's voice.

I pull the stake from her chest. Blood gushes out, and I cover it quickly with my hands before grabbing the comforter and letting it take the spot my hands are covering. It soaks through. My hands are covered in her sweet blood, and the smell of it is filling my head with desires I shouldn't be having.

*Keep her alive, keep her alive.* I let Liddy's voice steady me.

I take a deep breath in. The wound in her chest starts to heal itself, but it's slow. I do the only other thing I can think might work. I take a knife from my nightstand and slash across the palm of my hand. My blood flows, and I hold the wound to her mouth, willing her to drink.

"Come on, Row, don't die on me." I plead with her, knowing she can't hear me. I've put on a hard front to protect both of us from spiraling, but I'm starting to lose it. I can't lose her too. I won't let Liddy down this way.

My blood pools in her mouth and the wound on her chest closes faster now. If I can get her to drink, I can nurse her back to health. I can give her safety. This will never happen again.

The wound finally closes, and I remove my hand. It takes me a few minutes of watching life come back into her flesh to feel comfortable enough to move away. I go to my bathroom to collect towels and washcloths soaked in warm water.

I gently wipe away the blood from her lips and cheeks. Her eyes look hollow. I wash away the dirt from her light brown hair and brush her bangs back into place. Her lips return to a pale pink, plush and downturned. Her cheeks are blooming red and filling back out. She looks broken, and I plan to piece her back together.

I'm not sure she would appreciate me undressing her, but she needs out of these clothes. I rip them off and clean the red staining her chest. There's a small scar near her left breast where the stake had planted itself. I run my fingers over it gently. It's the only imperfection on her porcelain skin—an imperfection I will cherish for keeping her alive. I replace her torn sweatshirt with one of my own and lay her on the pillows, tucking her into fresh blankets.

After Noah was taken down by one of the henchmen, I tried to get to him, but I saw the stake raised above Rowan's head, and my stomach dropped. I wasn't fast enough to stop him. They are faster and stronger than we are. I guess they've been around a lot longer than Rowan let on.

I raced as fast as I could for her. I took a small piece of flaming firewood and drove it into the back of the henchman killing Rowan. I drove it straight through his heart. The wood and fire set him to ashes. The last henchman left Noah to get me for what I did to his comrade, so I did the same to him—drove the splintering wood straight through him.

Though the burns on my hand still hurt, I yanked Noah free from the chains. Harris stopped his bleeding and tended to Noah's burns—feeding him blood and setting him straight. I rushed Rowan inside and let my brothers deal with the rest.

I don't know how we made it out of there with everyone alive, but I'm thankful for it. My brothers are my lifeline, the only true blood I have left in this world. And now, I have Rowan. The burden of keeping her safe felt too heavy when she first arrived at the ranch and heavier when she left. It took everything in me not to kill her in those first few hours after she freed us. When I tasted her blood, it was like nothing I've had before.

It gave me life and power. It heightened my senses. Her moan shook me out of the daydream that day and set me straight into a rage of emotions I've been trying to mask since.

It was a lustful want, a hunger I needed to rein in. I tried to distance myself and put up a hard front, but she saw right through it. She tried to get me to drink from her again, and I stormed out like a coward.

I settle on my bed next to her, the mattress groaning under my weight. I watch her breathe, hoping she wakes up. I want to help her find out who's doing this to us and how many more will be after us. I don't want to abandon the ranch, but if she's constantly in danger, we may need to find a new place to call home.

Working the ranch was never my dream, but I stuck by Noah. This is the life for him, and he was the one who took it over after our dad died. Harris and I couldn't leave him here alone. It's a lot of upkeep, even after cutting the cattle down by half. Keeping up the land is still as much work. I count us lucky Dad left behind enough money to keep things running without the cattle.

Now, I don't know what path to take. Nothing is sure to me anymore. Liddy and I had plans to settle down here. She loved the ranch and loved her life in this small town. That was enough reason to do this. I wanted that for her. A life, a wife, raising kids of our own. That has been taken away from me—her dreams taken from me—in a flash, and the unknown terrifies me. I've always been on the straight and narrow, always the one everyone can count on. "Mr. Perfect," Dad always said.

I'm not perfect, I know it, but I do try to be there for everyone. I do try to take accountability and be the best I can at what I do. There's no failing in my mind. But I feel like I've failed Liddy.

Seeing Rowan here next to me feels like a failure. Sure, I got her out, but she's not awake yet. My mind starts to swirl with endless possibilities. The bad spills in faster than the good. There are so many unknowns left to figure out. I hope Rowan is here to help us find information. She wants revenge for Liddy, but I'm not sure I do. I'm not sure I can be in this endless battle if it means everyone gets hurt.

I roll onto my back and close my eyes. Sleep comes fast, but it's not restful. Nightmares come and go of Liddy. My last moments with her. How I left her at home with Rowan, thinking they'd be safe and able to defend themselves. Rowan shouldn't have left her. I shouldn't have left her. I can feel my body thrashing on the mattress. I fight the demons who took my sweet girl. I fight Rowan for letting this happen. The rational part of me knows she's not to blame, but the rage inside me is coiled so tightly, it's hard to tell the difference.

A cold hand presses against the side of my face. I'm stuck inside this nightmare, trying to wake up.

*Sylas, wake up. Sylas.*

I'm reaching for the exit, but it keeps getting further away. The sight of my girl lying dead flashes past me as I run. I run faster trying to catch up.

*Sylas! Wake up!*

Water splashes over my face, and I shoot up in bed. My eyes flash open, and I bare my teeth, looking straight into Rowan's golden eyes. There's a look of horror painted over her features.

I'm still feeling the emotions of the nightmare, and I try to coil back into myself. Her cool palm reaches my face, and I still. It doesn't feel right to have her touch me. It feels too intimate.

I unclench my jaw and remove my face from her grip.

There's a pang in my heart knowing I hurt her again.

"Sorry, you were having a nightmare. It looked bad. Are you okay?" The sound of empathy in her voice makes me feel worse.

I give her a terse nod and leave the room. I should check on my brothers anyway.

I head back to the main room and let my brothers know Rowan's health status. I leave out that we slept next to each other; it doesn't seem important.

"Thank God she woke up," Noah says as I face him, rubbing my short beard.

"I know. I can't fuck this one up too." I pat my thigh and head to the kitchen to grab a beer.

They both give me knowing glances and sly smiles. Harris speaks up this time, rubbing the back of his neck like something is weighing on him. "Look, man, we never had the chance to talk about Liddy. I know y'all were in it for the long haul. You want to talk about it?"

I lean back onto the counter and cross my legs over each other, one hand in my belt loop and the other holding my beer. "I miss her so much, man, but I'm trying not to think about it. Every time I think of her, I get so angry, it's hard to stop that rage.

Noah slaps his hand on my shoulder. "You still need to process it, brother. It'll eat you alive one day if you don't."

I nod my head slowly. I know he's right, but the weight of losing her feels too heavy when I need to keep Rowan alive now.

I look up from my boots and give both of my brothers a look. Harris angles his head at me, wondering what I'm thinking. "I think she's been talking to me. I hear her in my head sometimes, telling me what to do."

Harris chuckles. "She's haunting you from the grave. I knew you were the submissive one."

I throw my fist out and jab Harris in the gut. "I'm fucking serious. She told me to keep Rowan alive."

"Man, I don't know about that, Sylas. That sounds like some voodoo shit."

I smooth my hair back and let my hand rub the nape of my neck. "Being a vampire is some voodoo shit. I think there's still a lot we don't know about it." They nod in agreement. We need to start figuring out our new life.

I hear a soft whisper behind me. When I turn around, no one is there.

I lay on the plush leather couch in the main living room to try and get some rest. The moment I close my eyes, I see her. She's talking to me, whispering in my ear, and I can hear it like a faint noise in the distance.

*Sylas, she's not safe. You have to protect her.*

I try to ask her questions, but it's not getting through.

*No one can protect her the way you can. Be her savior, be her protection now.*

*It has to be you.*

I reach my hand towards her, but when I sweep my hand out, there's nothing but bright mist, and she's gone.

# Chapter Fourteen

## ROWAN

THE ONLY THING I REMEMBER BEFORE SYLAS WOKE ME UP WAS THE WOODEN STAKE DRIVING INTO MY CHEST. By some miracle, I didn't die tonight. It's easy to assume Sylas fixed me up. I'm in his bed, clean, and wearing what seem to be his clothes. I didn't mean to scare him when I woke him up. He was thrashing his legs into the mattress and crying out for Liddy. I was terrified.

I need to talk to him and set things right. I just need a minute to process what I went through while I was unconscious.

I swear, I could hear her voice.

Begging me to wake up.

Begging me to live.

Begging me to stay with Sylas.

The last part confuses me the most. Stay with him for what reason? I didn't plan on leaving anytime soon, but I need to know what she means. Meant? This is getting harder.

No matter how hard I tried, I couldn't speak back. She's in my head with one-way communication. There's static on my end, but I hear her loud and clear.

Our sweet girl is guiding us through this. Always so selfless, even in death.

I repeat her words over and over.

*Rowan, wake up.*

*Rowan, you must survive this.*

*Rowan, stay with him. Stay with Sylas.*

I have to talk to him.

I steady myself to get out of bed, still feeling weak. I run my hand over the spot where the stake went into me. It's a small, jagged scar. Another imperfection on me.

Breathe in. Breathe out.

I push to stand on my legs and fall hard onto the cold hardwoods. My knees shake in pain.

Goddammit.

I hear the bedroom door open, and the voice is unmistakable.

"Are you okay?" Sylas helps me back on the bed.

"Yeah, just embarrassed. I've been a burden on you guys, and now I'm fucking helpless." I rub my face with my hands, holding them there for a moment before he pulls them away.

"You almost died. There's nothing to be embarrassed about. We'd rather have you here than dead," he says very certainly.

I meet his eyes and can't stop the tears from falling. He lets me sit in this moment for a while.

"I think she's talking to me. Maybe it was a coma dream, but...she was talking to me." I look at him, and to my surprise, his face is soft and easy.

"She talks to me too, Row." The side of his lips turns up.

I take in a steadying breath before telling him the rest. "She told me to stay with you. I just don't know what it means.

I don't know what any of this means. I thought I was doing all this for her. Now, it seems like we were meant to do something bigger."

He takes my hands in his. "We figure this out together. For Liddy, but for you also. You deserve to know the truth."

I nod and feel the tension ease away. Having someone on my side means the world to me. Having my darkest parts show and being accepted is all I want. I grasp this moment like it could be taken away in a heartbeat. I squeeze his hands in silent prayer.

"Well, Mr. Loughty, I'm going to need to eat first for anything to get figured out." I give him a pathetic smile.

His chuckle is deep and inviting. "Never call me that again, and you've got a deal." I drink in his wide smile and hold my hand out to shake in agreement. "I'll be right back with some food. Don't move."

"Sir, yes, sir!" I salute, but he's already halfway out the door.

He has been hearing her too. My first reaction was to feel relieved, but I'm terrified and confused about what all this means. I chew my lip and fall back on the pillows. Of course, she would be talking to us. Of course, she would stick me with her boyfriend to figure things out. It would be a lie if I said I wasn't glad to have him by my side. We're both going through a lot right now, but he's here for me. He's here for me like no one has been in the past—aside from Liddy.

She's the only one who knows who I truly am, the only one who was there for me when my parents died—when my parents were murdered. She made me talk through my feelings, never letting me bottle things up. I don't know if she was sent down by angels, but that girl had a deeper perception than anyone I've met in my life.

And now, she wants me to stick by Sylas. I'll listen. I do feel guilty for feeling so comfortable with him. It feels wrong. It feels wrong, yet I don't want it to stop. Maybe it's my fear of being alone.

I close my eyes, willing her to come back to me, willing her to give me some answers. Doesn't she know I need her just as much? I want her to tell me it's okay. I want her to tell me what's going on, but it's silent in my head. I feel insane for thinking my dead best friend would answer my thoughts.

Sylas comes back with a tray of food.

Cheeseburger.

Fries.

And a cup of deep red liquid in a glass.

"What is this?" I pick up the glass and smell it. "Blood?"

He nods. "Drink that first. You need to get your strength back. Harris and Noah are going around town to see if anyone else was hurt."

I empty the glass in three long gulps and lick the remainder from my lips.

"You're taking this vampire thing a little too well," I say to him, starting on my fries.

"Trust me, I'm not."

"I'm just saying, you haven't gone feral at any moment. You look so...restrained." I wave my fry at him in a circle.

He sits himself at the edge of the bed. His bed. "Believe me, I am barely holding myself together."

"Pft. Prove it. You've been Mr. Broody, get shit done,

bodyguard vampire."

He slicks his hair back with his hand and then massages his shoulder. I imagine those big hands on me but quickly shake the thought away. Having someone protect me is messing with my head. When he looks my way again, I quickly make myself busy with the fries on my plate. "Well, thank you for the food."

He gives me a strained smile, but I can see a battle in his eyes. He stands to leave, and before I can think too much about it, I open my mouth. "I think we need to talk."

He lets out a tired sigh. He has been through a lot in the last 24 hours, but I can't let this go on any longer.

I rub my hands over my thighs, my fingers dancing lightly over my knees.

"I'm sorry about what happened at my house. I was so disrespectful and out of line. I'm still trying to figure this thing out, and my emotions are so not what I need them to be right now. All that to say, I shouldn't have forced you like that." I can't meet his eyes.

It's quiet for a long while, long enough to make me think he either left or fell asleep.

"Row, I-It's not that I was mad. I'm not mad at you; how could I be? This is new for both of us. I just...I don't know where my head is either. Tasting you...Tasting your blood that first day, it's like nothing I've experienced. I didn't want to hurt you, and I still need time to figure this out." Both of his hands are on top of his head, and he's pacing like we just unlocked some new kind of stress for him. "And now we're hearing Liddy? What the fuck. I haven't even processed that."

I nod slowly. "There's a lot we need to figure out. As long

as you're ready to do this together, I don't have to ask you any more questions." I finally meet his gaze.

"Let's just try to find out what's going on first." He bites his bottom lip and nods aimlessly, like he's still in his head, and then walks out.

That didn't go how I planned it. I finish my food before showering and moving rooms. To my room, I guess. Someone has put my bags in the room and hung some of my things up. I smile to myself, knowing they unpacked me.

I feel welcome here.

Morning comes, and I feel well enough to get moving on my own. I wash my face to get a fresh start on things and put on real clothes. I open the bathroom window to air the room. The morning air is crisp and begs to be enjoyed. I inhale the fresh mountain breeze, longing for the snow to make its way towards us.

I look out the window and see the cattle still near the barn. They're all lying down in the grass. I don't know anything about cattle or ranching, so I can't tell if I should be worried. I know Noah brings them in during the colder months, but it seems early to do so.

I squint trying to see better. It's no use, the grass is too high to see anything. I need to head out there to see what's going on.

I dress quickly in warmer clothes, putting on jeans and a sweater. I add a coat to my layers and slip into my boots by the back door before grabbing my hat.

I walk onto the back porch, noting no one is around. I step into the grass and make my way to the barn. The quiet of the morning should relax me, but I'm getting uneasy, concern building in my stomach.

The closer I get to the cattle, the faster my breathing picks up. They aren't lying in the grass—they're dead.

A loud moan from one of the cows startles me, and I run towards the sound. The barn is straight ahead. I round the door and see Sylas on his knees, crouched over the animal. Feeding off her. Draining her.

My eyes are wide, and I take a step back to leave the barn, but he turns and meets my eyes. He looks feral. He looks dangerous.

We stare frozen in each other's gaze before his lips drop into a frown. He quickly looks between me and the cow holding onto its life. The sound of its pain brings tears to my eyes.

"I didn't mean to. I didn't mean to. I didn't mean to," he mutters to himself as he stands, walking slowly towards me.

I turn on my heels and run as fast as I can away from him.

# Chapter Fifteen

## SYLAS

Rowan shook me from myself. I'm crouched over one of our cattle, covered in blood—doing something so unspeakable, I don't think she'll ever forgive me. I don't think Noah will ever forgive me. What the fuck have I done?

I remove myself from the barn and try to walk towards her to explain or something. I don't know what to do. But she runs. She runs from me.

I'm supposed to protect her, but I'm starting to question my ability. I'm starting to crack.

I run after her, knowing I'll need to make this right. I need to talk to her and get this sorted.

"Rowan, wait!" I call out, but she's fast. She's heading towards the tree line. My impulses are pushing against my rationality, pushing against the voices telling me to stop running after her and give her space. I need to catch her.

The grass is crisp against my boots as I plant them into the ground, digging my feet into the hard soil, gaining speed on her.

She looks back to see where I am, her hair flying over her

face. She looks like a doe in the headlights, and I smirk, a crack in my rational thoughts giving space to an unknown instinct. I make a U-turn and head back to the barn. I don't have time to saddle my mare. I grab my rope and hop on her bareback. I kick my boots into her side, and we take off running. I'm sure I would have been faster on foot, but I want to make this fun. I'm going to make her listen to me.

I can see Rowan slow down and look back at me, confusion lacing her brows when she sees me on horseback. I'm getting closer, and that realization comes to her, setting her back into motion.

"I'm coming for you!" I hoot out and ready my rope. I've only ever done this with cattle, but I grew up on this ranch; I can lasso anything.

I hug my mare with strong thighs and start swinging the rope around my head. I call her name, and she looks back with wide eyes. I throw my rope, and it catches around her neck. I don't want to choke her, but I want to teach her a lesson in running.

I ride to her side and pull the rope tight, the rope around her neck looking good there. I yank up on it, and she meets my eyes from under her lashes. I can't help but plaster the biggest grin on my face.

"Row, you know better."

She grips the rope, but I have a strong hold on it. I'm sure she could rip it in half if she wanted to. I'm taking this as a sign to keep going.

"Let me go!" She tugs the rope again.

"Only if you take a ride with me." I extend my hand out for

her to take. I see a fire lighting those eyes, and it only makes me want this more. This feral beast inside me is taking over, and I'm letting him win.

She takes my hand and pulls me right to the ground, slamming my face in the mud. I feel her boot press against the side of my face. My hair is getting matted with dirt. She removes the rope from her neck, and I feel my arms pull towards my back. The rough rope wraps around my wrists several times before she ties it off.

"Ready for a ride, cowboy?" She gives me the most saccharine smile I've ever seen, and I know I'm about to lose.

"What are you talking about?" I try to ask, but she's already mounting my horse. "You can't just leave me here!" That's when I feel the tug against my arms. She has the rope in her hands, kicking her boots into my horse and taking off with me in tow.

My body is dragging against the field until I feel a change of ground. There are sticks and leaves digging into me. My nails are getting battered, and my pants are barely hanging on with this speed. She's bringing me higher into the mountain. The terrain quickly changes to frost and snow. There's a relief on my body when the cool ice hits my torn skin.

We slow to a stop, and she jumps off and tugs heavily at the rope.

"Maybe this will teach you a lesson, Sylas." She towers over me and reaches for my hands.

"Untie me," I spit out.

"I will." She smiles. "But not yet." She moves me to a thick tree frozen in the ground. I feel her wrapping the rope and knotting it at the base.

I snarl at her. "Rowan, get back here!"

She turns and narrows her eyes at me, and I'm suddenly scared shitless of her. "I think I'll leave you here for a while. Don't get too cold, asshole." She takes off towards the ranch.

My new bodily make-up keeps me warm enough in the cold, but it doesn't help that there are gashes down my back. The snow makes it harder to heal, and I want to clean the wounds first.

I know Rowan has a temper, and I don't think she's coming back for me. I pull my arms against the tree, but she tied it tight, and the direction my arms are in would pull my shoulder right off.

My jeans soak in the wet snow, and I'm getting colder as the time passes.

*You deserve this, you know.*

I look around trying to find where the voice is coming from, but there's no one around.

"Is someone there?" I see clouds of my breath in the air. My teeth are starting to chatter. I might be getting delusional.

A moment later, a form comes into view. It shimmers a cool blue, blurring at the edges, and I see Liddy come to life before me. The sight of her makes my body warm.

"Liddy, baby." I smile up at her. "I miss you."

*Cut the shit, Sylas. What do you think you're doing?*

The words sting. This is the first time I'm getting to talk to her since her death, and she's coming at me with daggers.

"I don't know what came over me." I wipe my tongue over my bottom lip and suck it in, turning over my thoughts. "That's a lie…"

She just nods.

"I've been so tightly wound, and I let this new craving get a hold of me. It felt so good, Liddy. It felt so good to let go for a minute. The hunt felt so natural."

She kneels before me and places her hand on my knees. All I can feel is a cold whisper against my leg, like she's just a breeze in the wind.

*You've always been so steady in your path, in what you want. I knew it would bite you back one day. You have to learn how to control this without it going too far, to learn to adapt.*

I sigh and hang my head. "I'm cracking, Liddy. I'm breaking. This is so much to take on. I don't understand how Rowan and my brothers just adapted to this shit."

I feel a cold whisper on the side of my face. I look up and see into her eyes—see through her eyes. I lose a tear at the sight of her.

*They have their own battles. Focus on yours. She can help you. You'll be good together in this fight.*

"How are you not mad about this? How can you watch us like this?"

She chuckles. Actually chuckles. *Sylas, I'm a ghost. This is your life to live now. I'll be by your side and hers when I'm needed, but I'm leaving for a while. I need you to be strong.*

And I will be. I will try to be strong for her. For Rowan. There must have been a heavy weight on my chest, because once she said she believed in me, once she said I could be what keeps us safe, I could breathe a little easier. I could think a little easier. I knew I had to be better, become a better version of this monster. If I keep my grief and anger bottled up like this any longer, it could be the final blow for all of us.

I want to be the one to walk Rowan through this treachery, as long as she can forgive me.

I deserve to be out on my ass in the snow. So, I sit for a while longer, taking in the chill and willing my body to warm, willing myself to fight through the monster inside me. I will curb this craving and emotional ruin, and I will come out victorious. For my girls.

I doze off and wake up when the sun is at its peak. I put all my strength into my arms and snap free of the ropes. It rips my shoulder out of the socket, but I place it back and shake off the cold. I head home.

When I get back inside the house, she's waiting for me on the worn leather sofa.

"That took you a lot longer than I expected. Ready to face the music?"

I scratch my beard and saunter towards her. I sit in the leather chair beside the couch and prop my arms on my knees. It takes me a minute to gain the courage, but I look at her and tell her everything I need to say.

"My brothers warned me not to bottle this shit up, and goddammit, Noah gave me one rule, and I broke it. I'm the one with my head on my shoulders, but it feels like I'm the only one cracking at the seams." I start to hold back my tears but let a few drip down my cheeks.

It feels like I've ripped my heart out and served it to her on a platter, but this is what I get for bottling things up. She grips my hands and squeezes.

"This isn't easy for any of us, despite how you feel. We can all get through this together and fight those monsters. We are not like them, Sylas. We are better than them, and we'll win." I don't understand how she says it with such surety, but it gives me the push I need and a bit of confidence. "But if you ever pull this shit again, I'll chain you outside for the crows."

"I don't know if I want to fight them, Rowan, I just want to keep everyone safe. I know you want revenge, but this is getting far out of our grasp."

"I can't ask you to take part in something you don't want to do, but for me, this is the only way I can move on." She clasps her hands together in her lap.

I nod not wanting to get into that conversation yet. "Well then, let me get this mess cleaned up before Noah gets back." I know that's going to be another battle I fight today. That part is weighing on me the most.

"I'll help. Can we do something with the dead cattle so they don't go to waste?" It's really killing me how she thinks of this shit. How is she so level-headed in these situations?

"We can load them into the trailer and bring them to a butcher down the street. They're familiar with us and won't ask any questions." I reach the back porch and settle my hat back on my head.

Rowan and I make quick work of cleaning up the barn and pasture. We finish just as my brothers pull back up to the house.

"Hey, man." I slip my hands into the front pockets of my jeans, "Listen, I can't tell you how sorry I am." Noah's face is painted with confusion. "I lost control today, and the cattle…" I don't get the chance to finish before he's running towards the barn.

"YOU FUCKER!" He throws his hat to the ground and runs up to me. I'm shoved to the ground, and his fists come flying into my face.

"You."

*punch.*

"Fucking."

*punch.*

"Asshole."

*punch.*

"This is everything I have!"

*punch.*

I deserve this. Harris eventually drags him off me and tells him to drive the cattle to the shady butcher.

He helps me off the ground, and I see a fucking smirk on her face. The 'I told you so, you got what was coming for you' face. She's right.

Despite the pain and torture she's putting me through, I hear her tell Harris she'll take care of me. This is possibly the lowest I've ever felt.

"Let's go get cleaned up, cowboy." She laces her arm with mine, allowing me to lean on her to get up the back steps and into the house. "On your stomach." She points to my bed. "We need to clean your wounds first so they can heal properly." I obey.

The alcohol stings. I wince at the pain but bite into my pillow so she can't hear me. She works on my back first and then my busted face.

"I cried and lost all control I had over myself the first few weeks I was home," she says, mindlessly wiping away the blood. "I felt uneasy in my skin, unsure of who I was. I still don't think I know who I am."

"I just bottled it up and took it out on the local wildlife."

Rowan chuckles. "We ate our pizza delivery guy."

"Okay, that might be worse."

Rowan rolls her eyes. "It was terrifying when it happened. I don't like killing people, but they do taste much better than animal blood…"

"I agree with you there."

"That's the hardest part for me. I know deep down, I don't want to harm people, but there's a devil on my shoulder, hungry to jump at the opportunity."

I don't have to think before responding, "The control is what I battle with. I've been keeping such a tight leash on it that it snaps under tension."

She nods and finishes cleaning me up, throwing the dirty towels in the hamper. She pauses there a moment, and I can tell she's weighing if she should walk out now or not. A small sigh leaves her lips, and my gaze falls to them. She chews her lip and decides to come sit on the edge of the bed.

"I don't know what to do just as much as you don't." Her hands fold into her lap, and she's picking at her nail. "We need to come up with a plan to get our freedom back, and we need to lay out rules. For us."

I can't think of anything to say right now, so I nod. She assures me Harris will bring me some blood to drink so I can heal and get rest.

I want to sleep, but I can't stop turning over ideas in my head of ways to get out of this. I want to show her that I'm in this, show her that I'm reliable and not a liability. I think of running far from Georgetown, leaving everything behind and hope they don't chase us. I think of the reporter who brushed her off—the reporter who knows more than she could say over the phone. I fall asleep knowing who we have to visit this week.

# Chapter Sixteen

## ROWAN

I spend the night tossing and turning. Once I see the clock hit 3 am, I decide that's enough. With the lamp on the nightstand casting a warm tone throughout the room, I start writing down everything I know to be true. If I'm going to figure this out, I need to get my thoughts straight. Writing it down always helps me sort through the chaotic noise in my head. That's what got me into journalism—writing and truths. Not understanding what happened to my parents sparked a light inside me. I started seeking meaning, the small details in stories that could change the trajectory of things. The school paper was the first place I started to really fall in love with it—pieces on the high school football team that almost got me suspended, an inside look at the cafeteria lunches that made the cooks give me dirty looks for the rest of the year.

I don't have much to go on right now. The henchmen were sent for me, but I still don't know why. I can't place why my parents would have been involved in this. They died when I was so young; it doesn't make rational sense, and I can't put a finger on anything worth noting before they were murdered. They used to exchange whispers once they thought I was asleep, but I never thought anything of it.

I lift the soft pillow to my face and scream into it. Turning into a vampire, I can do. Fighting the cravings lacing my blood, I can do. This constant state of unknown I continue to find myself in—this is what breaks me.

The wooden door slowly opens, and I see his slicked back blond hair curl loosely around his ears. He walks to my bed, and the mattress shifts under his weight. "What are you doing up?"

I lace my fingers over each other, tapping my thumb over the top of my hand. "I couldn't sleep."

"I couldn't get much either." He moves to lay on the bed next to me, stretching out his legs that meet the edge of the mattress.

I move the notepad and pen to the nightstand and mimic his position, laying my head on my own pillow. We lay in silence for long moments before he speaks again.

"I thought the hardest thing I had going for me was what I'd amount to in life. I had it all figured out, and now, everything is shit."

I turn my head towards him. "Funny how life can do that to us. I had nothing figured out, and now the uncertainty feels crushing."

"Liddy would have known what to do," he whispers.

"She did always push us towards a path, made us make decisions."

"I don't think it was always the right path she pushed us towards, though," he admits.

"I think she just didn't want us getting lost." Lost is exactly what I feel now without her.

He turns to face me and looks into my eyes. I want to know what he's thinking behind those golden flecks in his irises. My breathing becomes hitched the longer he looks at me. Something stirs in my chest, and I can't seem to remember the moment when we became this close. It has been easy, sharing the grief of losing Liddy, that I never stopped to think about this growing attachment. We haven't talked about her much, but I can see it in his eyes, that twinkle of understanding.

I feel his calloused palm squeeze my hand, and I pull away. The connection felt like more than a friendly touch, making guilt build in my gut. We've always had a good friendship in the time he was with Liddy—we were playful, and he looked after me even when I didn't ask him to. I knew he was someone we could rely on. Memories of us hanging out together surface, making me smile.

"Remember when Liddy locked us out of her house because we were fighting over pizza toppings? She wouldn't let us back in until we could get along."

Sylas laughs beside me. "Pineapple does *not* go on pizza. I will never budge on that one. We had to pretend to agree before we were let back inside."

"It does! I have a well-refined palate, something a caveman like you could never have." I jab my elbow into his side and laugh.

"Did you just call me a caveman?" He reciprocates with an elbow jab of his own. "This reminds me of the time she took us hiking in the pouring rain. Talk about a caveman."

"Don't you dare." I shoot daggers at him.

"You slid down that mudslide like it was your full-time job." He laughs so hard, tears form in the corner of his eyes. "You were covered, I mean covered, in mud."

I can't help but bust out laughing. "I can't believe she made us do that. It was a torrential downpour. Nothing could stop her when she had her mind made up."

"Nothing," he repeats back to me.

I clear my throat and decide we need to do something about food. "We can't keep up an all-animal diet if we're trying to get stronger. We should talk with Harris and Noah and decide what to do." A silent nod is all I receive before we head to the main room.

"I have a buddy down at the sheriff's office. He can get us the addresses of the criminals in town. If this is our life now, we might as well take out some of the bad guys." Noah shrugs and bites the inside of his cheek. It looks like he's waiting for approval.

"God, I can't believe this is what it's come to. I think it's our best option," Sylas says, looking at me. It seems like everyone here wants me to give the final opinion. They wonder if this is okay in my eyes, or if they want to make sure it won't ruin me.

I clap my hands. "Well, let's get that list then."

We're all sitting in the truck parked a block from the house of someone named Ryan Fitz. He is a listed sex offender in the area. Apparently, we've never heard of him because he has been hiding away in his house since the charge.

We got into a heated argument about how to handle this five minutes ago, and it has been silent since.

"Whatever, I'll do it. I'm fucking starving and I'm losing my edge." That earns me a snort from the gallery. I grab a pocket knife from the center console and slide it across my wrist before getting out.

I round the truck and head for the front door. I land three solid knocks on Ryan's door before it swings open. "I don't want visitors," he practically spits in my face before getting a good look at me. His smile turns slimy once he lays his eyes on me. "Well, are you lost, girl?"

Bile rises in my throat, and I remind myself that he is prey and I am his predator. "I got a little cut up, and I was hoping you had some Band-Aids." I roll up my sleeve to show a bloody gash across my wrist, quickly covering it before he can watch it heal.

He licks his bottom lip, the decision is weighing in his eyes. "Come in." The smile he gives me makes my blood boil.

I step inside his home, and it reeks. There's a dirty pipe and scattered residue on the coffee table, several discarded takeout boxes on the floor next to it. The couch looks crusted in God knows what. I keep looking around for the back door that the guys will be coming in from. I spot the movement outside and give them a nod signaling I'm ready.

Ryan rounds the corner with a Band-Aid and dirty rag. "Let's get you cleaned up. Why don't you take off that sweater?" He reaches for the hem and tries to tug it free from my body before I grab his wrist and snap his arm.

"In your dreams, you disgusting piece of shit," I grunt out, and he doubles over his newly broken arm, spitting out curses at me.

"Get the fuck out, bitch!"

"You wish this was the worst of it." My smile grows feral, and I can smell the iron in his blood dripping from the break—the bone ripped through skin.

His eyes widen at the sight of the Loughty brothers, who made their way in. Harris gives a final smile to Ryan, who tries to open his mouth to speak, but Harris snaps his neck before he has the chance.

"This place is disgusting." Noah covers his nose with his shirt.

I'm almost drooling, ready to get a taste. I lower to my knees in front of this vile piece of human garbage. "Ladies first, right?" I lick the blood off the broken bone sticking out of his arm.

"Fuck."

I sink my teeth deep into his flesh and start drinking. His blood tastes different from the other humans I've been drinking. A buzz goes through my body. My head spins, and I have to break the hold I have on him. I throw my head back, and a wicked laugh comes out of my mouth. I see Sylas dig into Ryan's neck a moment later. He comes up for a breath, panting. I look into his bloodshot eyes and take in the biggest grin I've seen on him.

I can see Harris talking to Noah, but I can't hear what they're saying through the adrenaline, the instant euphoria that hit me the moment I latched on to Ryan. I can see Sylas feels it too. He leans toward me, his mouth a breath away from mine.

I feel his tongue sweep out and lick the blood moving towards my chin. My body heats rapidly as I brush towards him and lick the blood from his lips.

"I need more," I whisper into him.

"Let's get you more, then." Our smiles widen as he takes my hand in his and pulls me from the floor. I hear Harris and Noah telling us to stop, but we are running out the front door and flying through the streets towards the next house.

I knock on the neighboring house, having no plan but to eat. The woman screams as soon as she opens the door and slams it in our faces. Sylas laughs, and I can see why she is afraid. He has blood splattered into his beard, and he looks absolutely feral. He kicks in the door, and I snap the woman's neck the moment I see her.

We both stare at her, limp on the ground, before consuming every last drop of blood from her body.

"It doesn't taste the same," I pant out.

"It doesn't taste the same," he repeats back to me.

Our eyes barely have time to lock before he's biting into my lip, trying to get any remnant from our last kill—to feel that buzz again.

Heavy footsteps sound behind us, but I'm too consumed in the feeling of having Sylas' lips pressed to my mouth to see who it is.

My arms are torn from him and shoved behind my back. There's a strong burn that reaches my wrists, and I scream out in pain.

"This is why we brought the chains with us. You guys are fucking idiots and high on whatever the fuck that guy was smoking," Harris grits through his teeth. His gloved hands reach to haul me up and drag us back to the truck.

I can hear Sylas fighting Noah and losing. The chains restrain our strength. We're thrown into the truck with unnecessary force, my body pushed up against his. I can still smell the blood on his mouth. His fangs peek out from his grin, and he lifts his mouth to the place above my collarbone, sinking his teeth in deep. I let out a moan. The drugs we unknowingly consumed give me tunnel vision. The world around us fades away as he feeds off me, begging to keep that high. He lets go, and I sweep my tongue over his lips and suck his bottom lip into my mouth.

He grunts, and I feel him growing harder against my thigh. We drown deep into a kiss and lose all sense of time. My head is swimming, and I feel completely intoxicated by him.

The moment is cut short when we reach the ranch. Harris and Noah tell us we need to get this out of our systems before we can go back inside. The silver chains burn when they yank us from the truck.

"Where are you taking us?" I trip over my legs and almost faceplant into the dirt.

"The barn," Harris says without looking at me. I can tell they are pissed. They didn't sign up for babysitting.

He shoves me to the ground and chains me to a beam in the barn. I'm going to burn this fucking place down. Sylas is chained to the beam across from me, close enough that I can reach him with my boot.

The heat is still low in my core and begs for release.

The barn doors swing shut, and we're left in the dark. The

only light is streaming in from the cracks between the wood panels of the barn walls.

He's eyeing me like he wants to eat me from the inside out. It only makes the heat inside me burn hotter.

I slide my boot across the concrete floor and press between his legs. He grunts, and I slide down further to settle it on the seam of his jeans. His length is hard against my foot.

He lets out a wicked laugh. "Watch it, Row."

I only smile wider, running my tongue over my fangs. I let my boot slide across his crotch, pressing into his balls, teasing him.

"Fuck." He grinds himself on the boot, taking what he needs.

The drugs running through my veins ease the burn on my wrists as my hands scratch against the worn wooden post and fresh hay lines the rough concrete floor under me. The scent of Sylas' heat overpowers the smell of our burning skin. His moans echo through the empty barn.

I hear the scratch of his boot against the concrete as he slides it forward and nudges the tip to slide under me. His boot settles under my ass and his leg presses between mine, giving me everything I need to grind against it.

I slide myself slowly up and down, our jeans creating sweet friction.

"You're the sweetest thing I've ever tasted, Row. I can't get you off my tongue."

That earns him a moan. My head slips back, and I lose myself in the rhythm. The pressure builds between us, and he presses further into me.

A whimper leaves my lips. "The way you look at me makes me melt."

My climax is building, and I look up to see him panting, violent with heat. I'm soaking through my jeans and staining his.

"I'm so close," I whisper.

"Come on my leg, Row," he says through his teeth. His cock is hard against my boot, begging to come undone.

"Sylas, Sylas…" I barely get the words out as my orgasm washes through me. The release makes my legs tremble.

I feel his cock twitch against me and see him finish in his jeans.

"Fuck, you make a mess of me." His hair falls to his brow and curves around his jaw. He looks disheveled with his release in his jeans. I can't help thinking this was a mistake.

The drugs in our system start to take over, and we pass out in the position we finished in. We're only awoken when Harris comes banging into the barn.

"I can see we didn't put you two far enough from each other." Harris cackles and unshackles us with gloved hands.

It takes a few minutes for me to stand. Where the chains were on my wrists now burn hot before cooling and healing.

Regret is starting to set in when I see Sylas and the results of our actions.

"Row-"

"I have to get cleaned up." My words are clipped.

I let the water wash over me for I don't know how long. I'm

overthinking the last few hours. The regret is pounding in my chest. I don't know how I'll face him, and I don't think I could ever face Liddy again—if she decides to show up anymore. I wouldn't blame her if she never came back to me. I wouldn't blame her if she never spoke to me again.

She told us to stick together, that we need each other to get through this. I doubt this is what she had in mind. She must be rolling in her grave. She must be wishing me damnation, if turning into a blood-sucking devil hasn't condemned me already.

Being attracted to Sylas was never an option for me, never a thought I fully formed in my mind, because he was never mine. It feels like my heart is playing tricks on me, deceiving me into thinking we're getting closer because pain has led us together. But the sickness I feel in my gut tells me this is wrong.

Guilt and shame fill my dead heart with unwavering pain. My loyalty to Liddy is slipping further away from me. I press my forehead into the cool tile and swear out loud to never let this happen again.

# Chapter Seventeen

## SYLAS

GUILT SETS IN THE MOMENT SHE WALKS AWAY. I let temptation lead me, and it was a mistake I can't take back. How could I do this to Liddy? I was out of my mind, sharing an experience we were never meant to have. I pace the barn, letting the pain of being unfaithful take over—trying to rationalize this situation, but I can't. If she wants to haunt me from beyond the grave, then I'll let her. I deserve how shitty I'm feeling.

My wrists stop stinging with pain, and I slam a fist into the barn wall before letting out a breath.

"I fucked everything up, man."

"You were both high out of your minds; you can get past this," Noah retorts.

"Don't think we haven't noticed the way you two have been looking at each other. This was going to happen eventually. What's so bad?" Harris gives his unsolicited input.

"What's so bad? Liddy just fucking died. I'm sure this isn't what she meant when she gave me her blessing and told me to stick by Rowan. It obviously spooked her. There's no telling what's going through her mind now." I take in a deep breath and continue pacing around the barn. "She needs some stability, and I don't fucking know what that just was."

"Either way, dude, you need a shower." Noah looks me up and down.

I look down at my jeans and clench my jaw. "Yeah."

I run into Rowan leaving the bathroom on my way to shower. She doesn't so much as look at me as she brushes past and closes the door to her room. Drugs or not, I fucked this up.

We never set any rules, and that makes this worse. We needed to talk before diving head-first into shit.

We should have been looking for the truth instead.

I get into the shower and press my forehead onto the cool tiles and let the water run down my back. I beg for Liddy to come to me, to give me some clarity. She never responds.

Liddy said she had her own things to take care of, but I can't help thinking this is my fault she won't return. I want to know if she has been talking to Rowan. I need to give Row her space. I'm struggling with it. I want to make it right. I want to go beg on my knees for forgiveness.

My head swims. I want to get on my knees for more than that. I want to sit between her pretty legs and worship what's between them. I picture her flushed cheeks in the dimly lit barn. I can hear her moaning my name and panting for release.

I fist my cock, heavy in my hand. She is consuming me. My thoughts, my taste. Everything in me screams for her.

I pump faster, thinking of her parted lips. Her new fangs peak out from them. She's incredible. I can't stop thinking about her boot pressed into my cock, the way we came undone around each other so fast.

My length is throbbing, and I finish on the shower wall. My shoulders slump down with immediate guilt. I don't know how I'll ever prove my worth to her now that I've made a mess of things between us.

The only thing that can give me redemption is finding out what these fucking henchmen want with *my girl*. Tomorrow, we'll go see the only person who saw what happened to her parents.

After I put on clothes, I go to Harris' room and knock on his door twice.

"Come in," he calls out.

"Hey, man. I have a favor to ask."

"Yeah, shoot."

"I need you to break into Rowan's work and steal a newspaper." I put on a smile, hoping he doesn't think I'm insane.

"What?" His brows rise.

"I want to meet with the woman she called, the one who saw her parents. She said she found the paper in a box in the back room. It's a small office, so it can't be too hard," I plead.

"Fine, but you owe me."

"Thanks, man. I'll get you the whiskey you like." I give him a wink and tell him the only details I know about the place. Hopefully, having the paper in hand will give us what we need to get this journalist on our side. I'm not opposed to playing dirty, but I don't want it to go that far with Rowan around. After what happened tonight, I want her to trust me more than anything.

When the sun rises the next morning, I let my feet lead me and don't bother overthinking the plan my brothers and I set in place last night.

I knock twice on Rowan's bedroom door before throwing out all pleasantries and walking inside.

"Get up! Big day, things to do. Let's get answers."

She groans and drags the blankets over her face.

I open her curtains and step to the foot of the bed. In one sweeping motion, I have the comforter off the bed, and I take a moment to appreciate the way her tank top is shifted to the side and her flimsy shorts bunch perfectly at her waist.

I grab her ankles and drag her off the bed, moving her to stand.

She looks pissed and lets me know. "You fucking asshole, you have no manners. What do you want?"

"Get dressed, we're leaving in 10. Meet us in the truck." I beam my best smile at her, trying not to drool at her lean body. I know she will forgive me for this once we're there.

I leave her room to let her dress. Harris already has the truck warming, but I notice Noah hanging back.

"What's going on? You're not going with us?" I settle my Stetson on my head and tug my boots on.

Noah scrubs at his freshly shaven face. Something is clearly weighing on him. "I'm going to head to the blood bank. In theory, being the town superheroes was great but we saw how well that went..." His head hangs low.

"The blood bank?" My brows knit together.

"I know it's not ethical, but I think it's the best way. Until we are in the clear with this, I'm going to steal some blood bags."

I see the exhaustion in his eyes. Although we aren't aging, he looks older. He looks beaten and torn. My body aches with what this has done to him. "I'm so sorry, Noah."

"This isn't on you, at least not all of it. Don't carry my weight on your shoulders; you already have enough to hang on to." He pats my shoulder and squeezes it softly before turning away. "Get this shit figured out," he calls from over his shoulder.

There are so many lost words between us. Safety and normalcy feel worlds away. It only drives me harder to try and fix this. I can fix this.

Rowan reaches the main room, and I follow her out to the truck. She looks so good in my hat. She's wearing a long black sweater and a plaid skirt that barely peeks out from under it, her legs covered in a soft material. Her boots give me a brief flashback that I shove far, far down.

"Noah isn't coming," I let Harris know.

"I know."

"Well, thanks for keeping me in the loop," I scoff and climb into the backseat, letting Rowan sit up front.

Harris drives away from the ranch towards Rose Creek. It's a forty-five-minute drive deeper into the mountains, where the trees already start to frost in the late November weather. The roads have sharp hairpin turns that take us higher in elevation.

"Are you seeing someone right now? I haven't seen anyone come by the ranch, probably for the best," Rowan chuckles.

Harris lets out a clipped laugh, "No, I've been out of the dating game for quite a while now."

"Harris would have bitten off her head by now," I say trying to join the conversation. She doesn't even glance in my direction.

They continue their conversation as if I wasn't here. Anger starts clouding my thoughts as I try to get back to my happy place. A world where this is no longer an issue. A world where monsters like us don't exist.

Gravel crunches under the tires as Harris turns into the parking lot. We've reached the news station where Marie Stellar works; I figured she can't tell us much over the phone, but we can be persistent enough to dig the truth out of her.

"What are we doing here?" She turns around, only to glare at me.

"We're going to dig some information out of Marie, see if she's more inclined to tell us what she knows now that we're here." I smile wide to show her my fangs.

"Put those away. We're not threatening her, Sylas."

"Only if it comes to it," I retort and exit the truck.

She shakes her head but follows me out. Harris goes inside first and keeps busy at the front desk so we can sneak in and find her. I found an older photo of her that we use to point her out.

"Back left, that has to be her," Rowan whispers to me. I nod and we walk over, trying our best to blend in. Rowan moves through the office like she owns the place, fitting in seamlessly. I look outright out of place with my cowboy hat. I should have left it in the truck.

We round the desk in the back corner. "Marie? Stellar, right?" Rowan's voice is full of hope.

The small, tan-skinned woman with chopped straight black hair sits behind her computer. Worry covers her features before she returns to a neutral expression. "Yes, that would be me. Can I help you?"

I lower my head to be sure no one can hear us. "This is about the vampire attack in Rose Creek." I steady my voice. I can see Marie's knuckles going white, her face giving no indication of acknowledgment. "Robert and Laney Watson. You wrote this article, right?" I pull the paper out from my coat.

"How did you get that?" Rowan says a little too loudly and heads start to turn our way. I give her a stern look that I'm hopeful translates to *I'll tell you later.*

"We should talk somewhere more private." Marie moves to stand and gestures for us to follow.

We wind through the back rooms until we reach what looks like a supply closet. When we get inside, there are several metal shelves stacked with boxes. There's a small table at the far wall, a dusty lamp hanging overhead. Suddenly, I'm all too aware of the small space we've placed ourselves in with a *human.* The control has gotten easier, merely an itch at the back of my throat instead of a primal need but, that doesn't stop the unwanted trickle of venom in my mouth. It doesn't mean I can let my guard down completely.

"Please, take a seat." We settle in, and Marie opens her mouth again but nothing comes out for a moment. "You're the girl who called me about this, aren't you? You're their daughter."

I can see Rowan swallowing a lump in her throat. "Yes."

The weight of the air hangs heavy in this dimly lit room. I place the paper on the table in front of us. I can see the worry in Rowan's eyes. I take her hand in mine from beneath the table and give her a gentle, knowing squeeze. She squeezes back.

"I was sent to the cabin your parents were at to report on the fire. No one told me it was a crime scene; they just wanted fire coverage. I had never done larger pieces, so when I showed up to the area surrounded in yellow tape, I was so excited to finally get my big break—a story worth writing." Her hands shake as she reaches toward the paper, tracing her name in the byline.

"You talked about seeing their bodies. Can you tell me what seemed wrong?" Rowan squeezes my hand tighter. The way she's trusting me, letting me see this vulnerable side to her, soothes the ache in my heart.

"I saw them outside the cabin. They had already moved their bodies from the front porch. I started asking the officers on the scene questions, but they brushed me off. They tried to move me away from the bodies, telling me they died in the fire, but it didn't add up. They said an animal must have found them afterward." She takes in a deep breath. "I was desperate to tell this story, to get the truth out…"

I start to get angry at how she's using their death as a way to push her career forward. I can feel Rowan's leg start bouncing under my hand in anticipation. I close my eyes for a moment and breathe in through my nose. I can't lose it in here and risk not getting the information Marie is telling us. I focus my energy on Rowan and steady my rage the best I can.

"I stayed behind and watched the officers inspect the

bodies. They were looking in their mouths, so I got as close as I could without drawing attention to myself. They were pulling on their teeth, and I couldn't understand why. From a distance, they looked ghostly pale, their eyes were hollowed in. There was nothing that would make me believe it was smoke inhalation."

"Did you ever get a closer look at them?" Rowan questions.

Marie nods. "After the fire was put out, they started searching the area around the cabin." Her eyes go wide as she looks at Rowan in contemplation. "They still hadn't put the bodies in the ambulance yet, so when they went behind the cabin, I ran over there to see them—your parents. I think the shock of seeing dead bodies went over my head, the adrenaline overpowering all my rationality."

Rowan stares at her with intense focus, waiting for the moment she tells her they were bitten. Waiting for the confirmation of what she thinks to be true. If her parents were killed by vampires, I know Rowan won't stop until she finds who did it. I want her to have those answers, but I don't want her hunting for things that could end up killing her.

"I searched their bodies. Their necks were torn into, so there wasn't a lot to go off of, but I thought it was weird. If an animal had attacked them, why would they have only gone for one part of them?"

Rowan released a shuddering breath.

"Oh, I'm so sorry. I'm being insensitive." Marie reaches toward Rowan.

"No, I need to know this. Please, anything else you have, I'll hear it."

Marie dips her chin and swallows. "I was starting to believe what the officers were telling me until I looked in their mouths. They had long, sharp canines. I know this must sound crazy. I didn't believe what I was seeing."

Rowan grips my hand tightly enough to make me wince. I stretch my fingers out to signal her to stop, but she keeps her hold on me.

"I know how this sounds, but after I saw that, I ran out of there as fast as I could. I published the piece, leaving out that singular detail. I spent months looking into what they could be, and-"

"Vampires," Rowan whispers.

"Y-yes." Marie's brows furrow, and awareness lights in her eyes. "I thought I had gone mad, but the details I saw had only led me in one direction. I read through every book in the library, scoured all the records at the station that could be similar, and the only explanation was vampires. After I left the scene that day, the cabin roof collapsed, and they were burned right there, all the evidence just gone. I almost lost my job searching for any other cases like theirs, but I never found any real evidence like I did that day. I went back to the Rose Creek police station to confront them about covering this up, and they laughed in my face. If I had the guts to publish a piece on this, I would have, but the station would never allow it, and I can't afford to lose my job."

I look to Rowan and see tears running down her cheeks, her face bright red, like she's trying to hold herself together.

"I'm so sorry," Marie continues, but Rowan races to the trash can next to the door and retches. "I really should get back to my desk," she says in a hurry.

"Wait. Just wait, please." Rowan slowly steps back towards the table, and I put my hand on her back to steady her into the chair. "On the phone, you said you received backlash. What did you mean?"

She clears her throat and looks towards the door, making sure no one is lurking by to hear. "The head of your town's station, Sam Morana, she crushed my story and threatened my career if I ever spoke of it again. If I'm being truthful, I believe she also threatened my life."

Rowan's lip trembles as she says, "Sam...Sam..." It's if she is unable to believe it herself.

Marie just gives us a nod and begs that we leave now, ushering us back to the front, where Harris is flirting with the receptionist.

I nod to him, and we walk back to the truck. Rowan slides into the backseat with me. Her eyes look glossed over, and her body is ice cold.

Once we hit the backroads back into Georgetown, Harris looks back toward us. "What happened in there? It looks like she's seen a ghost."

I open my mouth to speak, but it's Rowan who begins talking. "My parents were like us. They were vampires. And I think my boss knows."

"Shit, Rowan, I'm so sorry."

She sits wholly still until we reach the ranch. If only I could read the thoughts racing through her mind.

# Chapter Eighteen

## ROWAN

I FROZE AFTER HEARING WHAT MARIE HAD TO SAY. My body went cold, and when I spoke, it didn't sound like it was coming from my own mouth. I finally had some information, but it only led to more questions.

I was only 11 when they died, but how could I have not known? The memories I try to bring to the surface beg to stay hidden. I try to dig them out, and they sink deeper, deeper. Bile burns in my throat as my temperature rises.

I'm pacing around my room at the ranch, trying to gather myself, but I can't. My blood is boiling, and the tears start to fall down my cheeks. I don't want to cry, don't want to sit here like a useless fool who couldn't see what was right in front of her. I need answers. I *demand* answers. How could I have not known?

I scream as loud as I can, letting the anguish and hurt take control. I take the vases and candles from the wooden dresser and throw them as hard as I can. I let them smash to pieces. Glass flies towards me, leaving paper-thin cuts across my arm.

I grasp the fabric over my heart and pull tightly. The sobs

come with no control as I let myself fall to the floor. The dresser knobs push into my back, and I rest my head in my hands, letting it take me for a long while.

The door creaks open, but I don't lift my head. I already know who it is. Heavy footsteps pad across the wood floor and stop beside me. I hear him sit, the groan of the wood telling me he's close. His arm brushes mine before he takes me into his arms, positioning me to rest against his chest. I dig my face deep into his shirt and cry silently, the warmth of him thawing my ice-cold heart.

His hands make large strokes down my hair, not saying anything, just comforting me. Having him here makes me feel that much more guilty.

It should be Liddy here.

They should have taken me instead.

Everyone I love is dead because of me, and I don't know why.

I set my hands on Sylas' chest and grip the fabric hard. I raise my head to look into his eyes. The pain in my face is reflected at me.

"This is all my fault," I finally say aloud.

He wipes my tears away, his calloused hands framing my face and making me feel small. "Don't talk like that. You didn't know. This is not on you, Row. This is not on you." He catches a free-falling tear with his thumb and kisses my cheek.

"They were my parents. Mine. Now, they're after me. They killed Liddy over this. Whatever they were hiding is now mine to deal with. The burden they put on my shoulders is too heavy."

He tries to speak, but I shake my head. "I can't keep

putting you, Harris, and Noah through this. It's not fair to any of you." My voice starts to tremble, and I close my eyes to gain the strength to say my last words to him. "I have to fight this on my own now. I have to go."

"Look at me." His voice is soft, but there's an edge to it. I let my eyes rise to his. His light hair is slicked back, but a piece falls against his cheek, and I resist the impulse to slide it back in place. My breathing is shallow, and I think he can hear my heart beating through my chest. "I will not let you do this alone. I-I promised Liddy. She told me to stay by you, protect you. You don't have to do this alone. I'm here."

His words sink deep, turning to guilt, to anger toward my best friend. She couldn't have known and shouldn't have used Sylas like she did. "She had no right." It comes out sharper than I intended.

He moves his hands to grip mine in a loose embrace and rubs his thumbs across my palms. He dips his head to look at where our hands connect. "I will protect you with my life. Her word or not, Rowan, you're mine." The air between us grows heavy, and my breath hitches. "Let me protect you," he whispers into the space between us.

"Let me fight my own battles," I counter. I'm unsure if I could handle this on my own, but the comfort he's giving me is lined with guilt.

"They hurt us too, turned us into something we didn't ask for. I'm staying, whether you like it or not." He lifts his head and looks into my eyes with certainty.

The pain in my chest continues to burn, knowing I can't drag them into this.

The room has fallen dark, evening setting in as the short autumn days cover us in darkness.

"Let me stay with you tonight. We can talk about it in the morning, but I'm positive they're not letting you go off on your own again." He slides his thumb against my cheek, and I agree.

The pain hasn't stopped since the moment I found out my parents were vampires, the moment I realized I'll be fighting for my life until I end this—unless it ends me first. I've been fighting off my tears all night, grasping at the stabbing pain in my chest.

I need to let go of the human part of me before I destroy myself. The grief, the pain; I can't bear it. I dig deep into my mind and find the right nerves to switch off. I let those feelings wash away and dissipate into nothing, leaving me with only anger and euphoria.

Sylas fell asleep beside me hours ago. I didn't try to sleep; instead, I've been waiting for the right moment to leave. The angel and devil on my shoulders are battling whether to stay or go. It will hurt him to leave, but I have to cut them out of this battle, a fight my parents seem to have started and passed down to me.

I roll out of bed gently and pull on my socks, making sure my steps are light. I grab my clothes and find my car keys I haven't been touched in weeks. I don't need much; I leave the rest of my belongings.

The house is silent and dark. I carefully make my way to the door, boots in hand, ready to make a run for it. Our vampire hearing is dangerously accurate, but I'm hopeful Sylas sleeps like the dead.

I open the front door, my beating heart like an echo through the house. I'm halfway through the doorway when I turn and see Harris staring at me. We hold each other's gaze for a long moment before I shake my head from side to side. His only confirmation that he won't stop me is a shallow nod. I close the door, tug on my boots, and run to my car.

The plan I thought out doesn't take me farther than Sam's house, a black Victorian home with a bright red door. It stands out in the sea of blue and off-white houses. Dense trees line her yard, giving a sense of privacy. My car idles half a block from her front door. The clock on my car radio reads 1:30 AM. The only light I can see is a faint glow from the far window. I'll take my chances waking her up. With the absence of my feelings, rationality tells me the pros outweigh the cons, that my intent is pure. I leave my car and walk to her door, knocking twice.

There's no answer.

I knock again, a bit louder this time.

I hear the locks turning a moment later. Sam slowly opens the door, putting her arm against the frame, blocking the view inside. "Rowan? What are you doing here? This is completely unprofessional."

My voice gets caught in my throat as the devil on my shoulder reminds me she's our enemy. "You knew what my parents were."

If she's shocked, she doesn't show it. She lifts her chin even higher. "Give me a moment. Have a seat inside."

Before I've stepped through the door, she's nowhere to be

seen. I settle into a plush cream seat next to the couch. Her home is decorated in black and deep shades of red. Dried roses hang from the mantle of her brick fireplace. Her walls are painted the deepest crimson, and only spots of cream give light to this dark interior.

I watch her walk into the living room, buns adorning the top of her freshly brushed hair. She's wearing the same black silk robe as when she answered the door. Did she sneak away just to do her hair? It's the middle of the night, and yet she looks flawless, ageless, in no need of rest. I wonder-

Sam cuts off my train of thought when she speaks. "So, you know your parents were vampires."

Her blunt acknowledgment makes me pause, and where I'd usually feel the impulse to attack, emptiness lingers.

"Yes. I'm told you knew their secret. I'm here to find out what you know." I speak clearly and keep my chin up.

She clears her throat. "Well, that is what I know. I'm sorry it's not more."

I shake my head. That can't be all. "No, you fired me for looking at those papers. There has to be more."

She grits her teeth and purses her lips as if I'm annoying her. "Rowan, your parents were vampires, and I just wanted to protect you. That is all."

"You've known about vampires for this long? And you're just okay with it?" I know I'm coming on strong, but I can't understand how she's so calm about this.

"You certainly have a lot of questions this time of night." She stretches her neck and covers a yawn that looks entirely fabricated.

"I knew about them long before I knew about your parents." She runs a hand through her silken hair, as if this is a normal conversation, before her eyes narrow at me. "This stays between us. When I moved here to run our station, we had strange reports all the time about murders on the outskirts of town. I went to investigate the most recent one, and that's when I saw the bites. I went to more and more locations, and they were all the same—until the last one. A vampire had been killed. I know this because one of them visited me—threatened me—but I threatened to expose them. We came to a deal: they stay hidden, and I'll keep their secret."

"This entire time, you've been working with these monsters?"

"I've gotten quite close to them over the years. They're not monsters." Her words send chills down my spine. She's friends with these killers and has no remorse for it. She seems to enjoy it, even.

"Why are they after me then? The henchmen." I say it before I can think any better of it. Her eyes go wide.

"They're after you? You've seen them?" She whispers something under her breath that I can't quite make out.

"They had quite a bit to say…" I weigh my words carefully. "They were sent by the Vampire Queen to kill me, whoever that is." I can't help but laugh at the inquiry. "It seems as though you know them. What did they mean?"

Her eyes pin me with a stare. They've always been brown, but I can see flecks of red pulling through her irises. She notices where I'm looking and blinks away, turning her head to the side. "Vampires can't bear children without the magic of witches, and that's utterly forbidden." She continues when I don't offer any words. "Children born from vampire parents can have certain abilities that threaten the balance of their kind. It seems they've been sent to end the threat."

This is more outrageous than I could have thought up myself. Vampires? Special abilities? Is she talking about magic? There's far too much I don't know. I think Sam is holding back a lot more than I was led to believe.

"I don't understand. I don't have special abilities. Why are they still after me?" I bite my lip but quickly stop. I don't want to show her my fangs.

The question makes her lip quirk into a slight smile. "They can only appear once you've turned." She sits down across from me and lets her head rest on propped-up hands. "And as luck would have it, you're a vampire now." A beaming smile replaces her hard features.

The shock on my face is obvious, my mouth hanging open like a gasping fish. I don't know how I would hide it from anyone if Sam knew just by looking at me.

"Your secret's safe with me. How about you stay here tonight? It's late."

My gut turns at the invitation, but it's the safest option right now. "That would be so kind of you. Thank you."

She leads me through the kitchen and down a winding hallway. I look to my right and see the living room, as if we took the long way to the guest room. The hallway is painted the same shade of crimson, and sconces line the wall with red bulbs. The sight sends shivers down my spine. What felt cozy and intimate now feels like hell on Earth.

Sam opens the door to what I assume is the guest room. The curved door frame makes it feel like walking into a dungeon. The room is painted black; not just the walls, but the furniture too. The bed is to my left, centered on the wall, and has a giant curved headboard. Two large side tables cap the sides, adorned with gold lamps and candles. The wall across from the bed has a fireplace centered on the wall, a large mirror perched on the mantle. The wall surrounding the fireplace is filled with shelves and shelves of books, save for a door at the far end.

"Well, this is the nicest guest room I've ever seen." I sound breathless.

"That bathroom is through that door." She points to the far right corner. "And if you need anything, just call. Have a good night." A tense smile is on her lips.

I take a step into the room, and she swings the door closed, instantly darkening the space. It looks clean, but it smells musty, as if no one has slept in here in years. I step further inside, and the wood creaks under my weight as I walk toward a lamp, turning it on to light the room. It's quiet in here, and the foreign space makes me feel like I don't belong. I rub my hands over my arms and step towards the fireplace but see no logs or matches.

I run my hand over the spines of the books until I stop to pull one out. I flip through the pages, but they're all empty. I take another, only to find its pages are empty too. I try not to panic. These must be for decoration. Surely, no one would have this many real, empty books.

I check a few more within arm's reach, all empty.

There's a ladder pushed towards the end of the wall. I

wrap my hand around the blackened wood and slowly drag it to the center of the bookshelf. I don't want Sam to think I'm snooping—I don't want Sam to *know* I'm snooping.

I remove my boots and gently start to climb. I'm four steps up the rungs when I finally see books with spine markings. Most of these look normal, but I spot one high up simply titled *Georgetown*. Dust falls on my face and sleeve when I remove the book. It looks older than the others in here.

Slowly, I climb back down and make myself comfortable on the bed to read.

The lamps on either side offer a soothing glow, and the chill in my bones starts to ease. Not wanting to get dust on her sheets, I wipe the cover with my sleeve. I stare at the cover for a long time, unsure what I'll find. It feels wrong to look through this book, one hidden amongst fakes and decoys.

*Georgetown.*

It's probably just a history text.

# Chapter Nineteen

## SYLAS

Rowan wakes me from my sleep with hands pressed on either side of my face. She's giving me deep, slow kisses, and I run my hands from her hips to trace her ribs.

I'm already so hard, my sweatpants hiding nothing. I can feel her trail her fingers down to my erection and palm my length. Her fingertips are begging the waistband to lower.

I need more of her.

I lift her thigh and swing her leg over my torso. The heat radiating from her is intoxicating. She takes what she needs, grinding herself over me. I reach where her panties connect with my sweats. The thin lace hides nothing; she's soaking wet.

I move the thin fabric to the side and slowly pull down the waistband of my pants.

A loud bang on my door pulls me out of what had to be the most vivid dream I've ever had as Harris busts through the door. "Heyo, brother. Thought you'd want to know, Rowan left last night." He eyes me. "That's a big tent you set up!" His shit-eating grin takes up his entire face.

I throw a pillow at the door before shooting straight out of bed and processing what he just told me. I adjust myself in my pants, pull on a sweater, and run out of the room.

"What the fuck do you mean *she left*?"

"Well, she left. Didn't say anything, so I didn't ask. I figured you fucked up." He tips his hat down at me and exits through the back door, leaving me reeling.

I run to the bedroom and shuffle her things around. It doesn't look like she took anything but her keys. That might mean she's coming back.

She wouldn't have left unannounced in the middle of the night if she was coming back.

I don't know how I could have stopped her, but God, I need to get her back.

I can't lose Rowan too. This feeling of abandonment hits too close to home, and my chest aches. I have to find her.

I spot the notebook on her nightstand and flip through it before I can let it hang over my consciousness. It's blank. I look in the trash beside the dresser and see a few scrap pieces crumbled at the bottom. It looks like she tried to hide them with a few tissues. I dig three of them out.

The first one looks like notes for research. The second one is a crumpled photo of us with Liddy from the time we went on a mud-filled hike. I straighten the photograph and set it back on the nightstand. The third just says *Sam??*

I'm taking my mare out for a ride to clear my head. Noah is getting me an address, but I don't want to come on too strong. I know she left because she doesn't want me. She doesn't want me just like our mom didn't want us.

I thought I'd be racing out of here to find her, but this ache is pulling me into myself. The pain is clouding my thoughts.

I let my mare run to the back of the property, straight into the mountains. The sun hasn't risen yet and the air is crisp. We're moving into winter, and snow has started to litter the ground closer to home. Once we're out of the pastures, we make our way down a trail covered with trees. It's the darkest part of this trail, and we ride through in silence, with only the sound of pounding hooves and birds flying from the trees to surround us.

This has always been my favorite trail on our property. My mom would take us riding while my dad was working the land and taking care of the cattle. She told me that through the darkness, you can always find the light. The light after this dark trail appears as a giant lake surrounded by mountains and tall trees. When the sun is up, you can see the trees reflecting on the water, making it look endless—endless light after the cover of darkness.

The water is frozen, and the trees are coated in a light layer of snow. I slide down onto my feet and perch on a rock overlooking the lake. On a hot summer day, we would have brought a picnic basket full of turkey sandwiches and homemade cherry pie.

The summer of my fifteenth birthday was the last time I had that pie.

My mother left.

She sat in my bed before I fell asleep and told me we had nothing left to learn from her. She told me how proud she was that I grew up to be strong and independent. I was beaming with pride by the time she walked out. I didn't realize until morning, when all her belongings were gone, that she was telling me goodbye.

I don't know where she went or where she is now. I never tried to find her. She didn't want us any longer, and I tell myself I didn't need her.

Noah took the news the worst. He begged Dad for a reason, but he didn't have any to give. Our dad went on like nothing was different. He had to have been hurting, but I think it helped us get through it a little easier.

Dad passed away from stage four cancer when I was 23. That one hurt like hell. I was always the steady rock in the family, and I continued to be that for my brothers long after he died. This is the first time I've fallen apart. Thirty-two years on Earth, and I'm finally folding like a house of cards.

The vibration in my pocket tells me Noah texted me the address. I could let Rowan leave us like my mom did, but I want to fight for her. I won't let her slip through my fingers.

# *Chapter Twenty*

## ROWAN

THE PAGES IN THE BOOK ARE WORN. There's a lot of basic information about Georgetown in the front, nothing worth noting or hiding. I flip through the pages, looking for any information I could use. It's not until halfway through that the mention of vampires appears. I backtrack to see the title: *Georgetown After Dark*. It sounds like a tourist headline.

Vampires founded the mountain town, settled here and brought it to life. It was built and marketed as a small, quiet city, a way to live in peace with the luxury of community and convenience. Georgetown grew, and the original vampires had their pick of meals. They did it slowly so no one would notice. They would follow people out of town and kill them beyond our city limits, keeping Georgetown out of the press and the residents calm.

A tear falls from the corner of my eye and soaks into the text—a sliver of my humanity slipping through the switch I flicked off. This is exactly what they did to my parents. They were vampires and still had this horrific death that was made out to be an accident.

I continue reading, trying to toughen myself and remember what I'm here for.

Recognition coils tight in me as I read the title of the next page: *The Vampire Queen*.

The Vampire Queen, the Devil in Disguise, rose from The Underground to bring us hell on Earth. I touch the words on the page as if they could talk to me, tell me who she is. She made rules to ensure safety of their kind and keep them in line.

They can only hunt after dark and outside the city limits—a rule they seem to be breaking these days.

They can't turn mortals unless that person is ready to take an oath and join the queen's army.

And they can't bear children without the magic of witches—the word *forbidden* is written in bold.

This confirms what I already knew. The Henchmen gave away this much information before the brothers killed them. I pinch my forehead between my finger and thumb; I need more. My eyes are growing heavy and start to water. I'm not comfortable sleeping, not when it feels so wrong here.

I hear faint whispers coming from the hallway but try to ignore it. This is Sam's house; the least I can do is afford her some privacy. I rub my hands together, breathing warmth into them before I flip the page. This room makes me feel cold, something I haven't felt in a while.

The illustration on this page shows the queen herself. She looks ethereal, unstoppable. She has long hair and piercing eyes. Small horns jut out from the top of her head. She looks like Sam, and it feels as if all the blood has drained from my body.

Before I can keep reading, the whispering picks up and trails past the door. I can make out 3 sets of footsteps, as if they're casually walking by. I hide the book under the pillows before gently stepping onto the floor. Pressing my ear to the door, I try and make out what they're saying, but it's nearly impossible. They sound farther away now, and before I can think better of it, I crack the door open to peek out.

The living room looks so far away from where I'm standing. When I was brought to this room, I saw it clear as day, right down the hall. Under the cover of the deep red lights, I slip into the hallway and try to get a closer look at who's in there with her. I take slow steps towards them, steadying my breathing, trying not to make a sound. Each step I take carries me farther from the living room. Nausea flows through me, and the red lights turn blinding. I try taking a few more steps, but the room isn't getting any closer. I have to get away from the lights, out of this hallway of nightmares. I pick up my pace until I'm at a full sprint. My third running step lands me in the middle of the living room—right in the middle of Sam and two hooded men.

"I'm so s-sorry." I press my hands into my stomach and take a few steps back.

"Don't be silly. Join us for some tea. You must be freezing." A small smile lines her lips, and I try to reciprocate the pleasantry.

We follow Sam into the dining room and sit at the large wood table. It's stained a deep cherry, red and black roses in crystal vases lining it end-to-end. Both men sit across from me and stare as if they're trying to burn holes through my flesh.

She returns with two tea cups and a teapot with a blooming flower inside. She pours our cups effortlessly and drops a single sugar cube in each. It seems rude to be ignoring the men sitting across from me; she didn't even bother serving them tea.

"Will you be serving them?" My head swivels towards the hooded men.

"I'm afraid they don't drink tea." She wears a warm smile on her lips, but it doesn't bring me any comfort.

I stir my tea, making sure the sugar cube is dissolved before taking a sip. I watch Sam take a drink from hers, letting a small moan drift from her throat. The tea goes down smoothly but turns acidic on my tongue. I can feel the warmth in my veins, and it takes all my concentration to set the cup down gently without shaking. I wipe a small bead of moisture off my lip. Through her smile is charming, I feel an uneasy tingle in my spine telling me to leave.

"I should probably get going. Thank you for letting me stay." I try to give her a smile, but the muscles in my face feel tight.

"Of course, Rowan. You can leave if you find your way out."

Confusion fills my mind—I can see the front door from here. I don't know why she's being so cryptic. It could be the company she's hosting. I glance back toward them, and they remove their hoods. Scars litter their shaved heads, and when they lift their faces, I'm met with blood-red eyes.

Every instinct is telling me to run. I move to stand, but my body feels like it's on fire, burning from the inside out. "What was in the tea?" I choke out, feeling my throat swell. I brace my hands on the table and press as hard as I can to stand up. My body fails me, though, and I collapse to my knees.

"Just a small dose of Holy Water, dear." I hear her laugh as she moves her chair to stand. I see her velvet red shoes stop in front of me. She lifts one foot and uses the point of her shoe to lift my chin, meeting her eyes. "I've been looking for you for so long, Rowan. You've been right under my nose this whole time."

"What-" is all I can get out. My throat feels like sandpaper, and I can barely breathe.

"The spell your parents used to hide you from me is broken now that you're a vampire. I guess we have Travis to thank for that; he did turn you, after all. Shame about him, though; he was such a good boy." She removes her shoe, and my head falls. "I had the witches cast out of Georgetown centuries ago for playing these vile tricks. Your parents always tried to undermine me. They couldn't just kneel for their queen. I had them killed, though—there was no other way. I knew you'd reveal yourself to me one day."

My body is a fire begging to be put out. I start to crawl towards the door, using every remaining muscle I have and a damn strong will to live. I didn't think I'd ever want to survive this much, never having enough to live for. I want to survive for the ones who didn't—survive for my parents, who gave up so much for my protection. My brain gets foggy, and I forget where I am. I try to look around, but I don't recognize it. Something grabs my wrist, and I'm dragged upward. The pain itself may kill me. My arm is throbbing, and I look up to see a shiny object in Sam's hand. Blood pours down my arm, and

I realize she cut me. Her lips wrap around the wound, and I want to be scared, but she's soft and warm. Her tongue glides over the cut, and it starts to heal, no longer a gash through my wrist.

I try to speak, ask her what happened or what she's doing, but nothing comes out. The men move to stand over Sam as she tilts her head back and lets their lips find hers—letting my blood mix with their saliva. They kiss her deeply, sucking it down like they'll never eat again. All three of them grunt out as if they might be in pain, but it doesn't take them to their knees like it did for me.

"They've tasted you. I've tasted you." She smiles, her teeth stained with my blood. "We will always be able to find you now."

The men look at me, and in unison, I see their mouths move before I hear them.

"Run."

I think it's shock that gets me to my feet. I don't feel my legs moving, only the jolting feeling every time I trip over my feet. My head is spinning, and I have to catch myself on a wall before vomiting. I don't chance looking back; I just move. I move towards where I think the door is, but I'm going in circles.

Ten steps, the living room comes into view.

Ten steps, the living room comes into view.

Ten steps.

I stop and take a gasping breath. I turn and run in the other direction, trying anything to get out. *No, no, no.* I'm confronted by the red lights lining the hallway. They seem brighter now, as if on fire. I can see the plush cream chair in the living room. I'm walking slowly with my hand braced on the wall, my fingers the only things keeping me up. The hallway stretches the farther I get. The lights start to blur, and all I see are streams of red lights blinding my vision. I trip over something, maybe my own feet, making me fall onto the cold floors.

Blood. I need blood. The burning coursing through my veins is replaced with a cold, hollow sensation. I lift my arm, but I can't see. I squeeze it with my other hand and feel a hard bone. I'm drying out; I need blood. I have to lay my head down.

I'm going in and out of consciousness. The next time I wake, I'm being dragged across the floor by my ankles. "Stop. Stop, stop!" My voice is barely a breath.

"I guess you didn't run fast enough."

I kick and dig my nails into the floor, but there's nothing to grab onto. The light fades, and I'm gone again.

My muscles ache enough to not risk moving. I blink a few times, trying to open my eyes, but my lids feel like cement. I keep making stupid decisions that end up with me in these places. I think this is hell. I finally made it; this is where I've belonged all along. I got my parents killed, and then I got Liddy killed. Now, I'm something designed to kill—so I'll do everything in my power to get revenge.

I'm back in the guest room at Sam's house. My arms are tied to the bed, and I'm assuming my legs are too, since I still can't move them. A shimmering figure crosses the room, and I feel the nip of frost on my chest. Liddy looks into my eyes. "It's been so long." I give her a soft smile.

She rubs small circles on my chest. The cold of her hand makes me shiver. "Liddy, how did we get here? This isn't how it was supposed to go." The cold spreads to my stomach and bites at my legs.

"Hey, Liddy?" She doesn't answer. I can't feel my toes. Her shimmering form hovers over my lips, offering connection, relief. All I receive is a mouth full of frostbite. She leaves the bed and walks straight through the door, and it's like she was never here, save for the unrelenting cold surfacing over me. Shimmers of frost coat my body, making me look luminescent. The tips of my fingers brush my thigh, and I pull off a sliver of frost. Piece by piece, I remove what's freezing me in place. Piece by piece, I can see myself again.

Warmth washes over me. I'm floating in a pool of bliss, letting the water pour over my limbs and wash away the pain. My muscles ease and my eyes blink open, no longer weighed down. My blurred vision begins to clear, and I sit up, finding no shackles on my wrists. I rub my eyes and rest my head in my arms. Whatever I was given must have made me hallucinate. I can't tell what really happened from what I imagined, but I slip my hand under the pillow and pull out the book. At least this much I know is true.

I tiptoe out of bed as something pulls me toward the bathroom at the far end of the room. I open the door and step in front of the mirror to see what damage has been done, but I find a pair of eyes looking back at me from the bath. "Sylas," I try to say in a low scream. I turn on my heels and remove the gag from his mouth. "What are you doing here? What happened?" I have to stop finding him like this. He looks dirty and exhausted. It makes me wonder how long I was lying on that bed.

"I came here to find you." His eyes are locked on mine. "I don't know what happened. Someone grabbed me, and I thought I saw Liddy, but I woke up here."

"We're not safe here. We need to leave." I help him stand and step out of the tub. His balance is compromised, and I can't hold him for long. We make it out of the bathroom but only as far as the bed before my muscles strain and I need to set him down. "I need more strength to get out of here." I eye his neck, and he follows my gaze. The squeeze of my hand is the only consent I need before sinking my teeth into his neck. Power fills my veins and clarity wraps around me. The shock that follows is crippling. "It's Sam." The words are barely a whisper from my lips.

I drink only enough of his blood to gain the energy to leave.

"It's Sam," I say again as realization flashes in his eyes. "We need to go."

He grips my hand hard, leading me to the bedroom door, but I tug his arm to a stop.

"Every time I try to leave, I go in circles. I focus on the door, and I never make it." I bite my lip trying to think. "We keep our eyes down. Focus on our steps. We pass two doors in the hallway and then turn left. That should be the door."

"I won't lose you again, Row," he whispers. Before I have time to respond, his lips are on mine. I revel in the sweet taste of blood and saliva mixing, in the warmth that takes over my body. My heart sinks at the emptiness that fills its place when he stops kissing me.

"Let's go," is all I can offer.

I pull the hood of my jacket over my head; I haven't seen my hat since I've been here. I shove *Georgetown After Dark* into my bag and secure it to my back.

# Chapter Twenty-One

## SYLAS

I'M GRIPPING ROWAN'S HAND SO HARD THAT IF SHE WAS A MORTAL, IT WOULD BE BROKEN. We walk slowly, keeping our eyes down at our feet. We pass the first door, and I stop to check for any noise, but there is none. I won't risk asking Rowan if she's sure no one's home. We continue walking and pass the second door. Still, there is no noise or whispers. It's too quiet. I don't hear the heater running, don't feel a buzz in the walls. There's only the sound of us breathing.

The wall stops, and there's an opening to the left, just as she said there would be. We walk as close to the wall as we can and scan the floor for anything concerning. I take a step toward the door, my grip on her hand holding steady. I take a second step, and we don't move. Our feet move, sure, but we stay in the same position—not covering any ground.

I can hear a defeated sigh leave her mouth. "The back door. We can try the back door." I hear the shake in her voice. She turns and guides me this time. We go through what looks like the main room. We pass a large table and a broken glass on the floor next to it. I don't know what she has been through since getting here, but I hope this wasn't from her, though I have a sinking feeling that it is.

We come to a stop, and I look up. Her hand is flat against a glass door, and I can see her face reflecting in the glass. She looks too scared this won't work. I'm terrified we won't make it out of here. I keep my hand grasped around hers while my other hand moves to the lock. I turn it and slide the door open. I swear, I can hear a cry of relief, but I move us out of the house so quickly, I don't find out. We push off the back patio and clear the steps in a matter of seconds.

I stop suddenly, and Rowan runs straight into my back. She removes her hand from mine and steps around me, seeing what I see.

The yard is full of tombstones. The early morning fog covers the ground under our feet and large trees canopy over the ground. "Rowan, we should leave. Now." She doesn't listen but instead walks further into the fog. I quickly catch up, trying to grab her arm and bring her home myself, but she stops. I follow her eyes and look at the tombstone she's stopped in front of.

"It's them. My parents." Her hand follows the curve of the porcelain stone and traces the letters in their name. I watch the single tear that falls to her cheek. "I didn't see them. I didn't see their bodies at the funeral. I was told they burned in the fire. I only got their ashes. I never looked inside to confirm what it was; I didn't think I needed to." Her glossy eyes search my face, but I have no resolve to give her. I wish I had all the answers for her. I wish I could ease all her pain. The best I can do is be here for her.

"I see you found my secret garden," a voice booms from the

house, and we jump back. "I was hoping you'd never have to see this, Rowan. Not yet." A woman appears from the shadows. Not a woman: a monster. A monster with iridescent red hair that falls to her waist and two horns adorning her head. This must be Sam. She laughs a wicked laugh, and I see a row of razor-sharp teeth.

Rowan grips the back of my jacket and raises her chin to Sam. "I knew it was you. The Vampire Queen. The Devil in Disguise." I can tell she's terrified. We should be running, but Rowan is being stupid enough to stand up to this she-devil. "You've hidden it quite well."

The devil laughs again. "You've been hiding yourself. I could smell you the moment you turned. A sweet, delicious smell. You're mine."

"We need to run. Now." I am begging her. This is enough terror to last a lifetime—a lifetime that has now been extended for God knows how long.

"You should listen to your plaything." She licks her teeth, and I shudder at the sight. "Your parents there." Her slender finger points to the tombstone. "They hid you from me, didn't want you to rule next to me. You have a gift, Rowan, a gift that could change our kind. A gift that could rule my hell on Earth. We could be unstoppable, darling!"

"I will never be on your side. I will never be yours. You don't own me. You took my family from me, and I'll be damned if you take me too." I can feel the rage radiating off her skin.

I bare my fangs at this monster in front of us. She won't be taking Rowan from me today. "I'll kill you if you touch her again."

She gives me a soft smile. "I know where to find you, darling." She melts away into the dirt, smoke curling where she once stood. We step back as the smoke disperses around us.

A cold terror that has been lacing my bones finally settles, and I let out a heavy breath. Before she can think about running from me, I grab her hand and run for her car. Her body is still on fire. I guide her into the passenger seat and drive towards the ranch.

"There are more henchmen. They've tasted my blood and know how to track me. I don't think the ranch is safe anymore. I don't think anywhere is safe now." She fidgets with her nails.

"Is there anything we should get from your house? I know a place we can go." I can only hope the cabin in far enough away to buy us some time. I let my hand squeeze her thigh and rub gently. I know it won't fix everything, but I want her to know I'm here.

"Yes" is all she offers me in return.

She gets back into the car holding an ornate vase with a lid, which I assume holds her parents' ashes. I watch her open the lid and stare blankly at the contents.

"What is it?"

"Sand." Her voice is hoarse and shaking. Her knuckles are stark white from gripping it so hard.

"You're going to break it if you keep squeezing it..." I try to offer, but she squeezes harder, baring her teeth. It crumbles under her pressure.

"It's fucking sand!" she screams so loudly, my eardrums

beg her to stop.

I see a small piece of gold in her lap covered by the sand spilling to the car floor. This will never fully come out. I slowly reach to grab it before she snatches my wrist and gives me a growl. "In your lap. There's something in the sand."

Reluctantly, she removes her grip and picks up the slim piece of gold inlaid with three small black and red gems—a ring. "I don't get it." She takes a closer look at the jewelry. "There's something engraved on the inside. *To the brightest star in the darkest world.* I don't know what it means." She sniffles, but no tears come this time.

"It's for you. They're talking about you." A smile spreads over my face, and I grip her chin between my fingers, turning her head to face me. I let my thumb run over her jaw. "You are the brightest star in this dark world. Your parents knew how unstoppable you would be."

"I don't feel very unstoppable." Her eyes glass over as the tears begin to form. My heart aches for her inability to see how bright she shines. She could bring me to my knees with a look.

I let my hand fall from her face and give her an easy smile. "We'll see about that."

Our ranch has a cabin at the back of the property, built into the mountainside. It's nothing fancy, a small wood log cabin with moss coating the roof. It's hidden by dense trees and not officially registered with the city of Georgetown. Our dad built the cabin for his hunting trips, ones my brothers and I only joined him for a few times. The trip out there was hard on us when we were younger. It takes several hours by horseback to reach the cabin, and we have to cross over a river that will be ice cold by now.

I called my brothers while Rowan was inside her house. They are setting up the cabin right now, stocking the small fridge with blood bags. I don't know how long we will stay in the cabin, if we will try to outrun this or stay and fight, though I'd prefer the former. We can only hide for so long if they're tracking her. I worry my lip, wondering if this is even worth it. They'll find her eventually, and I don't think they'll take their time. There's so much we need to talk about, so much that hasn't been said. I don't want to overwhelm her or seem insensitive to the trauma she endured, but we need to talk.

We make it back to the ranch, and I park her car out of plain sight. I know it won't do much in this situation, but Harris said the sheriff has been sniffing around town after our murder spree, and we don't want that kind of trouble coming our way.

I packed a few bags with clothes and some of Rowan's things I think she'll want out there. I walk off the back porch and find her feeding my mare a cherry red apple. She giggles as my horse wraps her tongue around the entire fruit and swallows it down. Horses have a way of knowing who is good and pure of heart. "You'll be riding her. She seems to like you." I pet my mare's nose in long strokes.

"I never asked her name." Her eyes shift to mine, and I almost lose myself in her beauty.

"Teddy." My mare bobs her head in response.

Rowan places a kiss on top of her nose. "Teddy," she

whispers. I let my eyes hover over the genuine smile on her lips.

I finish packing our saddles and finally replace the hoods of our jackets with new Stetsons. Her bangs peek out from the rim of the hat; it looks so natural on her. My vampire girl pulls off cowgirl so well. I bend down close to her ear and whisper that it's time to go. We mount our horses and head for the tree line.

Teddy makes her ride look easy, but Rowan looks like a natural, taking the lead like she knows where we're headed. Once we hit the trees, she slows and lets me take over navigation.

"I can't believe you grew up here—all this land. It's beautiful."

"Just remember that when you see the cabin. Beautiful is not what I'd it." I chuckle to myself. She's probably going to hate it and give me shit for it.

The path isn't very clear in the snow, but we follow the tracks from my brothers' trip and weave through the dense trees. My dad never cleared this area for fields, said it would be a pain in the ass. I think he just wanted to keep it for personal hunting grounds but couldn't tell my mother that.

We reach a clearing that stretches for about a mile. We're still at a walking pace, so I slow my speed and ride next to her. I loop a finger through her jeans and pull her towards me. I pinch her side, and she slaps my arm in turn.

"This is no time for that! We're fleeing multiple crime scenes and the actual devil." She laughs, but I'm not getting what's funny. She reads the confusion in my face. "Never did I think those words would come from my mouth. This has to be some sort of fever dream."

I can feel the words playing in her tone and see the panic in her eyes. "Do you ever regret it? Coming to the ranch? Travis… If you hadn't been there that day…" She stops me.

"He would have found me either way. He wanted to keep me, own me. Everyone seems to think I'm some sort of possession they can fight over." She looks up at the sky for a moment before the glare of the sun becomes too much on her eyes. "I still feel guilt pressing into my chest every time I think of Liddy. She should be the one here with you. I don't deserve what you've done for me."

I squeeze her thigh just above the knee. "You put yourself down too much. Liddy doesn't blame you. If anything, she would kick my ass for letting this happen to you. You are so much stronger than you realize. Liddy and I both know it." I swallow down the words I really want to say to her.

We reach the cabin, and I see the look of uncertainty on her face. The inside of the cabin is big enough to fit a sofa that wraps around a wood-burning fireplace and rocking chair. There's a compact kitchen in the back, with a gas stove and small fridge, cast iron pans and a few spoons hanging over the counter. A tiny bathroom juts out from the living room, just big enough to include a tub.

"Is there a bedroom?" She removes her hat and brushes her hair back with her fingers.

I point to a thin wooden ladder near the front door. It disappears into a platform above our heads. "It's just a giant mattress up there, but the view is incredible." The view from the top window peeks just above most of the trees and overlooks the land we just traveled.

I leave her to check out the cabin while I unpack the horses and thank my brothers for getting this ready. "Call me if anything happens at the ranch. I don't know how long we can hide here, and we'll need all the time we can get." I tell them I'll talk to Rowan tonight about what we decide to do and send them off. They are the one thing I can always count on.

I secure the horses in the small barn and make sure they have enough hay and blankets, another thing my brothers thought of that I hadn't. I look at my clothes still covered in dirt and realize how rancid I smell. Deciding that a bath is desperately needed, I head into the cabin with a few logs of firewood. I place them neatly next to our roaring fire before I walk into the bathroom.

I don't think to check where Rowan is before walking straight into the room, and I see her soaking in the wide tub. My instincts have me closing the door and spitting out an apology. I wish I had walked in and sat next to her. After what happened in the barn, I'm hesitant. I wait at the door for a moment, contemplating going back in. I feel such a strong pull, a tug inside my heart that calls me to her. "Do you want company?"

A smile plays on her lips. "Will you wash my hair?"

"Of course." I slide off my boots before padding over to the end of the tub. Her light brown strands curl at the end, and I spy clusters of knots. I make sure to grab her brush. She dips her head back into the water, her eyes closed but the side of her mouth upturned in bliss. I massage the shampoo into her hair, running firm circles into her scalp. I make lazy strokes at her neck and temples. A barely audible moan ensures me I'm doing an okay job. "Dip your head back." I guide her head into the water and let my hands go back to work rinsing the shampoo. I layer a generous amount of conditioner in her hair and slowly start brushing out the tangles and knots in her silky strands. Once I've washed the conditioner out, I put it in a loose braid, something I learned from my mother.

I stand from where I was working on her hair and notice the dirt around her knees that she hasn't touched yet. I remove my jeans and jacket, leaving me in boxers and a plain white T-shirt. I walk to the opposite end and slide into the tub. The water rocks and splashes outside the tub as I settle in.

"What are you doing?" she whispers.

I gently run my thumb over the mud on her knee. "Cleaning you up. Is that okay?" A slow nod accompanies a solemn look on her face.

I gather soap in my hands and start at her feet, gently removing any trace of the bad memories. I move to work her calves, digging into the muscles and kissing the rough spots that adorn her body. My hands slide up her thighs, and she tenses for a moment before relaxing her muscles. Slow and steady, I reach the top of her thighs where they meet her hips. My fingers dance past the delicate littering of hair between her thighs. My dick is hard beneath my boxers. The soap and water hide it enough that I continue without wavering.

Her breath is heavy, and I can feel her heart thundering as I reach her waist and add more soap to her chest. I run my thumb gently over the scar next to the smooth peak of her breast. I pass over them gently before moving onto her arms. I rest her hands on my shoulders to move up and down them. I set them back into the warm water and turn into the tub before getting out. I reach for a towel and wrap it around my body before leaving.

I let my back sink against the wall next to the bathroom door. The pouring of water coming from my clothes makes a puddle around me. I use the towel to clean it up and undress before replacing my wet clothes with sweats and a hoodie.

I don't know what I just did. I couldn't resist touching her. I couldn't resist kissing each healing mark that littered her skin. My cock is still throbbing through my sweatpants. I splash cold water onto my face in the kitchen sink to take me back to reality—the terrifying reality that I have no idea what we're going to do. I could run with her forever. I wouldn't tire of her in a thousand lifetimes. I'm not sure when it happened, but I'd give anything to save her. Liddy's word or not, I'd give anything to keep her safe. I'm terrified of a world that could take her from me too soon.

# *Chapter Twenty-Two*

## ROWAN

I'M LEFT A SOAPY MESS ONCE HE LEAVES THE ROOM. I can't stop thinking about his shirt molded to his firm chest, how his biceps begged to be free of the fabric as they washed me of yesterday's sins. I know I should feel guilty for the way I see him now, but that little switch I flicked off in my brain stops the feeling from fully forming. We keep pushing the lines and blurring them further. Logic tells me it's wrong, but my heart continues to warm for him. My body is still familiar with the heartbreak of her death, and feelings of betrayal trying to inch their way in, but I have it on a tightening leash. He makes me feel wanted and protected. I've always been deeply independent—not by choice—but it's shaped me to be who I am today.

I try to cool my ache and desire before leaving the bathtub, not allowing myself to reach my hand below the water. The thin walls don't leave much to the imagination. I heard Sylas propped against the wall, his clothes dripping water until he removed them. Once I know he's gone, I force myself to get out.

The wood floors are cold, ripping a sharp hiss from me when the warmth from the bath is replaced with a chill. I didn't bring any clothes in here with me, so I wrap the towel tightly around my body. The hem of the damp material reaches just below my ass. I step slowly out of the room, trying not to show too much. The fire in the main room is roaring and offers sweet relief to my frozen features. The biting frost that has taken over my toes begins to burn and soften as they warm up. I don't see Sylas, so I give in and sit in the rocking chair in front of the fire. I should search for my clothes, but the heat against my skin is inviting.

I let my head fall back onto the wood of the chair. My body is in a daze of relief and hard-to-come-by comfort, swaying me gently in the chair. I get lost in bliss, lost in my thoughts. My head is still cloudy from the bath, my hair still braided loosely over my shoulder. I can feel his touch against my skin. He was gentle but commanding, making me ease into him and lose all grip I had on reality. I feel him working my thighs, wishing he would move his fingers further, silently begging him with my eyes to move his fingers through the trim curls between my legs. I let out a groan and scrub my hands over my temples.

Soft footsteps fall behind me, making me realize that he has been here the entire time. He stills when he sees me. "Sorry, I didn't mean to interrupt." He moves to turn away.

"No, I should be getting dressed." The floor groans under the weight of the chair as I stand and walk toward the ladder leading to the bed. My bare shoulder unintentionally brushes his arm as I walk by. I take the steps of the ladder one at a time, and I can feel the heat of his gaze when I climb higher and the towel struggles to keep me covered. I don't chance a look in his direction. I don't trust myself not to invite him up. It would be so easy to remove this thin fabric and fall into his lap. Tucked away in the woods with the devil on my shoulder is not ideal.

I dress quickly before I have time to change my mind, my morals slipping through the cracks of my humanity. The book made it seem so easy to turn off your emotions, to let go of everything that made you more human than monster. Something inside me stirs and pushes against that mental gate, as if I forgot to turn the key and lock it. I reach into my bag and pull out the book I stole from Sam's house. I know enough about my fate to work on finding out more about vampires and what kills them—what kills me. The events of Sam's house waver in and out of my consciousness enough that I don't remember how she knocked me out so quickly. Aside from being a vampire, it seemed like she had powers. The M-word begs to surface. Magic shouldn't be a surprise after turning into a vampire, but it still makes no sense to me. It makes me wonder if I've ever met a real witch and didn't know it—everything hiding in plain sight. I flip through the pages, noting Sam's depiction, trying to find any meaning or reason to the fate chosen for me.

Sylas swiftly climbs the ladder holding two mugs in his right hand. "I brought tea." His smile is small and genuine. I grasp the warm ceramic and let out a sigh.

"Thank you." I offer a smile in return. The air up here gets thick when he moves to sit next to me. Our backs rest against the wood panels at the end of the mattress. The view looks over the trees and into the fields around the ranch house. The trees are covered in snow, and then hills of green are replaced with a blanket of white. "Your dad built this in the perfect spot." My gaze stays on the wall of windows.

"What are you looking for?" He faces me and sees the confusion in my brows. "In the book," he clarifies.

"Anything, really," I sigh. Sam told me what she gave me. She told me, and yet I can't find the memory. "I just want to know how to stop her. Stop them. She's taken so many people who didn't deserve it."

He takes the book from my hands and starts searching the pages without a word. His brows knit, and his focus is sharp on the words in front of him. I can see the muscles in his jaw tighten. "Fucking bitch," he mutters, barely audible. I can see his gaze slowly pass over the same paragraph a few times. I lean into his space and read what has him so intrigued. He stills when my chest presses into him. It feels like he stops breathing altogether until he lets out a loud sigh.

I ignore the tension that seeks to swallow us whole and focus my attention on the pages. He's reading a section with a sketched replica of the church beside it. I didn't peg them for the kind to worship anyone other than her. I read more, and my gaze stops halfway down the page. "Holy water," I mutter. "Holy water," I say louder this time, gaining his attention.

"That's what she gave you? You're sure?" His grip is on my arm, holding me tighter than we both expected. I nod. The smile that takes residence on his face turns feral. "Good."

Good? I'm at a loss for words as he continues to smile at me, giving me genuine concern. How could any of this be good? They used holy water to poison me—poison me because now I'm in the hands of the devil. I'm a demon, a creation made to kill. There's nothing good about this. There's nothing good about the realization that something holy can kill me. I will always be the bad guy, always be a killer. My heart races, and I tear from the bed, down the ladder, and out the door. I'm moving too fast, and my foot gets stuck in the snow. I fall hard into the fresh powder and roll onto my back, letting out the loudest laugh I can manage. I forgot my hat when I ran out, and I have to shield my eyes from the sun starting to set. I can't do anything right, not even run away. I would know, considering I've tried twice now.

I see him stand above me, not sure how to feel about the woman laughing like a maniac in the snow. He finally lays next to me and stays there while I laugh through my pain. He lets the back of his hand circle lazily on mine in comfort. I roll to face him like I do every time my world seems to be crashing down in front of me. The sunset glows around his face. The sting in my eyes is worth seeing his beauty. My eyes trace his features before I have to shield them from the glare.

I feel him move before he removes my hands from my face. He's so close that it blocks out the sun, so close that our breath mingles together in the small space between us. He doesn't say anything to me; he just looks at where his hand meets mine. His fingers slip between mine, and he pulls them to his mouth, where I feel the gentle kiss he whispers onto them. I let my eyes close and ground myself in the feeling, in the relief his body offers me and the comfort of his steady breathing. We lay like this until the sun is set, and I'm sure the frostbite on my toes has set in. When I open my eyes, I notice our legs twisted together and his lips a breath away. He's close enough that if I move an inch, I'm done for. There's a longing in his eyes that tells me he's thinking it too. My lips part slightly, and he tilts his head closer.

There's a shimmer that starts to form in the corner of my eye, and I shoot up. In front of me, Liddy comes into view like she never left—like she was never taken. Sylas stills beside me, realizing she caught us tangled in each other's embrace. "Liddy…" It's barely a whisper from me.

Sylas still looks like a deer in the headlights when she begins to speak.

*I only have a moment, but I came to warn you.*

Her ghostly form kneels in front of me, and I feel the blanket of chill she leaves on my body where her hand touches me.

*You need to fight. Don't stop until it's finished, Rowan. You hold the power to stop her.*

I feel defeated, knowing she's wrong. I want to fight for her—*she* wants me to fight for her. "I love you. I want to fight for you, but I don't have the power to stop her."

*You are more powerful than you think. You need to act fast, though.*

She looks at Sylas and gives him a nod, along with a glare that tells him he better obey.

*This is the last time you'll see me like this. My time here is coming to an end.*

Her hands wrap around mine, and I wish I could squeeze them.

*When the time comes, don't hesitate. Fight for yourself, Rowan.*

Warmth begins to slide down my face and is replaced with

a chill when she wipes them away. "You have my word." She always knew more than I did, always perceived the world a little differently. If she thinks I can do this, I'll try like hell to uphold that.

She moves to stand, and I see her light begin to dim. She's leaving us for the last time, and I know I can't stop it. I try to dig deep and feel grateful for the extra time we had with her, but selfishly, I'm heartbroken all over again.

A smile spreads over her face, and she waves her finger between us.

*I like you together. You make a good team.*

She winks, and her form fades away.

I take my time to defrost in front of the fire. Thanks to our icy skin, it's a slow process. I can finally feel my fingers and toes, my body starting to soothe. My mind is reeling after what Liddy said. Ever since turning off my humanity, I haven't felt the guilt of my growing feelings towards him so much, but her certainty etches confusion in my brain. She likes us together? Is that supposed to make feel like this isn't wrong? She's gone for good now, I don't feel guilt for the comfort he gives me, and yet I need more time to piece it together. The fire of my want and need for him burns hotter than ever.

I haven't seen him at all since we got back inside. He set up the fire for me and walked away. I don't know what's going through his head, but it can't be easy having your love ripped away from you again. We both know we had more time with her than we were supposed to after her death. Her unconditional love feels like it's strangling, waiting for me to break, waiting for us to be stupid enough to toe over that line of possibility.

I want to toe that line. I want our edges to blur and melt into each other.

I want to own everything he wants to give me.

That cowboy is mine.

# Chapter Twenty-Three

## SYLAS

I give Rowan the space she needs to process Liddy's words. I knew all along that we were gravitating towards each other, my feelings for her growing each day. I know she needs more time to get over Liddy's death, and this time, it isn't any easier. The guilt was hard for me to overcome, but I think Liddy understands. Sometimes, I think my heart froze over with how quickly I was able to move on. I wouldn't be honest if I said there weren't feelings there. I've always felt the need to protect her. Rowan came into my heart out of nowhere and filled it three times over. My love for her pools inside me, waiting to give her a small taste. She needs more time, but I don't want to wait any longer.

I let myself back inside the cabin and see Rowan still by the fireplace. She looks deep in thought, so I gently pad over and drop to my knees in front of her. "What are you thinking about?"

She peers down at me and gives a small smile. "We make a good team."

My smile grows, and I bite down on my lip to stop from

overdoing it. If she can see how great of a team we are, she can see that we're meant to go down this path together. I start to massage her calves, thinking about how smooth her skin was in the bath and needing more. "You ran off earlier before I could tell you what I was smiling about."

"What?" Her brows knit together. Her skin heats under my touch, and her eyes don't leave my face.

My heart rate picks up the further up her leg I touch. She lets out small moans while I work her muscles. Her eyes are watching my hands move in small, steady circles around her thighs. She was so stubborn earlier, running away before I could tell her how absolutely genius she is, how we found the exact way to stop the queen from destroying this town—the town we call home. The town I want to worship this woman in for the rest of our immortal lives.

Her gaze heats me to my core, my erection growing freely inside my sweats. I'm not hiding it from her this time. I want her to know what she does to me, how she makes me feel— completely ravaged and delirious.

I play with her waistband, tracing it with my fingers and letting them trail inside the hem. Her hips rise in offering. I don't think twice before pulling the band over her waist and down her legs. I press gentle kisses over her knees while I push them apart. "Tell me to stop now, and I will." I look into her eyes glazed over with heat.

"No," is all she offers me. The side of my mouth tips up before I graze my teeth right above her knee and take a shallow bite. A whimper leaves her throat, and I let her blood pool in my mouth. Gently sucking, I clear the blood from the wound.

"I'm going to ask you a question, and for every wrong answer, I'm going to bite you just like that." I run the pad of my thumb over the two shallow wounds I just left on her and watch them slowly heal.

Her tongue slides over her bottom lip before biting down. "I might answer wrong on purpose." Her laugh is deep and warm.

"Be a good girl for me, Rowan." I continue to massage her thighs, and she lets her head fall back onto the chair. The motion sets the chair gently rocking, and I let that momentum drive my hands over her skin. "Now, tell me how we can use holy water."

"Wh- I don't know," she breathes out.

"Wrong answer." I trail my mouth farther up her thigh and sink my teeth deeper.

"Fuck." She lifts her hips, and her hand drags through my hair. I suck the skin around the bite before leaving kisses around the quickly healing wound.

"Think about it, Row. You know this."

"I can't think with you distracting me." Her mouth parts as she lets out shallow pants. I can feel the heat building between her legs, can smell her arousal.

I let my hands drag further up and kiss her right where her thighs meet the dark curls between her legs. Her legs fall further apart in silent begging. I won't give her what she wants until she gives me what I need. "Try again."

"Please, I- It's poison." Her hips slide forward.

"And what do we do with poison? How can we use it, Row?" I give her a gentle bite at the apex of her thighs. Her moans get louder, and I'm starting to lose control. I need to taste the wetness gathering in her flushed cunt. My fingers trace the outline of her sex and through the scattering of hair. Her grip tightens against my scalp.

"We poison them. We feed them holy water. Drown them." Her breathing is unsteady as her chest heaves.

"That's my girl," I praise before letting myself drag my tongue straight through her cunt. Reveling in the sweet taste of her, I flatten my tongue on the small bundle of nerves and gently rock the chair, giving extra friction against my tongue.

Her hips move in time with the sway of the chair. "More."

"Tell me how we'll do it, and I'll add a finger." I let my finger trace the spot she's aching to have me.

"Please," she's begging me, turning into putty in my mouth. I remove my tongue and give her a gentle bite on her other thigh. She laughs with pleasure and pain. I give in and bite her again. My head is yanked back, and she brings our eyes to meet. "Stop playing with me." Her cheeks are flushed, and the hard lines of her mouth part.

Her grip loosens, and I run my tongue along her cunt, letting it slide inside her and giving her a taste of what she could have if she would just answer me. She knows what to do; she's smart. I need her to get out of her head and think.

"You know the answer," I whisper into her skin. She uses her legs to make the chair rock again, making my tongue pierce inside of her with the rhythm. I grip the arm of the chair and stop its movement, not letting her have this release until I'm ready.

She lets out an audible groan and stares at me with

determination. I swirl my tongue against her clit, begging her to think.

"If everyone drinks it, they can't feed. They'll burn." She pants out the words.

I smile into her skin and let my finger slide into her with ease. "You're so wet for me, so ready." I let the chair rock back and forth, my finger sliding in and out and my tongue soaking up her heat. Her hands fall back into my hair, and her hips grind against the grit of my beard. I add a second finger, and her legs shake. My tongue flattens against her clit in small circles, and I move my fingers faster.

My cock strains against the soft fabric of my sweats, and I'm doing everything I can not to blow in my pants in front of this woman again. She lets her leg fall between mine, and my cock presses against it.

"So. Close," she moans as she grips the chair above her head.

I work her faster, moving my fingers harder. My hand slides beneath her sweater and grips her full breast, trailing my thumb over her hard nipple. She's a puddle of lust and want. She melts into my hand before I feel her core tighten. "That's right, come on my fingers."

"Sylas." Her release spirals, and I keep a steady movement, letting her ride out her orgasm. When her body falls and her hand slides down to cup my face, I remove my fingers and wrap my mouth around them. I taste her release and groan at the disheveled beauty in front of me.

I see her eyes widen, and she shoots up. "You knew this whole time how to stop them, and you made me beg for it." I love the fire I see in her eyes. I can't help but smile. I know she hates it.

"You're so capable and you know what to do. I wanted you to think about it."

"But where do we get enough holy water?"

We started the trek into town this morning under thick hoods, hoping not to be seen. I spent the past few nights tossing and turning on our shared mattress, listening to the sounds of the woods. I called my brothers to set up this meeting at the church so we could be in and out. I've kept my fair share of distance from Rowan the past few days, letting her sort out her head, giving her room to decide if this is what she really wants.

We blew through the blood supply at the cabin and had to resort to hunting animals. Our speed and strength left them entirely defenseless. Catching them was easy; getting her to eat was hard.

"Animal blood doesn't taste as good, and you know it doesn't make us as strong."

"We need to stop feeding solely off each other," I counter.

She rolls her eyes and eats with a scowl on her face.

We need our strength for today in case things don't go our way. I can always see the battle in her eyes. She thinks she can school her face, but her eyes say everything. The amount of death she has seen has hardened her, but I can see how much it's tearing her apart. She's not a monster, but it will take a lot of convincing for her to see that.

It takes a few hours to ride back to the farm where my

brothers are waiting with the truck. They're coming along for backup, and I can't thank them enough for keeping us afloat. We're meeting the priest of the town's only church. It has been around since the birth of this town, seemingly the only place in Georgetown that hasn't been corrupted by the vampires.

The tension in the truck is thick, and Noah keeps looking between us like he knows what we did. The smirk and wink he gives me is telling enough. I shoot him a scowl. I don't want Rowan to feel any shame, since we haven't made anything official and haven't talked about what we did a few nights ago. I've been taking cold baths to tamp down the hunger I feel for her. My blood sings when I feed from her. My heart pounds when I play with her. I'll devour her when we can escape this war.

The church is old, the outside blackened with age, the white paint chipping away. The windows are stunning stained glass pieces that outshine the entire building. The artwork is preserved, but the budget hasn't allowed for repainting—a large argument amongst the town.

Stepping inside the church makes my lungs burn, like the air has been sucked right out of us by the looks on everyone's faces. A tingle starts to form in my chest. "Safe to say we're not wanted here..." I hear Rowan huff at that.

"We should make this quick," Harris gruffly states. I can see a bead of sweat forming above his brow.

We walk towards the back of the building. A short man comes out from a back room and smiles in greeting. Father Rice, I presume. I'm sure he won't be wearing that same smile shortly. I don't know what all my brothers told him to get him to agree to meet us, but I'm sure it wasn't the truth. The thin white band at his collar gives me a strange, uneasy feeling in my gut. I didn't grow up with religion, but I've never detested it. The room grows more suffocating the further we walk in. Rowan keeps her cool and holds her chin high despite it. Her strength pulls at my heart.

"Father," she says before offering her hand in greeting. "Thank you for meeting with us. I hope our request isn't too much to ask for."

"There's no such thing. I'm at your disposal." His smile is tense.

We get talking through our request, and he happily obliges. We brought enough large jars to fill with holy water to distribute throughout the Georgetown restaurants and shops. It's just enough that everyone should have it in their system, giving the queen and her henchmen enough time to get out of town or perish.

Father Rice blesses the baptism tub, and we fill our jars before loading them into the truck. We thank him profusely before we need to get out of there. My muscles are starting to ache, and we are all sweating. Stepping outside into the cold air is a sigh of relief, and I can start to release the tension I was holding in my shoulders.

We make quick work of distributing the jars, only giving enough information to the owners of the establishments. They've all been extremely understanding and have heard the rumors of death for years now. No one puts up a fight at washing away the sin of this town.

We make it back to the ranch with a jar of our own. Rowan is the only one to truly experience the effects of holy water in our system; my brothers and I want to taste it to be sure.

"I can do it since I already know what it's supposed to feel like," Rowan says before we raise our glasses to our lips.

"No, we need to know too. You don't have to go through that again." The pleading in my eyes is enough to get her to back off.

I lift the glass to my lips and take a deep drink. The moment it hits my tongue, I can feel my blood boil. My skin heats and my bones ache. I try to breathe through the pain, but it has no end. It feels like it's trying to release my soul from my own body, and my head spins.

"Fuck," I gasp before falling to my knees. My vision blurs around the edges; I don't have the strength to see how it affects my brothers. A firm hand is placed on my back. In any other situation, it would be a comfort, but no comfort comes from the touch. The room starts to sway and stretch with the burn.

The burn is endless, and darkness begs to consume me.

# Chapter Twenty-Four

## ROWAN

It's been an hour since Sylas and his brothers blacked out from the pain. They collapsed to the floor moments after taking a deep sip of holy water. I should have told them to limit their consumption, but I didn't have the chance before they went for it blindly. I tried to give them a soothing touch—ground them—but it didn't help. I'm getting anxious waiting for them to wake. We should be getting back to the cabin to hide and plan out our attack in case this doesn't go our way. I want another strategy. I want to be ready for anything. I don't think Sylas wants as much; if it was up to him, we'd run forever, but he's staying for me.

I pace the room, thinking, strategizing, pulling details from all the information we've found these past months. I've been a monster for several months now, and the change still feels foreign—like I've stepped out in someone else's body.

There are so many ways this could end. There are so many ways I could end them. We almost failed to take on three of the henchmen, and I can't wrap my head around how many more she will bring with her to find me. I didn't think I would make it this far; I thought they would have found me by now. The cabin felt far safer than here at the ranch house; the search should be harder for them.

Seeing him on the ground now makes my heart pull. The connection between us grows stronger every time I look into his eyes. When he touches me, it feels right. When he holds me, it feels meant to be. I start to wonder if we've always fit together like this. Liddy would drag us everywhere with her, and we always made the most of it together—making inside jokes, the arguments that were never really fights, the joy we shared over being around the person we loved.

It terrifies me now, terrifies me that I could lose him if this doesn't work. It terrifies me that I'm not able to give him what he truly desires. They'll be okay without me, but I won't be okay without him. I'd be dead without him. The queen—Sam—would still have me gripped in her claws. It sends chills down my spine.

I settle next to Sylas and prop his head in my lap. I run my fingers through his long blond hair. I let my fingers trail over his features, his strong jaw and firm cheekbones. We sit like this for a while, committing his face to my memory. His eyelids start to flutter as I place a steady hand on him and whisper sweet words in comfort. "Hey, relax," I try to calm him as he wakes.

"Fuck that," he grumbles, his voice is hoarse. "It's perfect." His laugh is dark and sultry. A laugh escapes me. It's a sweet relief after my anxiety has been running rampant these last few hours. I know exactly how he's feeling, and he must be incredibly hungry. I sweep my hair to the side and wrap my arms around his neck to guide him closer in offering.

"Please eat," I say calmly. His gaze lingers on my neck before meeting my eyes. He's studying me, and it makes my heart race. I hold his stare, making sure he knows this is okay. His tongue sweeps over his fangs, and he lowers his mouth on my neck. Kisses pepper my skin, leaving goosebumps in their wake. They travel up my neck, and his mouth slides over my jaw, making my breath hitch. His thumb grazes my bottom lip before his mouth meets mine and his beard tickles my skin.

"I'm so sorry this happened to you," he whispers against my tongue. He deepens our kisses, our tongues gliding over each other, feeling like static electricity in my blood. "I'll end them, every last one of them." His fangs bite into my lip, and I whimper. He only draws a little blood, sucking it clean. He certainly brings me relief.

My tongue darts over my lip, and I break our kiss to raise my fingers to the wound. I'm completely done for. The way he's looking at me with intense heat has me unraveling on the floor. I push down my desire and move his mouth towards my neck again, silently willing him to eat. "You need your strength back. Please."

"I love it when you beg for me." His laugh rumbles against my neck before the prick of his fangs fills my thoughts. This act fuels my blood with lust and connection. I haven't been able to read about vampire blood sharing, but there has to be something more to it. I don't feel this same connection with humans I've fed from. This is euphoric and otherworldly. I would chalk it up to my feelings towards him, but this feels something entirely different—a feeling lacing my blood. It's like feeding from each other intertwines us, creates a bond that can't be broken—if they're ever lost, I can find them.

Warmth begins to spread through me, his mouth giving me great reprieve from the demons battling in my head. My hand smooths through his hair before I curl my fist around it. My other hand trails up his shirt and presses against hard, smooth skin. I try to muffle the sound of my moan in his hair so Harris and Noah don't wake.

"You taste so sweet. Look what you do to me." He slides my hand from his abs to his jeans, where I feel his hard erection. I want to slip my hand under the rough material and feel his smooth length.

"Get a room!" Harris bellows mere feet away from us.

I quickly remove my hands and push Sylas from me. My eyes are wide in horror, not believing I actually let this happen in front of them.

"Jesus, I knew you were fucking, but not in front of us, alright?" Noah adds in.

"We are not!" I say, embarrassed and not entirely being truthful. It earns me an eye roll from the gallery.

"It's safe to say this shit works." Harris moves to stand and helps Noah to his feet. We all get up, Sylas adjusting himself. I hope they don't mention what just happened again. "This might be enough to take most of them out."

I know it's powerful, but I still think we need a backup. We need to be prepared for a fight; they're probably stronger than they've let on, and there are only four of us. They've been doing this far longer than we have, but from what I've seen, they haven't had to put up much of a fight. I won't put anyone's life in the hands of a maybe, especially not theirs.

"What are you thinking?" Sylas dips his head toward me.

"We need more. A back-up. This is going to piss them off more than anything, so we need to prepare for a fight." Saying it out loud gives me chills. I've never been to battle. I've never fought. My strength is all I have, and I know it's not enough to overpower someone who has decades on me, possibly even centuries. The warm press of his palm on my lower back steadies me from the spiral starting in my mind. Horrors beyond my imagination are happening right now, things I never believed to be true. This path has blurred edges, an endless road carved ahead. All I can hope for is that Sylas stays by me. I don't expect any of them to, but I hope for it. Fighting my own battle feels too heavy this time.

The moment the words come out of my mouth, Harris and Noah start spit-balling ideas, terrible ideas that make my gut turn. I look out the back windows of the house and see the barn that has little use now, the one where horrors have already occurred.

"The barn." I turn back to the men circling me. "If it comes to it, we draw them back to the barn. That thing needs to be burned anyway."

Harris gives me a vile smile. "Make them fight on our grounds, on our terms. You're getting somewhere here."

A weird sense of pride bubbles up through me. I don't want to be good at this, good at being a monster—being a killer—but the thought of succeeding gives me unsurmountable joy, a feeling I miss. It gives me the confidence to continue my line of thinking. When I tell them my plans for the barn, Harris is so overjoyed with my sick mind that he lifts and spins me around before planting a big kiss on my forehead. I tell him to gather as many silver chains as he can find.

"Vamp girl here really is going to pull this off, isn't she?" Noah beams at me. We might all be sick and twisted by the end of this. Together. We can get through this together.

"That's my girl," Sylas says before pulling me closer to him and covering my mouth with the most sinful kiss.

"That's our girl!" a ceremonious cheer comes from the brothers before Sylas turns and corrects them with a growl.

We make our way back to the cabin in the woods while the brothers set up the barn for our awaited war. The ride back gives me too much time to get lost in my thoughts. I shift the Stetson on my head and peer up at the sky. The sun is starting to set, and it stings my eyes. The beauty of it is one thing I never want to stop experiencing, no matter the short-lived pain it brings.

I look back towards the tree line and find him looking at me. He slows down his mare to walk next to me. We ride side by side in silence for a short while before he pulls me in for a kiss. The mares don't startle, and it gives me relief, allowing me to learn further into his kiss. After we pull away, his eyes are still on me. I can feel the heat in my cheeks, suddenly feeling shy under his gaze. "Tell me what you're thinking," I offer instead of cowering.

"I'm wondering how an idiot like me landed someone so beautiful and clever." His fangs snag on his lip when he smiles, and he looks unholy. I'm ready to sin for him any day. My skin flushes down my chest, my body reacting to the thoughts I'm having about him.

"You're the most level-headed one of the bunch." The side of my mouth twists up. He shifts in his saddle, and I give him a full grin at the sight of his erection. "Some men just have no self-control." His mouth gapes, and I laugh, flinging my head back.

I let out a sharp gasp when he pulls me from my mare and lifts me onto his saddle to face him. The small saddle doesn't offer us much room; I'm pressed completely into his front. "I can think of much better things for that mouth to do than mock me, sweetheart." It's my turn to leave my jaw hanging.

It doesn't stay like that for long. In moments, his mouth is back on mine. He nips at my bottom lip, making the heat in me burn hotter. We kiss deeply without end, gliding our tongues together in a dance, one completely sloppy and shaky. I let out a breathy gasp when he slides his hand under my shirt and rolls my hard nipple between his fingers. "Alright, cowboy. Now I see what all the fuss is about."

"Only now? Not when I had my mouth between your legs?" He bites my jaw and pulls on my nipple. "Not when you were begging me for more?" His hot breath meets my neck before he slides his tongue over the length of my ear. The sensation makes me shiver in pleasure.

"I don't beg," I lie.

"I'll change that."

He sinks his teeth into my shoulder, and I shudder. "Fuck." I grip his strong arms and lose myself in him.

His horse is startled, and I quickly realize we haven't been paying attention to where we're going. The realization doesn't come soon enough, though. We're thrown from the mare bucking us off. I land hard on my shoulder, or maybe his. My laugh is anything but soft. I can't stop the tears that come from how hard I'm laughing. I curl myself into his chest and feel the rumble of his laugh against my face.

Sylas starts to talk between cackles. "Maybe that wasn't the best place to devour you."

"You think?"

Our laughs continue in each other's arms for a short while longer. We have to find our hats in the growing darkness, and I search the ground for them while Sylas calls back our horses. They didn't go far without us.

I'm starting the fire in the cabin while he stables and feeds the horses. Life with him could be so beautiful. We've been dragged together in our grief and battles, but I don't know what life will look like when this war has passed. If he wants to stay here when the ranch is soaked in blood, if he'll want to stay with me when we no longer have to fight together. No one sticks with me long, and it's not like I make them want to stay. It's easier to keep my distance, easier to be on my own. Except now, I'm weighing if that has ever been true. If I was alone right now, I wouldn't have made it. He saves me in every sense of the word. He saves me, and I'll let him. He's worth the risk of heartbreak. I just hope he feels the same.

His arms wrap around my shoulders, and I lean back into

his touch. I'm done feeling guilty for the comfort he brings me. I tuck that feeling deep behind the gates of my mind. I revel in the feeling he gives me. We start to sway in our hold, swaying to music that doesn't exist. His hands fall to mine, and he spins me out. I land with a thud against his chest, our hands still locked together.

"I might not be the best dancer," he says into my hair.

"I won't tell anyone."

We sway and move to the rhythm, our steps messy and uncoordinated. Shameless giggles bubble out of me every time I step on his foot. He spins me and dips me back before lifting me. It's the only time our hands ever leave one another.

Our steps slow, and I rest my head on his chest, letting his heartbeat set the pace for our slow movements. He lays kisses into my hair, and I breathe in his scent of bergamot and rosemary. The thought of not having moments like this creeps in, and before talking myself out of it, I ask him. "Where do you want to be when this is over? When we don't have to fight or hide." I give him the space to answer the question, to think about it, but he doesn't need time. He replies within a heartbeat.

"Right here, with you. I'm not letting you escape me anymore, darling." He holds me tighter. My vision starts to blur with the tears starting to build. His words stab right into my chest and take hold. Fat drops of liquid fall down my cheeks before he lifts my chin and kisses them away. "I'm not going anywhere without you, Rowan Watson. If you want to run, I'll run. If you want to fight, I'll fight." I barely let him finish before lifting to my toes and kissing him deeply.

"Thank you," I whisper and place my hands on his firm chest. The fabric curls into my fists, willing him to stay like this with me. I feel his hands slide to the base of my neck and pull my hair tightly through his fingers, forcing my head back and exposing my throat. He hums kisses from my chin down to my collar. I lose myself in his embrace. My tongue sweeps over my fangs, and my body sings to get a taste of him. When he loosens his grip, I don't waste any time going for the soft skin at the base of his neck. I suck and tease him with the graze of my teeth before sinking them in deep. His blood flows into my mouth, and my hum of pleasure vibrates against his skin.

"Tell me how I taste," he grunts out in pleasure.

His blood is coursing through my body, intertwining us. I feel the power it gives me, the strength and clarity. "Like mine."

# Chapter Twenty-Five

## SYLAS

THOSE WORDS ARE ENOUGH TO SET ME ON EDGE, TO THROW ME INTO A BLAZING HEAT. It's enough for me to lift her and drag her up the stairs to our left, leading to the bed. Her mouth stays on the tender spot where her teeth sank deep. She peppers kisses around the wound, licking up any remaining blood and watching the bite disappear.

My hands roam her body freely, giving in to every impulse I've had when it comes to her. Her skin is smooth beneath her shirt, her waist perfect in my hands. I drop my head to give her kisses above her belly button, trailing them under her full breasts. I can feel her chest rise and fall in rapid motion. I unbutton her shirt slowly, keeping my eyes on hers the entire time. I want her to see me devour her, consume her completely. She hurriedly grasps at the button on her pants, and I lay my hand on top of hers.

"Slow down. We have time." Her smile melts my heart.

When I reach the last button of her shirt, I slide it over her shoulders and off her arms, exposing her soft cotton bra. Her nipples peek through, and I drag my teeth along them, biting through the fabric with a pinch. She slides her head further back on the pillows, her soft lips parting for me. "Absolutely stunning, darling." I kiss down the length of her body until my lips meet her pants and slowly pull with my teeth until they unbutton. Her pants slide off effortlessly, her legs smooth under my touch. These legs have been burned into my memory. I kiss down her entire form. I will worship her the way she deserves, slowly and completely.

Her panties are soaked through and absolutely ruined. I nip at her through the thin cotton.

"Sylas." Her voice is breathy and wild.

"Rowan," I counter, playing with the hem of her underwear. She lifts her hips in offering, but I waste no time breaking them free of her body. Her milky skin glows and vibrates under my touch. I start slowly dragging my fingers through the soft curls between her legs, slipping my finger through the wet folds of her pink pussy. Her hands fall to my shoulders and her nails dig in deep. I sink the tip of my finger into her and bring it to my mouth to taste.

She bites her lip, but I see the smile playing on her face.

I slide my finger in deeper, slowly pushing in and out.

In and out.

Her breath hitches, and she arches into my touch.

My cock is begging to be freed, begging to replace my finger just like she will be begging me soon. I fist my hard length in my other hand, feeling a bead of liquid drag out. I collect the bead of pre-cum with my finger and drag it across her lips. She wraps her mouth around the digit and moans at the taste, my finger leaving her mouth with a pop. The giggle that comes out of her makes me want to do this over and over again.

I pull the soft fabric of her bra over her breasts, letting them free, allowing me to drag my mouth over the sensitive skin. She likes it when I bite down; it makes her squirm.

"I need more. I need you."

"Such a needy thing. Beg for it." I kiss her, letting our tongues play.

"Please."

I add a second finger in and pump faster, curling my fingers upward, dragging a guttural gasp from her.

"Fuck. More," she says into my mouth.

"What's the magic word?"

She bites my lip hard, drawing blood she wastes no time cleaning off me. "Please."

"That's my girl." My smile plays against her lips. I release our kiss and pull my pants down over my hips, my cock springing out as I fist my length. She sits up on her elbows and reaches out to touch me. Her hand wraps around me and moves slowly. "God, yes." My head falls back, and I take in her touch, warm and soft.

I let my body fall to hers, holding myself above her with my hands on either side of her head. "Your touch drives me mad," I huff out. My cock rests on her abdomen, and I feel like I'm going to combust. I move to rub the head of my dick slowly over her clit, dragging it in circles and nudging her entrance.

"You're teasing me," she groans. Her tongue darts over her lips, and I might beg her to let me slip my cock between her perfect pout.

"You're quivering with pleasure. You make me so fucking hard." I tease her more, reveling in the mess she's becoming before me. "Fuck, I don't have a condom. Are you on birth control?"

"I can't...I don't think we need that anymore."

Something stirs in my chest, but it's all the confirmation I need. I slide my cock in slowly, letting her adjust to my size. Her mouth gapes open, assuring me I'll definitely be begging later.

I pump inside her slowly, letting my hips squeeze at the top. I don't want to just fuck her; I want to make love to her. She will be worshipped under my touch. I guide her legs to my shoulders, letting me go deeper. I press my weight into them and grip the back of her thigh. I pick up my pace, unable to stop as she unravels under me, taking in every inch.

"More. Please give me more," she begs and pants.

I drive into her harder and faster, her hips meeting my pace every time, trying to take all of me. I let my fingers circle her clit, feeling her pussy tighten around me. "You take me so good, darling." I won't last much longer.

"I'm s-so close." Her moans are deep and sultry. She looks so sinful under my touch, taking me so well. I move my fingers faster in time with my thrusts.

Her eyes roll, and she arches back violently. "Yes, yes..." I feel her pussy pulse against me. "I'm coming!" Her legs shake around me, and I lose it. I pump faster, only getting in a few final strokes before my release spirals into her. I slow my pace, drawing out our releases together, easing her orgasm to the end.

"Wow, that was... Wow." She runs her fingers through her hair and gazes up at me with what I can only describe as admiration. I let my body fall on the mattress next to her. I fold her into me and tuck her head beneath my chin.

"Are you ready to do it in the bath now? I can't stop thinking how good you looked, soapy and panting." I run my hand over her bare skin, goosebumps forming where my touch meets her. She practically drags me out of bed to sprint for the bathroom. I'm in awe at the life that has sparked in her skin.

I lower her into the large tub, her back pressing against my cock that's already hard again. I wrap my arms around her and kiss her exposed neck. When I lift my face again, I can see a grim expression on hers, like she's questioning something, like she's in pain. "What are you thinking?"

She's silent for a long moment, her hands fidgeting in her lap. "The look you had on your face earlier." My brows knit together, not understanding what she could mean. I let her get her bearings, and she moves to face me, sorrow filling her eyes. Dread fills my gut. "When I reminded you I can't get pregnant anymore."

I should have known. I should have pieced it together, but I didn't. Vampires can't have children without the help of magic, and still, I didn't connect the dots.

"I'm sorry." She's breathing heavily and can't meet my eyes. "I've never been able to conceive, even before turning. I used to think of it as a good thing, but now, with you... I know you and Liddy had that all planned out." Her thoughts trail off. Her words are like a punch to my gut. "I'm so sorry," she whispers.

It wasn't always my plan to have kids, not until the decision was made for me. It always seemed like the right thing to do, but now, I'm not certain if it's what I truly wanted or if I was just doing what I thought was expected of me. I struggled with this lack of perfection, and now, I'm being sliced open again. "I wanted that for so long, Rowan."

Fat tears stream down her cheeks, and my heart aches at the sight. I feel like I'm being torn apart. I thought I had a good handle on change, but something deep in me sobs and strains against it.

"I'm falling in love with you." Her voice shakes with honesty and regret. "I tried to stop it. I've never let myself get attached so deeply. It's so different with you. I didn't want you to leave. I understand if being with me is not what you need." She buries her head in my chest, her shoulders shaking with her silent cries.

My hand wraps around the base of her neck, and I smooth her hair over her back. I'm deeply confused, though I can't help but comfort her. I remind myself this is about her too, that she hurts too. I smooth her hair and run my fingers in light circles against her skin until the water runs cold and she shakes against the chill. I lift her out of the tub and carry us to bed. I hold her until her sobs soften and she falls asleep.

She's falling in love with me, but I already love her. I love her so unconditionally that I know this won't make me leave. I couldn't give her that truth, though, not until I sort out the pain deep inside my bones. My life has changed so thoroughly in the last month that I thought I could handle this with ease. The thought of losing her strikes deeper than my want for a child. She is all I need to be complete and whole. She has dragged a deep-seated love from me that no one has given me before.

My thoughts keep me from sleeping. I move to the main floor and sit in front of the fire with *Georgetown After Dark*, hoping to find more answers to our new life. My fingers feel rough on the worn pages as I flip through the text I've already been over. I come across a page with a dried spot of blood. I run my thumb over it and see the page titled *The Blood Bond*.

A blood bond can only be created between vampires turned by the same one. When you share blood, it mixes in the veins, tethering you to one another.

My blood begins to boil knowing Harris fed from her that same night. He will never sink his teeth into her again. I will never allow that bond between them, not when she's mine. It explains the deep pull I experience when I'm looking for her, how I can read her expressions so well. We're linked, for better or worse. I search the pages to find more information.

Sharing blood for long enough will expand the bond. You will feel their emotions, their pain. It can be hard to tell your own thoughts and feelings from theirs. The Blood Bond can be deepened through Soul Binding.

Turning the pages faster, I continue to scan the pages.

Soul Binding allows you to draw power from the bond, but it can be deadly. If you die, your soul dies, and your bound partner will die. A soul bond is very powerful and gives both individuals immense power.

A chill goes down my spine.

I glance at the next heading: *Bloodstones*. Still, I can't focus enough to comprehend the words in front of me.

I can't help but think this is what Liddy means. We already have a blood bond. I'm the only one who can bind my soul to Rowan, the only one who can give her the power she needs to stop the queen. She wasn't encouraging our lust; she was encouraging our power. We could be deadly together, lethal. Binding myself to her was always the final play to win. This was always the path chosen for us.

My skin is on fire, and my heart could be pounding through my chest. It was so easy to get lost in her touch, get lost exploring her body. This makes things so real. My ears buzz, and I can only hear the sound of my thundering heart. My palms itch; I feel like a fraud. It's not that I don't love Rowan, but I feel like Liddy used me. I would have done the same for Rowan. I would put everything on the line for her. I will put everything on the line for her.

As if she can hear my screaming thoughts, she finds her place next to me. I can't hear her steps over the panic rising in me. Her hand lands on my shoulder, and she gives it a reassuring squeeze.

"You're tense. What are you doing awake?" I know she's feeling concerned, that she's wondering if this is because of what she told me. There's no point in being dishonest anymore. If I'm going to show her these words, I need to be certain.

"I was stuck in my head and decided to do some reading. Honestly, it didn't help at all." I look at her.

She grabs my chin gently and places a kiss on either side

of my mouth. "Show me." Without missing a beat, she slides into my lap and curls into me, leaving just enough room for the book between us.

I'm silent as she reads, letting her take in the information and draw what she wants from it. I don't want to come on too strong and tell her I'm ready to bind myself to her if she's not there yet. I don't want to scare her by saying I'm ready to live an eternity with her.

She shakes her head. "This all makes so much sense now." Her smile is light, and it fills me with hope. "I had a good feeling there was more than the satisfaction of feeding between us." She smooths my hair behind my ear to lay a tender kiss on my temple.

"Did you read this part?" My fingers trace the Soul Binding section. She shakes her head no. My impulse has been one son of a bitch lately; it takes over again, and I know I let it. "Let me tell you first: I'm ready."

# Chapter Twenty-Six

## ROWAN

My eyes move back to the pages, and I see *The Binding of Souls*. I scan the text, weighing his words while I dig deeper into the book. I read the same sentence over three times.

*A blood ritual to bind souls, immense power, bound for life and death.*

I'm breathing heavily remembering his words. *I'm ready.*

After I just shattered a dream of his, he wants to be bound to me for life? He wants to intertwine our souls? I want to say yes. My answer is yes. It took him no time at all to come to his decision. I didn't know he felt so strongly.

"You don't have to decide right now." His whisper tickles my ear.

"Yes." Our eyes meet, his glossy and mine filling with tears. "Yes."

He kisses me deeply without haste, and my mouth parts for him. Our tongues dance in harmony and love. I love him. I don't know when it happened or how he wormed his way into my dead heart, but God, I love him. Hell must be freezing over.

I break the kiss first, still having questions I need answers to. I will give him my soul, but I need to know he's okay first. "This is really what you want? Even if I can't give you children, a family?" I can feel the sides of my mouth turn downward.

"You're all I need." His thumb brushes my cheek. "Anything that comes our way, we'll take it on together."

My eyes gloss with tears, but a smile lines my lips. I slide my hands over where his are cradling my face. "That's all I needed to hear."

"I love you, Row."

"I love you, cowboy."

Our moment is cut short when Harris bursts through the door of the cabin, huffing like he just ran here. "It worked and they're pissed." We're already standing, letting him catch his breath. "Everyone in town knows there are vampires. The henchmen are pissed; they're snapping necks instead."

"Shit!" I thought it would deter them. I didn't think about them going after the town. They have to know it was us. "We need to get back. Now." My head is spinning, and I just want one thing to go as planned. We give Harris one of the horses to ride back on so all his energy isn't lost in transit. Sylas and I will ride back on the larger mare.

"We should do it now." I pierce him with my eyes, determined to use everything we can to fight this.

He chuckles, and it's almost infuriating. "This is so not romantic."

When we look back on this moment, I want it to be a happy memory, even if the events following are pure horror. I scan the cabin, finding a few candles and a lighter, and I grab the sharpest knife I can find. I place the candles in a small circle and light them one by one, watching the flames illuminate the room in a soft glow. I sit on one side of the circle, placing my knees on the floor and folding my legs underneath them before motioning for him to sit opposite me. The candles burn bright between us, his face contoured in the light and shadows playing at his features. I take a deep breath in and steady my hands. Flattening my palm above the flames, I raise the knife and slice my hand. The blood flows into my palm and around the slim gold band around my finger, pooling in the center of the candles. I don't hand him the knife yet. "I vow to protect our bond with my life," I say with my eyes on him. He's practically glowing.

I pass him the knife and watch as he repeats the action, his blood mixing with mine on the floor in front of us. "I vow to love you endlessly." Warmth wraps around my cold heart. His hand reaches towards me, and we join them, threading our fingers together. A sharp pain shoots down my finger, and I swear, I see the gold ring glow and hum before dimming again.

"Did you feel that too?" My gaze leaves our linked hands to study his face. "In your hand? I felt a shock go through me."

"No, just a tickle." He bites his lip but then thinks otherwise and gives a full smile. I can feel his joy coursing through my veins. I just hope he doesn't feel my confusion. I decide he doesn't when my senses fill with lust and I feel wetness growing between my legs.

Our grip stays tight when he lifts me to stand. He moves swiftly, and my back crashes into the wall behind us. Our lips crash in a hungry craze. I feel the same shock shoot through my hand again, but the lust filling my brain overpowers the feeling.

His thoughts fill my head like they are my own—unwavering love and lust, undeniably honest feelings and a flicker of horror. I wonder if he can sense how scared I am too, if my thoughts are flowing through his mind, mixing with his.

"You're scared," he says breathlessly.

"Terrified, and so are you." I smile, knowing exactly how he feels.

"Are you ready for this?" I nod and give him a final kiss.

We fix ourselves and move to leave. The candles are still burning by the time Sylas makes it past the doorway. I turn to blow them out, but something makes me focus on the glowing flames. I'm transfixed by their slight flicker, my head tilting slightly until they dissipate into smoke, as if they blew themselves out. My brows knit in confusion, and I feel a pulse around the finger where my ring lays. I don't have time to read into this, so I leave the cabin.

I lift my ring in the glow of the moonlight and study it on our way into town. The black and red stones seem to suck in all the darkness around them. I never looked too closely at the ring, only knowing that it was left for me instead of my parents' ashes. I only knew that someone wanted me to have it; now, I'm starting to question who.

We pass the ranch completely, deciding that riding the whole way would be fastest. We didn't tell his brothers about the soul bond we now share. They chalked up our tardiness to our lust—not completely untrue. When we reach town, everyone lets out a shocked gasp.

Fires are raging in homes along Main Street. The streets are filled with limp bodies—likely dead—and a hoard of henchmen are flowing through the streets in the most lethal dance. "I don't suppose you brought any weapons?" I look towards Harris, the one most likely to carry them. He hands me a small stake with a solemn look, telling me it's all we have.

Noah ties the horses to a tree off the trail to ensure we can get back home if fate allows. We step down the hill in the cover of shadows, hoping they can't see us, hoping they can't smell my blood.

"Take down as many as you can, by any means," I whisper into the shadows. A group of henchmen lock their red eyes on me and start for us. I waste no time running toward them, the stake gripped tightly in my hand. I have no fighting skills, instead relying only on my new instincts.

They charge for me, and only two of the seven leave the pack to go for Harris and Noah. I can hear Sylas' footsteps close behind me, and I'm thankful to have him at my back. The henchmen are faster, though, and circle us. I press my back against Sylas to steady me before charging toward the one straight ahead.

He dodges my first swing with ample ease. I swing again, and he shoves me to the ground, tackling me in a fit of rage. I strain against his heavy form, trying to free my arms or angle the stake upwards towards him. A row of sharp teeth reach for my neck, and I shove hard against him, making him release his tight grip for a moment. It's enough time to drive the stake through his chest. Shadow-like movement rushes towards me from the corner of my eye. I survey around me and see two more rushing forward. It takes several hard pulls to free the stake from the dead henchman's chest. A rippled gush of blood covers my front, the blood putrid. I hold my breath, careful not to vomit.

I don't know where Sylas is, and I don't have time to look. There are four more, and two are feet away from me now. I'm hopeful he's taking care of the others. They both gain on me faster than I can dodge, and their long nails slice the skin on my arm clean through my jacket. I let out a sharp yelp and swing again, again, missing each time. My breathing is ragged, the cold air harsh in my lungs. They lunge again, and the stake lands in the middle of one's chest while the other dodges the attack. It didn't hit his heart, so I don't dare hope that it keeps him down. I grip his throat in my teeth and pull back as hard as I can. The skin tears with incredible ease, and I spit out the flesh with a terribly deep laugh.

"You're next," I say with a smile to the remaining henchman in front of me.

I move faster than I ever have, my arm swinging the stake as I dodge his attacks and land shallow blows. The exhaustion that was starting to creep in dissipates quickly, and I charge at him straight on. He doesn't waver; he comes at me with matched speed. I raise the dagger and drive it straight through. The force was so strong, my hand buried itself with the stake. I stand with his limp body attached to me before wiggling my fingers free of the hold I had on the stake. I can feel his dying heart, the beat almost gone. I wrap my hand around it and pull it straight from his flesh, holding it up like a trophy. The blood drips down my fingers, and the shocks shoot down through my hand, making me drop it.

I take in my surroundings, seeing the street ruined in a sea of death. The men are huffing on their knees. They took out the last of the henchmen and all that lay in front of us are bloody bodies. The sweet smell of human blood mixes with the putrid smell of death.

There's no relief when a loud explosion sounds to our left and a fit of flames forms over the town. Blurs of shadows retreat into the woods and take off. The church is up in flames, crumbling to its demise. I fall to my knees and watch it burn, knowing I can't stop this. We have been victorious on the streets for mere moments, but they ensure we know just how much damage they can do.

A tall, red figure emerges from behind the flames. Sam is wearing a long satin dress that has slits going up both legs, leaving nothing to the imagination. A crown adorns her head, circling the horns that are red as blood. She looks like a queen in every sense of the word. She ends her steps in front of me, and I stand on unsteady legs, the brothers already at my side. She is more powerful than all four of us combined, but I won't back down. "Oh, Rowan, you won't win."

She makes my blood boil. "I will take you down even if it ends up killing me." I push down the thoughts of what will happen to Sylas if that happens. I don't let them surface or draw doubt.

"Even if it kills your new toy?" She raises an eyebrow at Sylas, and my mouth hangs in shock. "I know everything, dear. I am queen, after all." She laughs, and I glimpse the row of dagger-like teeth. "I hoped you would. You're playing into everything I planned for you. Shame, really, that you haven't learned how to use the most powerful gifts I've given you." Her gaze tracks to my hands, and I follow where they're pointed: the gold band wrapped around my finger. I try to pull it off, but it doesn't budge. I try again, and razor-sharp teeth bite at my finger and dig in. I grit my teeth and bite back a cry.

She takes a step toward me and lowers her head. My body goes rigid, and I'm locked in place. "I'll be seeing you soon," she whispers, sending a strong chill through my bones. Just as quickly as she appeared, she's gone.

# Chapter Twenty-Seven

## ROWAN

HER WORDS HAVE SUNKEN IN SO DEEP THAT I'M FROZEN IN PLACE, UNSURE WHAT TO DO OR HOW TO MOVE. I know Sylas carries me back to his mare and takes us back to the ranch; there's no point in hiding now. There's no telling how big of an army she's going to raise. We arrive at the ranch, and he carries me into the tub, setting me gently in the water spilling from the faucet.

There's no heat or desire in the way he's peeling my clothing off and washing my skin of enemy blood. The water runs red immediately, and I look to him for any sort of relief. "Your nose is bleeding."

He wipes at it, leaving a streak of red across his face as he studies his finger. "I'm okay." He's gentle with his words. He keeps such a calm demeanor after what happened. The hold I had on my humanity is slipping, letting pain leak through its cracks. It's a crushing weight to bear that I'm the reason for it. I want to be preparing for battle. I want a spine of steel that keeps me from crumbling. I want to be the one everyone says I am, with great power to end them all. Tears fill my eyes and make quick work of flowing down my cheeks. I feel far too soft for war.

The last of the blood is washed away, and he dresses me before laying me in bed. I feel so thoroughly beaten and exhausted that I fall asleep the moment my head hits the pillow.

The piercing glare of the sun reflects into my sleeping eyes and wakes me. The clock on the nightstand reads 9:30 am. I groan at the ache in my muscles and the pounding in my head—it feels like a hangover. Sylas moves into the room quietly, probably hearing me wake. I wouldn't be surprised if he had slept on the floor outside my door. "I brought you toast. We haven't eaten solid food in a while." I give him a soft smile that doesn't conceal the worry in my eyes.

"Thank you." I take the plate and bite into the warm, crusty bread. It's smeared with butter but doesn't give me the satisfaction it used to. As if reading my thoughts, he removes the plate from my hand and slides into the bed next to me.

"It's horrible, isn't it?" The corner of his mouth tips up.

"It's not. It's-"

"Come on, it's not very good. Not as good as blood. "He lifts his wrist to his mouth and pierces the skin with his teeth before settling the bite to my own lips.

I drink from him as if I was starving. I *was* starving. Fighting took so much out of me; I used more power than I had. I take deep drinks from his wrist, losing myself in the taste and strength it's giving me. Sylas relaxes his head on the pillow and slumps down. I see his skin pale, and I pull his wrist from my grip. "Oh God, I'm sorry. That was too much." The marks on his wrist have already disappeared.

"You needed it. I'll be fine. Lay down with me." His hand guides my head to the pillow next to him, and we thread our legs together before linking hands. Laying like this makes me feel safe and warm. I feel like we can whisper secrets in the space between us. No harm can come from me in his embrace.

The gold of my ring shimmers in the morning light. "I need to tell you something."

He tracks my gaze. "Do you know something about it?" His voice is a calm and steadying comfort.

"Not much, but when we left the cabin yesterday..." My chest rises, but he gives me confidence. "I think I put out the flames with my mind."

His eyes shoot up but soften quickly, willing me to go on. "I keep feeling this pain bolt through my hand where the ring sits. I don't know how I knew to do it; I just had a feeling. It was calling me to study the flames, and I was thinking about blowing them out, and then...they were out." I study his face.

"Have you tried it again?" A reasonable question, of course. There hasn't been any time between when I did it and now. I didn't have a chance to test mere theories when our lives were at stake. I shake my head. "Well then, I'll help you practice." A smile plays on his lips, and I stare in wonder. The panic in me always settles when he takes things with ease and guides me in the right direction.

"We don't know when she's coming." A rational thought on my part, I believe.

"Better start now, then." He kisses my lips and gets out of

bed. "Get dressed!" Way too cheery, I think.

Getting dressed feels like such a silly, minuscule task. I don't know if I should dress for comfort, for battle, for what I'll be wearing in my afterlife. I opt for black cargo pants that make my ass look good and laugh at how asinine I'm being. Practical and cute, I think. I put on a simple gray, fitted long sleeve and leave for the main room.

The blinds are drawn shut, and candles fill the room. This would be highly romantic under any other circumstance. He's waiting for me, seated on the floor in front of a small ring of candles. I take a seat across from him, mimicking our positions in the cabin. Flickers fill the room, and the flames behind him light the space around his form.

*Deep breath in.*

*And out.*

I cross my legs and sit with my palms facing up, resting them on my knees. I don't feel the same pull to the flames, but I focus on a single wick dancing under our breath. I study the fire hard, focusing all my will on wanting to see it burn out. There's no sense of urgency and no tingle of power. My brows crinkle. I send all my thoughts into the flame, and nothing.

Nothing happens.

I school my face into neutrality and think about everything making me break right now. Everything is riding on us and our success. I try again and again, and nothing. Not a flicker. I swear, it stands straighter with each attempt.

I try everything. I pretend not to look at it. I give it my anger, I plead. It takes nothing from me.

The candles have been burning for a while, and wax drips

down to the floors. I have nothing else to try and the feeling of defeat takes over. "Have you tried taking it off again?" he asks me, and I jump; I almost forgot he was there.

I hadn't tried again, but I feel the faint prick of the invisible prongs that dug into my skin when I tried last time. I wrap my fingers around the metal and gently tug at it with a groan. Apparently, it's not coming off.

"Okay, okay…" I can hear him thinking, his thoughts filling my head. "When did you first feel it? The power in the ring."

"When we bound our souls. When blood dripped down my hand." I can hear his mind turning just then, and we both look at each other in knowing and intrigue. He pierces his thumb with a fang, the blood beading out in a small bubble that sits atop it. I reach my hand over the flame and allow him to wipe the blood across the ring. That familiar shock courses through my hand and up my arm. What originally came to me as pain now gives me feelings of joy. A smile spreads wide across my face.

"Bloodstones?"

"I saw a section about this in the book, but I didn't look any further. I thought it was more voodoo shit, as Harris calls it," Sylas tells me with a solemn look on his face, as if he regrets not remembering the information.

"I *feel* it everywhere." I flex my hand and feel a hum go across my skin and travel down my spine. "There is so much *power* in blood." I look at the flames again and give my full attention to the one directly in front of me. I will it to go out; all I want is the flame to go up in smoke. I tilt my head the way I did in the cabin, and the flame goes out. The room is completely dark.

I hear Sylas move to stand, and then the blinds are open. I lift my head to survey the room, all the candles having burnt out. "Holy shit." His disbelief is exactly what I'm feeling right now. My jaw hangs low before curling into a smile. I run to grab him and pull him into a kiss. I feel hopeful for at least a chance in this fight because he believed in me.

I pull away and see a drop of blood flowing from his nose. I wipe it away. "Has this been happening often?" He shakes his head and kisses me again, completely ignoring the nosebleed. I can't help but think I'm causing it, but I don't want to press further. It's just a nosebleed.

His brothers return from whatever mischief they get into, and I have to put on a show. Every time they light a candle, I blow it out with my power. I have to admit, it's a fun party trick. Sylas looks more exhausted each time I look in his direction, though, so I cut the fun short.

We feed from blood bags they brought home and drink whiskey sours garnished with cherries in celebration. It's a sight to see Harris mixing up cocktails. Noah blasts music, and we dance until the sun starts to set. I soak in these moments with them, promising myself never to forget their faces and the love they've shown me.

By the time the sun is set, we're all on the cold hardwood of the main room. The guys are telling jokes and reminiscing on the good times they've had together. They poke fun at us for "getting hitched" without a word. I thought it would upset them, but it has been the complete opposite. They call me sister, and we all keel over laughing. I'm thankful for the stronger tolerance to alcohol.

The words die down, and reality sets back in. "I think we should just get on with it," I say, killing the mood.

"It would be easier than sitting here, anxiously waiting. The barn is ready; we just need to draw them here," Noah adds, and I'm grateful I'm not the only one thinking about it. Harris and Sylas agree, but I can see the worry in his eyes. I try to feel what he has going on in his head, but it's just...worry. I study his face and wonder if he's doing that on purpose so I won't feel his true emotions.

"Not tonight." His smile is terse and distant. "We need to sleep this off." We all part ways, and I drag him into my room. There's no point in sleeping apart now.

He's holding me tightly, and I still only sense worry. I think to ask him, but I would rather just ease his mind. I roll and swing my leg over his body as I move to straddle his waist. His hands go to my thighs, and he lifts to kiss me. I guide him back to the pillow and move my mouth down his body, leaving kisses in my wake. I whisper against his skin, hovering over his torso. "One last time before tomorrow."

"Oh, darling, this won't be the last."

My cheeks heat, and it drives me down his waist farther. I undo his pants torturously slowly and slip them down. He's already so hard for me. I marvel at the size and test the weight in my hands before flattening my tongue on his swollen tip. I slide my tongue up from the base and let his moans fill me with pleasure. I use my free hand to cup his balls, lightly squeezing and pulling. His cock twitches against me in pleasure. "Fuck, Rowan. Let me see your mouth around my cock."

"Look who's begging now." I smile against his length and graze my teeth up the side, teasing him. When I reach the swollen head, I part my lips and sink my mouth down his length as far as I can. I hollow my cheeks and find a rhythm that has him arching, thrusting into my mouth. He matches my pace and lays a hand on my head, gently moving his cock deeper. He hits the back of my throat when he picks up speed, and I keep my hand gripping his balls, edging him to his release.

I can feel him losing himself under my touch, his moans mixed with the wet sounds of my mouth sliding up and down. He grips my hair tight, and I know he's almost there. I can't help but smile, causing my teeth to graze him. It throws him over edge, and he shoves my mouth down hard onto him.

"You look so good with your mouth around my cock. Swallow me and tell me how I taste on your tongue." It doesn't take long before hot liquid fills my mouth. I swallow, keeping just his head around my lips while I draw out the last of his release. I suck hard and lift my head, licking the last of the cum as I hum with pleasure. "Tell me." He's panting.

"So, so good, cowboy." Before I can fully smile, his lips are on mine.

We don't fall asleep for hours, and with the noise we're making, I don't think his brothers do either.

# Chapter Twenty-Eight

## SYLAS

Rowan is fast asleep beside me, curled into my chest. Our bond has planted deep talons inside me, and I can sense her reaching out to gauge my feelings, so I hold strong to one and let it consume me. Worry. Because truthfully, that's what I feel most. I'm worried that the woman I love will be taken from me. *Again.* I'm worried because she thinks she can face this fight after blowing out a few candles. Instead of practicing her blood magic, she was consuming me, and I let her. I let her stray one last time because of the way her touch makes me so malleable. I've been stupid and reckless when it comes to her.

I watch her chest rise and fall—she looks entirely calm. I hate what I know tomorrow brings for us. I knew the moment she over-extended herself in town yesterday, the moment my nose started to bleed, that she would need to take all of me to be victorious. If a simple trick to blow out a few candles could make my nose bleed, I'll bleed out with the type of power she needs to stop the queen. I won't tell her. She deserves to be free and live a long life, long enough to replace me. I let the peace of my decision wash over me, calm my nerves, and float me to sleep.

"I'm going to check out the barn and make sure it's all set." She places a quick kiss on my mouth before running off.

"Woah, woah, slow your horses. I'm getting up," I groan and roll out of the bed. I see her eyes graze my body, realizing I'm still naked from last night. I wink at her and strut to my clothing to let her check out my gorgeous backside. She bends over in laughter, and I can't help but admire her. Her light bangs sweep over her brows, and her hair falls just past her shoulders. She's wearing something similar to yesterday: dark cargo pants and a tight-fitting black long-sleeve t-shirt. It looks like she's joining the Army but my god she makes it look appealing. I get dressed, not looking quite as ready for boot camp as she does, and pull her into a kiss. I grip her waist tight and let myself drown in her love for just another moment before reality sets in outside the walls of our room. She weaves her hand into mine, and we walk out to check the barn.

"Brother." Harris claps his hand on my shoulder. "You're moving the fuck out of here when this is over. You two are louder than skeletons fucking on a tin roof." I choke before tossing my head back and howling with laughter.

"How's it looking in there?" My chin raises towards the barn.

"Like a scene straight out of hell. But it'll work. Your girl had one hell of an idea." He scrubs at his long beard. I wish he would shave the damn thing off, but I can't say much with mine. My beard is short-cropped while his is growing like a damn weed.

I hear Rowan gasp from inside the barn, and I jog over to see if she's okay, but she's beaming. "I can't believe they pulled this off." Her excitement makes me feel like electricity is running through my bones.

Hanging from the ceiling of the barn are hundreds of thick silver chains with large hooks on the ends. The sun reflects off them, making the room dance with lights. I run my finger along the edge of one, and it cuts through my skin with ease. I suck the blood away. Weaving in and out of these could be dangerous if she's thinking of bringing them here.

"Watch this." She takes my hand and guides me to the far wall, where a lever sits. A hard pull down, and the chains hide in the ceiling beams above. "They won't even see it coming." Her laugh startles me, and I eat it up with a kiss.

"You're so twisted, darling. It's like you were made to do this." I kiss her again, but she pulls back. I can feel the nerve I just hit. Her pained emotions fill me with guilt. "That's not how I meant it."

"I hate that you can feel everything I feel now. I know what you mean, but fuck, it sounds like something Sam would say." She tucks her hair behind her ear and looks down, but I grab her chin and make her face me.

"You are so much more than a weapon. I will never let you forget that." Her hand meets mine, and she squeezes it in thanks. I let the love I feel for her pour into my body, into my mind. I want her to know just how truly deep I am in this.

*I love you. I will never leave.*

Tears swell in her eyes, and I kiss away the ones that start to pour down her face. She lets me know she hears my confession.

*I will love you to the end and forever after.*

She wipes the tears I didn't know strayed from my eyes. I throw my mental shield back up and give her a smile. These might be my final days with her.

Harris and Noah are arguing when we step back inside. We strip our coats before intervening.

"This is not just about you!" Harris is red in the face with anger towards Noah.

"I never wanted this! I've been dragged into your shit for years. This ranch has been my life, and it's fucking tainted now, ruined!" Noah's words hit us like a freight train. We haven't given any thought to what happens after. What happens once we've run everything to the ground fighting? We haven't given any thought to destroying the one piece of him that made him whole.

"Noah, I'm so sorry-"

He cuts me off. "Mr. Perfect is sorry, would you get a load of that!" Rowan goes rigid beside me when he turns to face her. "I'm sorry this is how your life ended up, but it can't be my cross to bear. I can't keep on like this and watch everything I've helped build crumble under your touch."

"Noah." She tries to reach a hand towards him, but he dodges her touch. Guilt pains me, and her sadness creeps in. "This isn't how I wanted things to go. I won't make you stay and fight my battles."

A pained laugh escapes him, and his tongue darts over his

lip. His fangs shine against his fake smile. "You want me to leave my own home, Rowan? Do you think I'm just running away? I want my ranch back." With a snarl, he turns to leave, slamming the door after him. I hear his truck start and drive away.

Harris has his elbows propped on the kitchen island, and his head hangs into his hands. He lets out a long sigh. "He's not coming back."

Rowan has been in her room for hours now since Noah left. She locked me out and won't answer me when I knock. The sun will start to set soon, and we're running out of time to form a plan that only involves the three of us.

Harris and I sit in silence in the main room for a long while, waiting for her to come out. He starts pacing, and I understand every bit of panic he's feeling. "I'm so fucking worried about him out there." He clasps his hands behind his head and blows out a breath.

"I'm worried too, but it's not him they want." I don't sound as convincing as I intended. "Let's finish this fight tonight, and then we'll go after him. We can rebuild the ranch and leave. If he truly doesn't want us here, we go." Chewing his lip, he nods in agreement.

I can't sit still, and my hands need something to do with all the anxiety. I go out back and start sharpening sticks. They will have to do since we couldn't find enough silver daggers. Harris was smart enough to have four commissioned. I hold onto Noah's in the hopes that he comes back. I don't blame him for leaving. We have been so caught up in keeping Rowan alive. I killed his cattle and we're destroying his barn. We are filling his land with bloodshed. It will take a lot of work to rebuild this ranch to what he spent years building it up to be, work that might be left for Harris to bear on his own.

The pile of stakes builds beside me as I watch the sun on the horizon slowly descend. My eyes burn, and it's not entirely from the sun. I let it sear into me, a reminder of the sacrifices I'm willing to make to protect her.

I feel a pull in my chest, an ache. It's not heartbreak or love that I feel—it's panic. I run back inside to find Rowan. I bang on her door, but there's no reply. I'm done with her hiding when everything is on the line. I silently apologize for what I'm about to do and then kick the door down. It splinters around my foot and shatters into the room. The empty room. It looks like someone broke in and ransacked her things. The pillows are ruined and things are smashed.

A cold breeze brushes past my face, and that's when I see the open window. My blood boils, and the leash I've been keeping my temper on snaps. How could she have been so dense to leave on her own again? I have half a mind to think she went after Noah. I told her not to. I told her to let him go, that we didn't need him to fight with us.

Harris rushes to my side and stills beside me. His fists clench at his side, and I get the sense he's thinking the same thing I am.

"Start the bonfire. I'm going to find her. We will end this—*tonight*," I grit out.

He doesn't argue.

# Chapter Twenty-Nine

## ROWAN

NOAH LEAVING SENT ME INTO A SPIRAL. I know it hasn't been easy for any of them, and this is exactly why I wanted to finish this myself. This is why I didn't want to involve them. My nightmares are coming alive right before my eyes.

I pace around my room for a few minutes, trying to think of any way to get him back, any way I can stop Sam myself. It feels entirely impossible. I don't know how many henchmen she has working for her, but I know it's too many for me to take on. I don't know how my blood magic works entirely. I have only been able to test it inside this house. I don't feel prepared for tonight. When I offered to settle the score, I didn't know how I'd do it beyond preparing weapons.

I press a hard finger into my top fang and let the blood bead on the tip before smoothing it across the ring on my hand. I buzz with power. I focus hard on my nightstand, on the lamp sitting there. The bulb flickers and lights, and I turn it off and back on again until I feel comfortable. I turn to the dresser and focus on the drawers, letting them slide open one by one. As impressed as I am, I need more. I need something bigger.

I turn to the bed and make the pillows hover. Taking a deep breath in, I focus on destroying them. They tear in half, and the feathers spill out, but I stop them from hitting the bed. Instead, I let them float mid-air amongst the destruction. The far bedpost groans and cracks under my gaze. I smile, taking in the chaos around me, the chaos I caused. "I did this," I whisper. "I can do this."

I let my magic slide open the window, and then, I run. I run to find Noah, run to draw the henchmen to their deaths.

The town is quiet, unmoving. Destruction and debris still line the streets. There are no cars in driveways and no lights on in homes. The sun starts to set, and I know my time is coming. I scan the streets for any sign of movement as I walk toward Sam's house. The only sound is the wind filtering through the streets.

When I don't see anything in front of me, doubt creeps in. They wouldn't have all left. They wouldn't have gone through all that trouble to just leave me here alive. My brows furrow, and I spin, checking the sky and listening for anything the wind could whisper. I settle my hat back in place and continue walking toward her street.

Down the hill, a shimmer of red glows in the distance. It grows slowly, moving toward me. I take a step closer, squinting against the setting sun. Closer and closer, it creeps up to me until figures take shape. Hundreds of red-hooded forms walk towards me, and a single man leads them my way.

My heart drops to my stomach, my blood ice cold. His eyes meet mine, and the world slows as I take in blood-red eyes and a sinister smile lining his face. It isn't like him to turn on his family, to turn to the enemy. This has to be Sam's doing.

I wait until they edge closer, and then, I run. I sprint back to the ranch and bring them to the trap we laid. I *will* find a way. This can't be Noah's end.

The wind whips my hair behind me, and I move faster than I thought my legs could go. My boots dig into the solid ground as I take off through the trees. The air gets colder as the sun dips below the horizon, the harsh bite filling my lungs and straining my breathing. I have to make it back.

I'm almost to the gate down the winding road to the ranch when I see Sylas running towards me. My breathing is ragged as I try to get out the words, "Noah."

He looks past me, and I turn around for the first time to find they're gaining on us. They're almost here. "She got to him. He's not himself anymore. He's one of them." The words shatter me as they leave my mouth.

He wastes no time deciding what to do, gripping my hand as we race back to the ranch. I can see smoke billowing behind the barn. Three of us against an army of them; the odds are not in our favor, no matter how much magic I can draw up.

It's a short sigh of relief to see Harris before we draw him close and quickly get him up to speed. The rage in his eyes is reflected in our own. I let him feel it, let us all feel it, let the rage ebb and flow between us. I gather a stake in one hand and palm the short silver dagger in the other. Before they draw closer, I make a cut across my palm, letting fresh blood flow to my ring as I look between the two men who have stayed by my side. "We kill as many as we can and draw the rest to the barn."

"Leave Noah to me," Harris grits, his jaw clenching.

I feel Sylas' true emotions as he lets the wall slip briefly when Noah comes into view. It's not the feeling that he's giving up, but he's resigned, as if he thinks this is his last fight. I feel the flicker of our bond telling me as much. Too much power could take him from me and drag me down along with it. We knew what we were doing when we bonded; I just hoped it would never come true. I look at the ring I thought to be a gift and shudder at its glare. "Sylas." I turn toward him, but before I can say it, he kisses me deeply. My mouth parts for him, and our tongues glide against each other's in knowing.

He pulls back and grips the base of my neck. "You do what you need to do, Rowan. You fight with everything you have without looking back. I will love you to the end."

"And forever after." The tears fill my eyes before steeling my spine and turning towards the fight ahead.

Beneath their red cloaks, I see glimmers of silver chains and black leather gloves. They can dress up however they like, but in the end, they're just demons doing someone else's bidding. I don't see Sam in the sea of red, but I know she'll turn up to collect her prize at the end.

The fire is blazing, and Noah leads them closer into our trap. If his mind was his own, he would know not to lead them here. The three of us get into position, and I grip the handle of the dagger tight at my side. They aren't running toward us; no, they're walking in perfect sync until they slow and stand before us.

"One last chance, Rowan. Come with me, or die here."

The voice coming from his mouth is not his own, something foreign and deadly as his red eyes glow against the flames.

"This ends here," I shout, and in the blink of an eye, they charge.

The henchmen gather chains from beneath their red cloaks and twist them around their leather-gloved hands. They start to whip and swing them. I take a few steps back and dip the end of my stake in the fire roaring next to me. The sharp end catches, and I throw it as hard as I can towards the group moving towards me. It lands in the shoulder of one and burns through his cloak. He removes it with a snap and gets back up. I let the anger fuel me, let my blood run hot, and pick up another stake.

The flames burn around it, and I throw it hard. It hits the henchman straight in the chest, and he lets out a piercing scream as he turns to ash on the spot. More flaming stakes are thrown into the crowd of demons, flying past me on both sides. They gain on us, swarming until we're caged in with the bonfire roaring at our backs. I throw my next stake with a fury, and it shreds through the chest of two henchmen. They scream and crumble to ash, two more immediately taking their place.

I can feel the heat against my back, and sweat drips down my neck. The pile of sharpened wood grows thin, and my first instinct is to panic, but I push it down. I grit my teeth and stare at the demon in front of me, putting all my thoughts and strength into his destruction. I twist my head with a smile, the snap of bones like music to my ears as his neck breaks and he collapses to his knees without a sound. "Demon bastards." I smile at the next one, who looks at me with large eyes. I'm guessing she didn't tell them what I would become. She kept that a secret. They all turn to face me with fury in their eyes, and I laugh mindlessly before snapping ten of their necks at once. I watch them fall to their demise, the power jolting through my body, begging for more.

I give in to exactly what it begs of me. I push my hands out in front of me, one open and the other still gripping the dagger, my fingers tightly coiled around its hilt. I push magic and energy into my hands, and a spark shoots through my palms as they warm. My mind and body focus on lifting a dozen henchmen into the air, and I grit my teeth, holding on to the weight of the magic before snapping their spines and swinging my arms down. The men slam into the hard, frosted ground, the air filled only with the sounds of snapping bones.

I send as much of that power through the dagger gripped in my hand as I can, thirsty for the chance to use it to the fullest. I walk toward the line of henchmen forming before me. My boot splashes in a pool of blood, stepping over their corpses. I swing the dagger with all my power as it slices and decapitates the demon in front of me. I turn to the next and slice his head clean off.

Two more come at me. I swing with my dagger and send my hand straight through the chest of the second. I grip his heart in my hand, his blood sending a shock down my arm before I pull it straight from his body. He crumbles to nothing as I hold his heart high above my head.

"I will end you. All of you." I squeeze tightly and let the organ burst in my hand, blood coating my arm and dripping down my face.

"You play a dangerous game, bitch. The queen will end you if we don't." He lunges at me, and I sink the dagger deep into his chest, pushing it upward before pulling out.

There are still at least a hundred henchmen around us. Harris and Sylas are slicing and gutting each one they can, but they're pushing us closer and closer to the fire. Noah is nowhere I can see. It's time to end this before they close in. "Now!" I scream as loud as I can as I turn, running toward the barn.

I cut and push my way past the line of henchmen closing in. I swing my dagger, and it lands hard into a chest, but I can't get it free. I leave it and keep running. A sharp, burning pain slices through the back of my arm. One of them got my dagger and is swinging it at me. I dodge his swings and slam my foot into his knee. It cracks, and he swings hard before falling. It lands in my shoulder, and I gasp at the pain. I can feel the blood spilling out of my arm as I yank it free. The silver blade is causing the wound to stay open. I run as fast as I can to the barn, watching Harris and Sylas make their way in.

I just have to make it to the barn.

The loss of blood is making me dizzy, blackness begging to creep in around me. I fight against it as I run straight through the barn to the edge, and they swarm in like moths to a flame.

I look to Harris, and he lifts the lever. The chains drop with a thud, and I have to duck to avoid getting hit. They swing and shine in the moonlight, a glorious death trap.

The henchmen try to leave the barn, but Sylas locks the doors. They inch towards me, bloodthirsty smiles on their faces as they lick their teeth in desire. They won't get to taste my blood today. I grasp the silver hook in my hand, and it burns in my palm. I shove the sharp hook into the back of one demon, driving it in as far as I can muster.

I grab another, shoving it deep into the chest of the next. Like a perfect dance of death, one by one, sharp hooks dig deep into their flesh and latch on like talons. Blood pools at my feet, the putrid tang of iron hitting my nose, putting me in a deep frenzy.

I work the hooks into more and more henchmen. Their screams echo off the worn wood as their feet slip in the blood below them. They grip onto each other trying to pull free, but the hooks stay and dig deeper.

Harris runs towards the lever and smashes it down. As quickly as they come down, they draw back up. The hooks slice through their bodies, blood splashes to the floor, and I shield my face with an arm. Their organs spill from the large gashes, some falling off the hook completely with a loud thud and splash. Their bodies reek, and I move around their hanging corpses, moving limbs out of my way and stepping over spilled body parts. I unlatch the lock and open the barn doors.

The sight of death filling the field in front of me suddenly makes my gut turn. I clutch my stomach before I fall to my knees and vomit violently. Sylas is quickly by my side, panting heavily and holding my hair back. "It's done." He rubs small circles on my back, and I rise back up with nothing left in me. His nose is bleeding in twin streams down his chin.

"I hurt you." I grab his face in my hands, studying the blood running down his face. "How bad is it?"

"I'm okay." He surveys my body, and his gaze lands on my

shoulder and the cut down my arm.

"I'm okay too." My voice is hoarse.

I move from his touch and grab the jug of gasoline. I step carefully into the massacre and start dousing it. I work my way backward, leaving no spot untouched until the jug is empty. I step back through the doors and give Harris a nod. He lights a match and tosses it into the barn. We run as far back as we can before the match hits the floor. With a bang, it goes up in flames, making the bonfire look measly. I take a step back and twist my head up to take in the sight. The fire is hot on my face, even from a distance away.

I want to release the pent-up anxiety and anger I've been feeling, but the relief doesn't come. There are two faces that remain hidden, two faces that need to find their justice.

As if I called him from the shadows, Noah walks into view. "It seems you've found your power, dear Rowan. How delightful." His voice still isn't his own but *hers*. "It's a pity you're choosing this gangly man over the hell you could be ruling beside me."

"You're pathetic. You couldn't show up on your own. You have to use him as a puppet. You're a coward of a queen, and I would never serve beside you."

Noah laughs—*she* laughs. "Poor Noah ran off because of you. I merely saved him. He's the perfect puppet to prove my point." A foul smile spreads across his face, and it boils my blood. "If you won't come with me, I'll pick off your precious men one by one."

"Do not touch him," a growl from Harris next to me.

"He did it to himself," he says—Sam says. Noah reaches

a hand over his chest before plunging it in and ripping out his own heart.

"*No!*" I scream and run for him. We all run for him. The world starts spinning in slow motion, and I can't get to him fast enough. The world turns quiet, only the rushing of my blood and pounding of my heart filling the gaps. I take his heart in my hand and try to push it back inside his chest. I don't know how much healing we can do, if he can repair his heart. His blood is pooling out too fast. Everything is happening too fast. I press his heart back inside, willing him to live. I push my magic into him, and it winks out. I try again and again to give him everything I have. I know I don't have the power to heal, but I keep trying, try to stop the blood from flowing freely and try to hold him together. "I can't lose you too." The tears stream down my face and land on his chest. My vision is so cloudy, I can't see my own hands working.

"That's enough, Row. He's gone," Sylas gasps beside me. I turn to face him and see a blur of blood sliding down his face and across his lips. I've used too much; I'm hurting him too. The ache in my muscles starts to take form, and Sylas' exhaustion wipes over me, reminding me that I'll take us both down if I push too hard. Everything I touch turns to ruin.

# Chapter Thirty

## ROWAN

SNOW BEGINS TO FALL. Noah's lips turned purple hours ago, his body now stiff from the sub-freezing temperatures. The snowflakes land in his hair and gently coat his body until I can't see him beneath the white. I lost feeling in my fingers and knees hours ago. The weight of my decision has been hanging heavy between us, and I couldn't leave him here alone. Harris and Sylas take turns bringing me blankets and coffee, sitting with me for a while before going inside. They've been arguing for the better part of the night.

The barn is now mere embers, melting the snow that falls just around it.

The entire town should be getting ready for Christmas, caroling, filling the streets with shopping and lights. But no one is here—we turned Georgetown into a ghost town. The small city was so full of life, and I sucked it right out in just over a month. The angel on my shoulder tells me it's Sam's fault, but the devil has his pitchfork aimed at me—and rightfully so. My parents brought this fight onto me, and I know they did what they could to shield me from the world, but the wall had to come tumbling down someday. I just didn't think it would take so many people with it.

Glowing light shifts and hums in front of me. "Liddy?"

The form takes shape, and I see him. "Noah."

*Rowan.*

"I'm so, so sorry. I tried to piece you back together." The tears I thought had run out start flowing freely from my eyes. I'm prepared to take the verbal beating I know he should give me.

*What's done is done.*

I reach out my hand and hope he'll grab on. His eyes shift back and forth between my hand and his form under the snow. Reluctantly it seems, he reaches and touches my hand. I don't feel the chill in my hand, but rather, my soul. "I don't deserve to live in a world where you're gone. I'm sorry I took this from you."

*Rowan, I won't say this again: it's not your fault.*

"What if he blames me…"

*Sylas will be fine. Do what needs to be done and end her.*

"She won't live another day," My body runs hot with rage. I need to stop blaming myself, stop putting on this pity party of grief to sulk in alone. I will destroy her. I will bring that evil bitch to her knees, and she will beg me for mercy.

*I did come with a request.*

"Anything."

*Burn my body. Make sure it can never be used against you again.*

I nod my head and push to stand. My legs are wobbly, and my knees ache at the sudden movement. I stand to face him, eye to eye. "Anything for you, brother."

He nods back, and the glow fades before he's gone.

Harris gets the bonfire started once more, and I gather a few of Noah's personal things to burn with him. The least we can do is send him off properly. We gather around the fire, and I motion to them to say a few words.

Harris clears his throat. "Noah, you were the glue all along. This place was so much more than home for you, and I'm sorry we ruined that. I'm sorry we failed you, brother." He chokes out the last few words but holds his chin high.

"Brother, I will miss you so much. You deserved the world, and I wish I could have given it to you. Say hi to Dad for us." Sylas has tears streaking down his face, laced with blood.

I already said my peace to Noah, but I give him one final parting message as I throw his things into the fire. "I will watch the vile bitch burn in hell for what she did to you." Sylas wraps his body around mine, and I soak in the smell of him, the closeness of him. I can't lose him too.

I don't have the stomach to watch his body burn to ash, so I go inside and prepare myself for her. I'm done wasting time.

# Chapter Thirty-One

## SYLAS

I can feel in my chest that she thinks I blame her for this. Noah dying hit me harder than I could have imagined. I know he ran away of his own accord, but it was because of *us*. I thought it would be me dying today, but instead, I saw my world crash around me. I have no time to mend the hole in my heart before we head for more bloodshed.

Rowan plans to confront Sam tonight, but we are both drained of power. We drained a few blood bags each once we were back inside, but I still think she needs to sit down and rest for a moment. This is our last stop before freedom, and I don't want to blow our chances by being unprepared. "Sleep tonight, please. We're going to need the energy."

Her eyes turn molten, and she looks me dead in the eyes. "You should be angrier about this. You should be begging me to follow you to her doorstep for what she's done." Hurt flashes through me, and I steady my face, but I know she reads the emotion straight through me. She smirks, knowing she struck home.

She's so infuriating, so headstrong, it's driving me mad.

She does not bend to my words; she does as she wants. I'll make her listen, make her bend. "We'll go if you can get past me." I give her my best sugary smile laced with poison.

"You're childish. Blocking the door? Really?" She tries to run past me, but I stop her with a hand to her chest. I press against her and walk her to the wall until she's flat against it, shoulder blades digging into the drywall.

I dip my head down and graze my mouth along her ear. I feel her shiver against my touch. "I'm going to fuck you until you remember who you are."

"I haven't lost myself. I'm just angry." She pushes against me, and I catch her hands before our feet tangle and we fall to the floor. I cradle her head in my hand before we hit the hardwoods. She breathes heavily underneath me and grits her teeth, giving me a dark stare.

"You and I are not so different. We take calculated steps, we think, and we plan. You're being impulsive, and you've seen where that got me." I level my eyes on her and let myself feel warmth and comfort. I want that feeling to seep into her bones and fill her up.

She's struggling against my grip. She's strong, but I'm bigger than she is. I grip a handful of hair and pull down, exposing her neck. I scrape my teeth against her throat and feel it bob underneath my touch. I nip at her shoulder and tease the sensitive skin below her jaw before sinking my teeth in. She lets out a sharp gasp, and her hands freeze on my chest. Her blood fills my mouth, and I moan at the sweet taste. I take my time letting it slide over my tongue and coat the inside of my mouth. I drink her in and feel my strength coming back. I don't bother cleaning the wound I left, instead kissing her deeply, making her taste how sweet she is on my tongue.

Her legs part, and I wrap them around my waist. I let my hips dip towards her and move across her core as I stare down at her bleary eyes, at the mess of blood on her face, her hair tangled in my grip. "You look like heaven to me."

Without warning, she holds my waist tighter between her thighs, grabs onto my neck, and rolls me onto my back. "I'm about to give you hell." Her smile tips up on one side, and it's not because she's about to run from me. She's about to use me in the best way possible.

"Do your worst, darling." I kiss the words into her mouth, and she shoves me back to the ground. She rips my shirt in half and peels it off my body before her tongue wraps around my nipple, giving it a tug. My hips lift into hers in response.

"You're such a needy boy." Her laugh tickles my chest, and I laugh back. I love seeing her in control. I love watching her take what's hers instead of cowering in the dark. This is where her true power lies.

She takes my hands in her grip and lifts them above my head, holding them there as she kisses down my neck. She nips my ear, and I almost lose it. I easily slip my hands from her grip and shred her shirt straight down the middle. Her bra breaks at the same moment, and her full breasts bounce free. I grip them both in my hands, smoothing my thumbs over her hard nipples in small circles. She moans in pleasure as I lift my mouth to run my tongue around each of her sensitive peaks. "You bend so easily under my touch." I kiss between her breasts and run my hands up her back.

I see the scowl on her face when she pushes my body back to the floor, my back slamming into the hard surface. "I won't be bending to anyone ever again. I will not break again," she says with clarity. It makes my smile grow wider, and I can tell my smile is confusing her, setting her on edge. She moves down my legs and unbuttons my pants before pulling them too hard. They bust at the seams and hang shredded around my legs. She's gentler with my boxers, sliding them down slowly and palming my hard length as it jerks free.

Her mouth lowers around the swollen tip of my cock, and I slide my hands into her hair. I can't hold back when her perfect lips are wrapped around me. I move my hips, shoving myself deeper and deeper down her throat. Her lips part so wide for me a she lets me fill her mouth and slam my cock into the back of her throat. She takes me so well. "That perfect fucking mouth on my cock, baby. So good." I feel her head press hard against my hand, and she removes her mouth from me suddenly. She meets my gaze with a smile before moving to straddle me. I make quick work of removing her pants. It's not graceful, and she won't be able to wear them again, but the sight of the slinky pink thong between her legs practically makes me vibrate. "You wore that to go on a killing spree?"

"You don't like it?" A fake pout lines her face.

"It's a shame you won't be able to wear it again." I pull hard on the thin bands wrapping around her hips, and they snap. I pull the fabric from between her legs and discard it. Her mouth hangs open in shock before sucking her tongue through her teeth. Her pussy sits flush to my abdomen, and my dick presses hard into her ass. "Fuck me, Rowan. Put me inside you." I grip her thighs tight, my nails dig into her skin. She lifts her hips, and I feel her hand wrap around my length before dragging it through her wet pussy and nudging at her entrance. Her hand leaves me missing her touch just as she starts lowering herself onto me. I push her down the rest of my length with a hard thrust and let her take over the pace.

She rocks back and forth, taking what she needs, rising and lowering herself. I watch her head tilt back, and her moans only make me harder. I won't last much longer with the sounds she's making. I tighten my grip on her hips and slam myself into her over and over. A hand braces on my chest, and she grinds against me as I pick up my pace. "Don't stop. I'm going to—"

I don't let her finish the thought before I move my hand towards her ass. I slide my finger into her tight pussy, soaking my hand in her pleasure before I slide it around the tight pink muscle on her backside. I tease and circle it before pressing my finger in to the tip.

She tightens and writhes against me, and my own release takes over as I pump into her, letting us ride it out together. I hold her close to my chest, running my hands down her back and over her ass. My hands roam her body freely, I feel her muscles relax with each stroke.

I move us to the shower and kiss her over and over while washing her body. The cuts on her arm are almost fully healed, and the dried blood is being washed down the drain. She agrees to sleep tonight, and I can finally let out a breath for that.

"Thank you for today. For all of it." She sighs next to me in the bed. I pull her closer and wrap myself around her.

"It was never a question for me. I will always be by your side. Always." I murmur the words into her hair.

"I love you," she whispers, her eyes fluttering shut.

"To the end. And forever after." I close my eyes and hold her tight, afraid to let go.

# Chapter Thirty-Two

## ROWAN

*Rowan... Rowan... Come to me...*

I sit up with a start. Sylas is still asleep next to me, and I don't hear anything. Assuming it was a dream, I lay my head back down next to his. I don't close my eyes; instead, I let them wander over his face, the face I've come to love and cherish deeply. A faint red glow covers him, and I turn towards the window to see the night sky lit under a full red moon. We must have slept for an entire day.

*Rowan... Come to me... I have your parents.* The sultry voice makes me still—her voice.

"Sylas, wake up." I nudge him hard with my hand. "Wake up!"

His eyes shoot open in a panic. "What is it?"

"She's calling for me. Sam. Like a whisper in my head. She said she has my parents." I know it's untrue. She has them in a grave in her backyard like fucking trophies. I know she's baiting me. I look towards the clock—9 p.m. I give him an apologetic look.

"Are you sure about this?

His hands grip the side of my face. "It would take an army to remove me from your side." His mouth moves to my jaw as he licks and kisses his way to my neck. I wait for his fangs to dig in, but he only lays gentle kisses on my skin. Goosebumps cover my body, and my lip quivers with hurt and wanting.

I pull back, cupping his face in my hands as I make him hold my gaze. "I can't take any more heartache. If anything happened to you, it would be too much."

"I'll fight for you until my dying breath."

We embrace in a desperate kiss before I move to dress.

"I'll find Harris. God knows he'd be pissed if we went to see the bitch queen without him," His mouth tips up, and he walks down the hallway.

Exhaustion lingers in my bones as I slide my body into clothes and slip a long hood over me. I swiped one from the henchmen before coming inside last night. Their bodies are still littering the yard beneath the snow.

I hear the guys talking in the hallway, so I move toward them, and they still at my appearance. "That's the exact reaction I wanted." I give them a smile and go to the kitchen. I drain several blood bags and finally feel strong enough to make this visit. I make them do the same.

I slide my starry night boots onto my feet and scuff away any lingering blood spots. They've been my good luck charm through this all. Not everything has gone to plan, but I'm here, alive, ready to avenge my family.

She knows we're coming, so there's no use in hiding our arrival. Running down the wooded path is our fastest option but the blood moon makes me anxious about what we'll encounter. We haven't come across any other creatures in the months since turning, but I'm sure they won't keep themselves hidden tonight. Harris covers us from behind as Sylas and I take the lead through the woods.

The frigid air is a relief to my boiling skin. My rage burns hotter with each stride towards Sam. We have no plans beyond killing her. We have no plans because we thought she'd show up to the party we threw for her. Tonight, I will rely on my instincts and the cowboys who chose to fight with me—the rugged cowboys now flanking my sides and running toward the battle.

Thumping footsteps sound beside us, animal-like. I don't stop running as I twist my head in each direction, trying to pinpoint where they are. My eyes meet twin bright green ones. I shift my focus and see several pairs that match. Werewolves. I gasp, but they don't move towards us. They aren't hunting us but running with us. The wolf closest to me dips his head, and I mimic his show of support. We aren't the only ones who wronged by the vampire queen, it seems. I wonder if they've been watching us, wonder how long I've been walking among them. We pick up our pace, and they match it with ease.

The blinding red door to Sam's house only glows brighter under the blood moon. The snow on the ground glows the same shade of red. There's a reason she chose tonight, and I get the feeling it's not just about the scenery. I look to Sylas and see his hands clenching at his sides. I take them into my own and squeeze them tightly.

"I'm not letting you back inside that house."

The memories I tried to block out of what happened in this

house begin to surface, and I want to push them down, but I let them rise. I let the thoughts of what she did to us feed the rage inside me. "No, we won't be going inside." I nod to Harris and then the werewolves who followed us here. I lead us into the backyard, into her makeshift graveyard. If she thinks my dead parents will make me turn and run, she's dead wrong.

"I was wondering when you'd stop chatting at my door. And you brought friends! The more the merrier." The bitch purrs her amusement.

"You summoned me?" I give her a deep curtsey.

"It's almost Christmas. I have a present for you!" She smiles and shows off her pointed teeth. Sylas brushes his hand against mine, telling me he's right here with me.

"There's nothing you can give me, nothing I want from you."

"Not even your parents?" She takes three steps towards us.

"They're dead," I spit out. He slides his hand to the small of my back, and I lean into his touch.

"Oh, they'll be here soon, dear. The blood moon offers us so much." She slides her fingers over her horns and through her silky red hair.

My heart rate picks up faster, if that's even possible. I open my mouth to speak, but nothing comes out.

"That's always my favorite reaction." She steps closer but moves towards her graveyard. She lifts her hands beside her, palms facing toward the sky, and takes a deep inhale. "I'm so glad I get to show you my best trick." She slides a dagger from her thigh and slices across each palm. I can't hear what she's saying under her breath, but it looks like a chant. Her blood drips down her arms and onto the ground below them.

The ground below my feet shifts, and I grip Sylas' arm to steady myself. I look at everyone around me, but they're just as confused.

"Rise, my loves." She turns to face the graveyard.

The ground shifts and rumbles until shredded hands shoot up from the graves behind her. I hold Sylas tighter as my knees begin to give out. She can't be doing this. Out of everything I've come to know is truly real, this can't be. My eyes shift to where I know my parents' graves are, and they begin climbing out. Their hands scratch at the snow and soil beneath, and their bodies fight to push them out of their graves. I know she's powerful, but I didn't expect to relive my horrors tonight.

"You can't do this." My voice shakes.

"I already did. I thought you'd be happy?" She gives me a fake pout.

"Stop this, stop this!" I scream to no one in particular. I see them all rise from their graves on unsteady legs, all dressed in red cloaks with large hoods to conceal their faces. All at once, they remove their hoods, and I see them. I see my parents, I see Liddy. It looks like them, but their faces are warped and rotted, their eyes blood red. "No, no, no..."

"This power could be yours. You could have had all this, spoken to them one last time. Too bad you're just a stubborn girl." She raises her chin and faces her zombies, giving a dip of her head, and then they start moving towards us.

Their steps are slow, but their eyes are focused on me. I make a quick slice into my palm once more letting the blood flow onto my ring. The pain shoots through my body, and it's stronger tonight, stronger under this blood moon. I know in my mind that I need to kill them, kill my parents and my best friend. My heart aches and lurches at the idea.

Slim daggers slide into the zombie's hands from beneath their cloaks as they get closer. No one makes a move. Sylas keeps his hand on my back, and the wolves growl towards them. Nothing in the world could have prepared me for this moment. It's hard enough fighting for my life, but this is disgusting. She knew exactly what strings to pull to get me to falter.

They get closer and closer, and still, no one moves. "Mom, Dad?" I try to snap them out of this, if it's even possible. "It's Rowan, your daughter!" They give nothing away that says they remember me or that they have any control over what they're doing. "Mom!" I scream at her. I need them to give me something to tell me they're under there somewhere, but it never comes.

"We're going to have to kill them again," Harris grits out from beside me. Any strength I have left turns to fiery rage. If she thinks this will get me to fold, she's wrong.

"Do it," I say to my group, the ones who willingly stayed to fight with me as we all run towards them.

The zombies raise their daggers to swing, but it's weak. I kick one down and take the dagger before the next charges toward me. I throw my elbow into the next one, and they fall to the ground with a hollow thump. I have to dodge another dagger that flies towards me, but I don't duck far enough, and sharp metal grazes my cheek as it flies past me. My fingers touch the skin, and the cut is already healed. The daggers must not be silver.

My parents move closer to me, their eyes only set on one goal. Sylas arrives at my side, panting, but free of any blood that I can see. "You don't have to do this." He looks deep into my eyes.

"I'm okay." It doesn't sound convincing, even to me. I steady the dagger in my hand and watch as they inch closer and faster until they're a breath away.

With a dagger raised in both hands, they swing hard for me, and I freeze as the world slows. I thought I would be able to do this; I already made my peace with them being gone so I could stop them. Still, I thought it would be easier. Slowly ,their arms swing toward me and still, I can't move.

A hard body slams into me, and I see Sylas swing his arm to cover me, his other arm raising across his body as he slices hard at my parents, leaving them without heads and crumbling to the ground.

"No!" There's no amount of planning and recovery that could have prepared me for this loss again. My legs become so weak, I want to crumble right here along with them. Sylas wraps himself around me and holds me steady on my feet as I let my body lean into him.

"*No, Liddy,*" Sylas yells toward her, and red eyes meet ours, marching forward with vigorous determination.

I regain my legs and steel myself for what I have to do now. I place my palm on his chest and force so much love through our bond, giving him some sense of peace before what he's about to see.

Liddy charges at me, and I try to fight her off, I block each attempt she throws at me. My arms groan with exhaustion, but

I push it away, fight harder, delaying the inevitable. Her dagger slices the air in front of me. I breathe in, and on my breath out, I shove the dagger deep into her heart. Her rotting body sags around the blade, and I let my tears flow silently.

Sylas starts to melt to his knees, but I don't let him. I make him continue the fight like he did for me. We kill everything in our path with revenge-fueled blood.

I see the wolves snarling toward more undead, pouncing and tearing their bodies apart. Sam set this up as a trap. I look in front of me, and her smile is so broad, it takes up half her face.

"That little trick is my favorite."

"Too bad tonight's the last time you get to use it," I say through my teeth and march towards her. She's done torturing me, done killing the ones I love. I feel Sylas and Harris at my side, the wolves stalking closely behind. My body hums with magic that begs to be released. She doesn't back down or flinch as we circle her, a wide smile on her face.

She lifts her hand and presses two fingers together. With a snap, she disappears from the circle and laughs behind me. I turn to her and run. My speed gets me to her in a blink, but she snaps again and stands in the center of the graveyard. I focus all my magic on her hand, and before I approach, I twist my head. Bones snap, leaving her hand hanging limp on her arm. She screams out in pain, and it's my turn to smile at her. I bare my fangs and charge at her once more. I keep a steady gaze on her and focus my magic on keeping her pinned in place. I can feel her struggling against it, like she's trying to break through a wall in my mind.

"I'm so much stronger than you. Are you sure you want to play this game?"

"I want this more than you. Let's see who comes out victorious today, bitch," I snarl in her face. I push and push against the daggers she's throwing into my mind. I can see the wolves circling her again, waiting to sink their teeth into her. "I will let them tear you limb from limb. I will tear your heart out myself and feed it to them."

Her laugh is shards of glass in my spine. Her daggers shoot through my mind faster. I scream and my knees buckle, but I don't fall. I can't fall. I try to patch the tear in my mind and push her out.

"You're killing him," Harris says from beside me, and I look down at where Sylas is on his knees, grasping at his throat. Blood flows fast down his face, covering his chin as he reaches towards me on his hands and knees.

"Kill her," he grunts out, barely able to speak. Is it worth his death? If she's dead, I'll welcome my own, but is she worth the death of the man I love?

She pushes harder at the tear in my mind. "You'll kill him, just like you had everyone around you murdered. You can't handle this. You're weak, girl." Her voice turns deep, and it sends shivers down my spine. She holds her hand out in front of her, slipping free of my hold. The ground rumbles beneath my feet, but I pay no attention to it; it's just another illusion. The earth between us breaks and opens to a pit of flames that rise higher and higher. It's not an illusion; this is real, the flames heating my skin and boiling the ground beneath my boots.

She slips farther from my grasp until I let go completely,

gasping for air. Sylas heaves next to me, and I can't stop the quiver starting on my lips. Each step forward takes me so far backward. My anger has gotten us here; my fight for vengeance has hurt us all, and I thought if I gave everything I had, I could stop her.

"I would never take your place. I would never bring this hell on Earth as you desire. I will destroy you and everything you've made."

"How?" She shifts her head, waiting for my response. The problem is, I don't know how anymore.

Hell blazes between us, and I focus on the flames dancing in front of me. I close my eyes and think of everything good I've had in my life. I focus on my parents, who fought for me, on Liddy, who continued to guide me even after her death. I focus on Sylas, who through all his grief, chose me, stayed by me. I can hear Sylas next to me, fighting the power I'm using. Harris has him in his arms, doing anything he can to stop his pain. I just hope he can hold on long enough to let me do this. I let him feel my emotions, let them wash through me and into him. I need him to know I'm doing this for both of us. For Noah and Liddy and everyone she has hurt. My face starts to chill with the winter air. I crack my eyes open and watch the ground below me piece back together step by step, carving out a path straight to her.

I open my eyes and pin her in place, dredging up every last bit of energy I have. I focus on her throat, I choke her, all the air leaving her lungs. She grasps onto her neck, and I lift her from the ground.

"You have taken everything from me, and this moment

will be carved into my memory as such a happy day." My smile holds genuine. I nod to the wolves walking the path behind me, and no second is wasted as they tear her legs from her body, her flesh getting stuck in their jaws as blood sprays the ground, hitting my boots.

No sounds leave her body as her legs are gnawed straight off, and my grip on her neck holds. "Goodbye, Sam," I say before I slowly shove my hand into her chest and tightly grip her heart. I let the hold on her throat lessen, and she screams. I want her to look me in the eyes as I end her, her red ones on my golden. I pull hard, and her back arches at the pain before her head hangs limp. Her pulse dies out, and I take a bite from the bloody heart in my hand, relishing in the sweet taste of victory before throwing it to the wolves.

Suddenly, there's a sharp burning in my left arm that makes me gasp. "Wait," I say to the wolves.

They stop and back away, jaws dripping in her blood. The symbol on her left arm slowly disappears and reappears on my own arm. I rub and scratch at it, trying to stop the mark from forming on my skin, but it doesn't stop. The Vampire Queen's mark is now burned into my arm—an upturned crescent moon with a silver dagger going straight through it. The symbol of dark power. I feel it hum and groan, every sense of exhaustion and pain wiped away entirely. I think about the remaining hole in the Earth, and it closes on my command.

I hear Sylas move to his feet, and I run towards him. I grasp onto him hard, wiping the blood that stains him and looking him over. Nothing is broken, and there's no more bleeding. I still feel the soul bond between us, so I know it hasn't been broken. That's when I look in his eyes and notice bright red.

"That ain't good," Harris says as he looks between us. He looks into my eyes and back into Sylas'. My brows arch into each other. "Yours too, Row…" he says, looking me dead in the eyes. My heart lurches into my throat. I grab his hand and drag him to the back window of the house and look at our reflections. Twin pairs of red eyes stare at us in the glass.

"Sylas, I'm so sorry…" I open my mouth to say more, but I don't know what to say.

His voice is hoarse and raspy. "I feel good, Row." His smile broadens, and I try to read his eyes. He lifts the left sleeve of his jacket to reveal a matching symbol engraved onto his skin. He dips his head low as he kisses me deep. "I guess this makes me the vampire king." He breathes it into our kiss, and it sends shivers down my arms, though I can't help but laugh.

"I guess it does, cowboy." I run my fingers through his hair and hold him tight. For the first time, I know he's not going anywhere.

# Chapter Thirty-Three

## SYLAS

Harris stays back to help the werewolves clean up. They did most of it, but he burns what's left of her.

I take Rowan's hand in mine, and we slowly walk back to the ranch. We don't take the forest path but instead, we walk through the streets. We've turned into real monsters tonight, but I won't let it stop us from enjoying the victory. We pass all the snow-covered houses that are supposed to be decorated in flashing lights and decorations. It's a small loss we have to endure.

"Can we stop at Liddy's house? I haven't been back since that day I found your hat." She looks up at me with kind eyes and an easy smile. I love seeing her so at ease after months of torture—years, to be honest. I squeeze her hand and turn us towards the road.

"Did you really think I killed her?"

"Not for a second," she admits and chews her bottom lip. Her pointed fangs stick out over her lip, and I admire how perfectly they suit her. "But I did think you were a huge asshole." I can see her trying to hold back her laughter. I nudge her hip, and my laughter comes just as easy.

We make it to the front door of Liddy's house still lined in police tape. Rowan stares at the house with sadness in her eyes before moving to the back gate.

"You're a queen now, but I think breaking and entering is still illegal."

"There's a key, dumbass," she laughs over her shoulder and unlocks the back door.

It's just as cold inside as it is outside, and the lights don't turn on. It makes sense that everything would have been shut off here. I never saw how the house was left after she was murdered, since I was chained and turned. I still don't understand why they thought we'd join their army—why'd they risk giving Rowan allies if it didn't pan out. Maybe they just planned on killing us if it didn't.

I let the thought travel through my mind as I look around the room. Everything looks normal and in place. Liddy was so organized and precise with everything in her life. I loved that about her. She knew what she wanted, and I followed her lead. I let her guide my life because I didn't have any direction. All I had was the need to be perfect, so I followed her, let her guide my life in the right direction. I got so used to it that once she died, I had nowhere to turn. I didn't know what to do next. We were going to build a house on the ranch and raise our children together and live happily in Georgetown. Rowan threw me for such a loop. She held me accountable and forced me to make my own decisions.

I loved Liddy, and I love her even more now that she led me to Rowan. I didn't feel lost in the moment, in the year we spent together, planning a life. It was once I didn't have her to lean into that my world started to drift. I was going to be the perfect cowboy for her. Now, all I want is to be the king to my otherworldly queen. Rowan gave me the space to find myself, and then she gave me more than I could have possibly wished for.

I move to the living room and see the dishes knocked to the floor, food molding on the carpet. I can smell her blood dried to the couch cushions. I drag my finger through the blood, and it's like a flash of a memory shoots through me at the touch. I see Liddy sleeping on the couch. It looks like the night she was killed—she's still dolled up in her makeup and blonde curls. I'm looking at her through someone else's eyes, but I don't know who. They look at Liddy for a while and smooth her hair down. I can see the thick tendons flexing in the man's wrist as he strokes her hair again. Liddy comes to her senses and jolts up. "Travis?" Her words are a shrill scream, trying to fight, but she doesn't stand a chance as a mortal.

I weigh telling Rowan what really happened, but it doesn't change the outcome. It would only hurt her more.

My eyelids grow heavy and fill with tears at the memory. Every time I think I'm over the hill of grief, shit like this gets me. I move to her bookshelf and trace my fingers over each picture she has of us together and each she has with Rowan. They look so happy and carefree, wrapped in each other's arms. Rowan's face is full of life and joy despite all she has been through. I take the frame from the bookshelf to keep for Rowan; I know she'd want it.

I hear rustling from the bedroom and call out for her, but

she doesn't answer. I walk through the doorway, and at the same time, Rowan comes out with a bag of things. "Don't give me that look," she whispers, though not very well.

"It looks like you're robbing the place." I give her a smirk and take the bag from her to hitch over my shoulder.

"That's exactly what we're doing." She cracks up, and we leave through the back. I lock the door and place the key under the mat as we head back home.

I tug her into my side as we take the long winding roads back. The sun will rise soon and I plan to burn my eyes watching each sunset and sunrise with the woman I bound my soul to.

# Epilogue

## ROWAN

**4 months later...**

"It's PERFECT. Your mom picked the right spot." I squeeze Sylas' hand and rest my head on his shoulder. I stare across the lake surrounded by a large mountain, tall trees circling it. The spring breeze is cold up here, and I inhale, allowing the fresh air to fill my lungs. My fork slices into the cherry pie I brought, the tangy fruit melting with the buttery crust.

"The blueprints were sent to me this morning." I can hear the smile in his voice. "Our room will face the mountain, just like you want, and I'm thinking of a big bathtub right about there." He points to the clearing to the left of the lake, where we're building our future home.

"It's perfect." I lean back, and his mouth takes mine in a deep kiss.

There isn't a road leading to our new home yet, and we're thinking of not having one laid down. The seclusion is a nice change of pace, and I'd say we thrive in our own little world.

The beating of hooves makes my head turn, and I see

Harris and his girlfriend, Tess, ride up to the lake. "Sorry to interrupt, lovebirds," Tess quips.

I smile at her broadly. She has quickly become a part of our family here. Harris still hasn't given us the full story of how they met, but I'm happy for him either way. She was here for most of the aftermath—helping rebuild the barn and clean up the ranch. The new barn is something Noah would have marveled at. We've been able to house new cattle Harris and Sylas have committed to keeping alive no matter who stays to keep it running.

"People are starting to come back into town." Harris looks me in the eye. That's my cue to handle it. They turn and ride back to the ranch.

"Do you want to try it one more time?" Sylas brushes his thumb against my chin.

"Just once more." I smile and show him my palm. He makes a shallow cut, and the blood flows around my fingers and across my ring. The cut closes, and I shake my hand at the buzzing sensation. "You're as stubborn as a mule." I can't stop the giggle that bubbles out of me.

"That is not fair-" His words are cut short as I stare deeply into his eyes and allow my power to snake around the memory I gave him, slowly pulling it out.

"And? What did I just tell you?"

"You're devious. I don't have a clue. I hope it was about how great my butt looks in these jeans." He laughs before pressing a kiss to my lips.

"Obviously."

Sylas settles himself in the saddle behind me and wraps his

strong arms tightly around mine. Grabbing the reins, he leads us towards town.

After cleaning the remains off the streets, the mayor hired contractors to rebuild. They finished last week, and we've been waiting for the town to begin to fill again.

They trickle in slowly throughout the day, and each time we see a car pass out the window of Bluebird, we follow them, and I drag their memories away. I leave only a whisper of what happened so they can prepare themselves if it happens again.

The baristas slip blood into my drinks from bags we've stocked for them, ensuring they'll be discreet. An exhaustion sweeps over me by nightfall that no amount of blood can cure. Midnight comes all too quickly, but everyone is back home safely, and we can return to the ranch.

Terror shakes through me as Sam grips my throat, her red eyes glaring through me as I thrash against her grip. Still, my body doesn't move. She dips her head, allowing her sharp teeth to graze my neck until her hand plunges through my chest and rips my heart from its cavity.

I sit straight up in bed, clutching at my chest and panting loudly, my eyes desperately trying to adjust to the dark room. A warm hand presses against my back, and I turn to see Sylas waking up beside me.

"I'm sorry, I'm okay. Go back to sleep." My voice is ragged.

"No, come here." He pulls me into his chest and weaves his hand around my head before pressing a kiss to my forehead. "The nightmares—are they getting worse?"

I offer a shallow nod, and he runs his hand through my hair, coaxing me back to sleep. They started the same night I killed her. For a while, she came to me every night, each time ripping my heart out the way I did her. Her wild red eyes remind me of my own that now haunt me each time I look in the mirror.

The first time I saw myself like this, I punched the mirror so hard, it shattered around my fist. As days pass, the red dims, and the gold resurfaces until anger or emotion sweeps through us and they blaze red as hell.

Most days, I look at myself in the mirror in disbelief that this is my life now. I cover the mark on my arm with bandages and sweaters, but it burns to remind me it's there, that my best friend is still gone—that Noah is still gone. I tried to bring them back, but even I don't have the power to do that.

Having all the power Sam did has proven a challenge. I've been able to try out my new tricks here and there, but there's so much more I have to learn.

We've laid low here, and nothing has come to our doorstep thus far. Tess is from Stanton, a few towns over from Georgetown, and says they all felt the shift of power when it happened. She doesn't think I can hold out much longer without running into someone who's after my title. With Sylas by my side, we pose a large threat to the balance of it all. There hasn't been a king in centuries, and the henchmen are getting restless. She told me it might not be wise to continue without issuing a statement to those who now answer to me. I have nothing to say to them. I know I'm queen—I'm now the devil walking this Earth—but I still haven't decided if I'll be honoring the title.

Every so often, I feel a tug to go back to Sam's house, some invisible thread begging me to take a look at what's inside. I haven't told Sylas about that feeling. I so badly want our lives to stay in this new normal, so I push away the thoughts of pulling the string to see where it leads. Some nights, it keeps me up, wondering what would happen if I just looked inside. Other times, it's a whisper in the wind, begging me to follow its voice. This morning is the strongest I've felt its call.

I wrap my arms around Sylas in our bed. "Good morning." I let my forehead fall to his and breathe him in. The loud sounds of rainfall hitting the window offer a good excuse not to leave bed today.

"This is the best part of my day." He squeezes me tight, and I wrap my legs around his middle. My soft edges melt into him as we kiss slowly until a hungry need takes over. We lose ourselves in pleasure and pain, feeding off each other, letting the hum of power flow through us both.

Sylas has gotten so strong—our bond has given him magic that feeds off my blood. The more he drinks, the stronger he is. I smooth my hand over his hard biceps and across his muscular back. My hand cups the back of his neck, and I groan. "I can't believe you cut your hair. There's nothing for me to grab now."

He laughs at me before plunging his hand into my hair and grabbing a handful. "What a shame. Thankfully, I still get to pull yours." He nips my throat, and I can't stop the moan that escapes me or my nipples that harden against his chest. "While I have you pinned down, I need to tell you something."

My body goes still, and it takes more effort than I care

to admit to soften and breathe. It's the feeling you get when everything is going too well and you're waiting for the other foot to drop. It doesn't matter that I have him naked in my bed or that he has given me a piece of him. He gave me his soul, yet I can't stop feeling helpless at this moment.

"I need to go into Sam's house." I try to lift myself, but he has my hair gripped tight. "I feel something in my chest pulling me there. When I pass by in town, the pull gets so strong, I think I'll be sucked right in." His grip loosens, and my brows are knit tightly together. I'm not surprised that he feels it too. I was hoping, since he didn't say anything, that it wasn't true, but I can't hide it any longer now.

I sit up and cover my chest with the bed sheet. "I feel it too." I let my gaze soften and trail my hand along his jaw. "It pulls and whispers, begging me to come closer." He threads his fingers through mine.

"If we go, it doesn't have to mean anything. We don't have to answer for our titles if you don't want to." His ruby and gold eyes study my face. "I need to know what else she hid and what waits for us inside."

As much as I don't want to step foot in there again, I agree. "Tomorrow."

He smiles and cups my face. "Tomorrow."

# Acknowledgments

To everyone who made my shift into writing enjoyable and backed by support, thank you. I couldn't have made it to the finish line without you.

To my husband, you helped make this dream come true for me. Your support is unmatched. Thank you for celebrating me at each milestone. I love you endlessly.

To my boys, you endured my writing schedule and begged me to tell you about my book. Your creativity and boldness inspire me every day. I love you both.

To my parents who will buy whatever I write no matter what's in it. Thank you for being supportive, I'm lucky to have such a friend in you. I love you.

To Molly and Michelle, you never questioned my change of career and cheered me on from the moment I broke the news. Your honesty and support will be something I hold dearly for life. Thank you with all my heart.

To my beta readers, Taylor and Molly, thank you for your hard work and for picking up on things I hadn't thought of myself.

To my developmental editor, Julia, you helped me make this book what it is today. Your honesty and deep dive into the world I built helped bring it to life. I will always be thankful for your work.

To my editor, Alexa, you shaped this into exactly what I hoped it would be. Thank you for having the audacity to work despite what life throws at us.

To my cover designer, Austin, who made my book dreams come true with this incredible art. You worked so hard with me on this and it's perfect. Your skills are unmatched, I couldn't thank you enough.

To my ARC readers, you make a huge difference in the launch of a book that I can't even begin to express my gratitude. I appreciate every one of you.

And finally, to my readers, thank you. Thank you for taking your chances on me and diving into this world. I hope I made your Edward and Damon hearts full.

# About the Author

Kira Bates is a mom and writer of stories that raise the heart rate. Her love of the paranormal is equaled only by her obsession with romance novels, so she decided to write books that bring them together. She loves spooky and gory stories but will make sure you're cozy for the ride.

Originally from Florida, Kira currently lives overseas and —when her nose isn't in a book — can be found bingeing TV shows, baking, and playing video games.

To stay up to date on Kira's upcoming projects, connect with her on social media @authorkirabates, sign up for her newsletter, or go to www.kirabates.com.